DATE DUE

THE BOOK OF ABSENT PEOPLE

THE BOOK
OF ABSENT
PEOPLE

Taghi Modarressi

DOUBLEDAY & COMPANY, INC.
GARDEN CITY, NEW YORK
1986

Library of Congress Cataloging in Publication Data
Modarressi, Taghi.
      The book of absent people.
      I. Title.
PR9507.M63B66   1986   823   85–12884
ISBN: 0-385-23042-7

Oh, may your journey to the border of Sheba be happy.
May your speaking the language of birds with Solomon be
happy.
Hold back the demon in chains and in prison
So you will be the keeper of the secret like Solomon.

Attar of Nishapur (1142–1220 A.D.)
The Conference of Birds

BOOK ONE

Dark Mirror

1

Three nights before he went to Ghaleh Bagh, my Khan Papa
Doctor sent a message for me to come see him later in the library.
After I got the message, I went out to the balcony and looked
down into the courtyard. Maybe he would appear and walk
around the flower beds and inspect his crossbred roses one by one.
With finicky care, he would clip the withered blooms and throw
them into the green plastic pail he'd bought after New Year's. He
would hold the fresh blooms between his fingers and draw back
and study them with the Heshmat Nezami pridefulness.

But in the courtyard not even a bird was flying. It wasn't dark
enough to turn on the lights yet. Only one lamp burned weakly in
the entrance hall of the library. I was about to give up when he
appeared from the direction of the orangery. He wore his white
coat. He was busy with some idea, and he paid no attention to his
surroundings. I ran to the opposite side of the courtyard. When I
reached the sealed room of his first wife, Homayundokht, God
forgive her soul, I put my hands behind my back and, walking
parallel to my Khan Papa Doctor, I goose-stepped like a soldier.
As we reached the end of the courtyard, I raised my chin. I

slapped my bare heels together hard and shouted from the depths of my throat, "Ten-SHUN!"

He noticed, but he continued walking. From his expression, it was clear he was displeased but not out of temper. He only threw a taunting, sidelong glance at me, as though to ask when I planned to give up my childish ways. For heaven's sake, I was twenty-three years old; when was I going to pull myself together and find a job worthy of me like most of the Heshmat Nezamis and enter the society of respectable people? Finally I drew up and yelled, "At eee-ase!"

He glared at me. He chewed a tip of his salt-and-pepper mustache. Close up, his face looked haggard and depressed. His white coat was gray with charcoal. With his sooty hands, he might have come from one of those whitesmith's shops where they enamel copperware. He gave off a smell I couldn't identify. It was something like a mixture of caraway seeds and potter's clay. He narrowed his eyes, and in an undertone he asked, "Rokni, do you hear something far, far away?"

I said, "No, I don't hear anything, Khan Papa Doctor."

"Listen carefully. See if you do."

I listened for a moment. Then I turned up my palms and said, "I swear by the Lord of the faithful, I don't hear so much as a fly. I only wondered why you wanted to talk to me."

He gestured for me to leave, saying, "First I have to wash. Come to the library in half an hour and I'll tell you."

Then he disappeared in the darkness of the orangery. I thought to myself how old age had changed his character. He behaved more like the Sardar Azhdari side of the family. He had become pale, melancholy, loose-lipped, and talked a lot of nonsense. His words would have sounded like gibberish even to a monkey.

As I was heading toward my room, I pricked up my ears and listened to the mysterious sounds of our old house. In my mind, I heard the flapping of a handful of wild birds.

When I entered the library, I was surprised. There were hardly any books on the shelves. The rugs had been rolled and they were leaning against the pillar near the dais. The floor was cluttered with cardboard boxes, bundles of old magazines, and lithograph books. He had found most of those books in the Shah's Mosque bookstores, in dusty storerooms that had never seen the light of day, and he'd spent a great deal of money on every one of them. Some of them were sent to him from India, Turkey, and Egypt— books about alchemy, botany, the summoning of spirits, and secret societies; books with strange Arabic titles like *Treasures of Secrets, Gardens of the Horrified,* Meghdadi's *Secrets of Numbers,* and *The Deleted Beginning.*

The twenty-pound dictionary lay open on his desk, next to the lamp with its shade from the Naser ed din Shah period. The lamplight yellowed the page with a circle the size of a palm. A cigarette butt that had just been stubbed out was smoking in a china ashtray. The ashtray was a high-heeled shoe that my Khan Papa Doctor's father, the late Heshmat Nezam, had brought for his wife, the Lady of Ladies, as a present from his last trip to Austria. Now, why he had brought an ashtray for the Lady of Ladies, who wouldn't even touch a cigarette to her lips, was beyond anybody's comprehension. We didn't dare ask Khan Papa Doctor about it, either. He wasn't the type to put up with any curiosity about the past.

I looked around at the walls and doors. Nothing had changed in that house for a century. Anyone else in Khan Papa Doctor's place, with his position and influence, would long ago have built a chic, new-style house on Pahlavi Street and put two of the latest-model cars in the garage and married a modern European wife. But my Khan Papa Doctor insisted that nothing should change in the house of his forefathers. Still the photographs of the late Sardar Azhdar and the late Heshmat Nezam remained on the walls behind the dais. The only new ornament in the library was Khan Papa Doctor's own full-length photograph above the mantel, the one that he'd had taken in his youth before his marriage to Homayundokht, God forgive her soul—wearing a wool Cossack hat and his military uniform, with a cape on his shoulders and his hand on the hilt of his sword. He was staring at a corner of the veranda as if he'd been called unexpectedly. His expression revealed a sort of absent-mindedness that was seldom seen on the face of a Heshmat Nezami. I stepped forward and stood in front of his photo. It came as a surprise; I said, "Good Lord, how much he takes after his late father! They're like two halves of an apple; they don't differ by a hair."

Steps approached from the hall behind me. I turned, shifting the paper tube I carried. It was Khan Papa Doctor. He was standing in the middle of his office doorway, slowly taking off his surgical gloves. He was still wearing a white coat, but this was a clean one, starched and ironed. From beneath the hollow arches of his eyebrows he fixed me with his gaze—a cold, magnetic, penetrating gaze that made him look distant and unreachable. I thought he might finally have decided to start talking about his marriage to his first wife, the late Homayundokht, God forgive her soul.

He came closer, with easy, sauntering steps. When he reached the center of the library, he threw the rubber gloves on his desk. He took a cigarette from a drawer and lit it with the gold lighter he'd brought from Germany. He blew into my face the voluminous, dense smoke of his first puff. He sat calmly in his chair, leaned back, and looked at me. Maybe because I was in a weak position, maybe because I was nervous, I smiled foolishly. I unrolled my sketch on the desk and said, "Here."

With a snap of his thumb, he flipped cigarette ashes into the late Heshmat Nezam's ashtray. He said, "Here what?"

I said, "I made this for you."

I showed him the sketch of the legendary bird Simorgh. He stubbed out his cigarette, leaned forward, and examined the sketch. He became absorbed and ran a finger around the outline of the bird. When he reached Simorgh's wide wings, he looked up and said, "These are flames, aren't they?"

I said, "What do you mean, flames, Khan Papa Doctor?"

"They say it burns up and then a thousand chicks will rise from its ashes."

"That's a phoenix. This one's Simorgh. Simorgh of Mount Ghoff. When it spreads its wings, the sky turns blue. When it opens its eyes, the sun or the moon shines."

I stretched out my arms like two wings, as if I were Simorgh circling the sky on my own, revolving and sightseeing and harming no one. My Khan Papa Doctor frowned and set aside the sketch. He stood up and started walking among the bookshelves with his hands clasped behind him. There were a few old books remaining. He lifted them off the shelves, dusted them, and put them in cardboard boxes. He was distracted and paid me no attention. I took my life in my hands and asked, "Didn't you send a message for me to come to the library?"

He paused and nodded. "Have patience," he said.

"Are you pleased with my sketch? Do you still say painting and sculpting won't make my bread and butter? Do you still think I'm wasting my life?"

"Rokni, stop this foolishness," he said. The tone of his voice had changed. His words echoed through the empty library as if he were talking in a Turkish bath. He gestured for me to sit on the leather chair in front of his desk. Without a care in my head I sat down, hoping he wanted to talk about Homayundokht, God forgive her soul. In recent weeks he had been behaving as though he was searching for a confidant. As though, finally, he was tired of thinking about Homayundokht, God rest her soul, and of all the events in the past. As though he wanted to open a conversation. But I knew I should watch myself. I should stay alert and act rational so I wouldn't annoy him. He set his heavy fists on the desk. He leaned forward and said, "I want to tell you something very important. Listen carefully."

I said, "All right, Khan Papa Doctor. Whatever you say."

He was silent. He looked disheveled, and the Heshmat Nezami confidence had gone from his eyes. The lamplight carved deep lines in his face so that he seemed awesome, like Boris Karloff. In a hushed, intimate tone he said, "Rokni, this afternoon I stopped practicing medicine. I've examined my last patient and lanced my last boil. Do you hear me?"

Humbly I said, "I'm listening."

He said, "Today is the last day of the month of Khordad. Isn't it?"

"Yes."

"I want to go to Ghaleh Bagh and look after my herb garden. I want to get away from here and spend all my time discovering an anticancer medicine. In ancient Iran they had a cure for cancer that's lost now, it's gone. . . ."

With a stroke of his hand he emphasized "gone." He pushed the dictionary toward me and with a palsied finger showed me pictures of wormwood, Mary's palm, Roman anise, and sweet marjoram. "The cure for cancer is among these plants. There are secrets in these herbs that nobody knows. Nobody understands them. Only the ancient Iranians guessed their uses. They knew long ago that the cure for cancer is not in the knife. You have to get to know cancer to uncover its mystery and halt it."

His eyes glittered. He looked at me triumphantly. Then he went to the next room and brought back a few small sugar pouches. These pouches were filled with the herbs he'd grown. He held one of them above my head and ordered, "Smell it, Rokni. See what kind of mood comes over you."

I said, "What is it, Khan Papa Doctor?"

He said, "Never mind. Put your nose close to the pouch and breathe deeply."

I rose from the leather chair to a half-standing position. I closed my eyes. I drew in a breath and waited for the effect. All of a sudden, in that hundred-degree summer heat I felt a kind of damp, sticky chill raising goose bumps on my arms. I thought, What if he wants to poison me? What if he's gone mad? Though this kind of personality change is very rare among the Heshmat Nezamis, anything is possible. It's the Sardar Azhdaris who have passionate dispositions. At around age thirty the hereditary melancholia afflicts their minds; their deaths occur on Thursdays that are even-numbered days of the month on the lunar calendar.

My Khan Papa Doctor said, "How are you feeling, Rokni?"

I said, "I don't know how to describe it for you."

"Aren't you getting dizzy?"

It's true, I was. I said, "Oh, my Lord, yes. My head is light as cotton, a puff of cotton. I'm spinning like a pinwheel. But I feel fine; there's nothing wrong with me. How cool it's turned in the library! Look how hollow and distorted the furniture has grown. What air, what cool and pleasant air—chilled and thin and brittle, just like a sheet of glass."

He said, "Prick up your ears and see if you hear the sound of singing far, far away."

I said, "Oh, my Lord, yes. How clearly I hear it, Khan Papa Doctor! Someone is singing far, far away. Oh, my Lord, that's not it. Someone is whistling. How well he's whistling, too! Like my

Cousin Masoud who used to go to the head of the alley every evening and lean against the lamppost and whistle for the neighbor girls. Do you remember, Khan Papa Doctor?"

He said, "Of course I remember."

I said, "Do you remember Homayundokht, God forgive her soul? After thirty-odd years, do you still think of her?"

I was speaking without fear now. I was picking up speed. I remembered the picture taken in Petersburg of Homayundokht, God forgive her soul, with her Dear Daddy, the late Mirza Yousef —the white shawl around her naked shoulders, and her pitchblack hair tossed and spreading on the lilac-white skin at the back of her neck, her swooning gaze turned to the sky. The photographer's backdrop shows a gray jetty in a stormy, raging sea. They have put a rattan chair in front of waves that are foaming at the mouth and tearing at their chains, and on the chair they've set Homayundokht, God forgive her soul, who is no older than thirteen.

My Khan Papa Doctor was taken aback by my question. He couldn't seem to think of an answer. I insisted: "Well, Khan Papa Doctor? What are you worried about?"

He set aside the sugar pouch. He sat down and said, "You puppy dog! This meddling doesn't become you."

I said, "Why not?"

"I asked you here so we could talk about your half brother Zia."

I was thunderstruck. I hadn't expected this. I opened my mouth but couldn't speak. He grumbled, "How come you've stopped talking?"

"You swore you'd never utter the name of my Khan Brother Zia," I said.

In protest, he raised both hands and said, "There has to be at least one person who will look after our business, who won't allow that inheritance we gathered with our heart's blood to get lost. When I go to Ghaleh Bagh, who will there be to care? The Sardar Azhdaris? Like hell they will. You, Your Excellency? You've always got your head up your ass. Who's left, then? Obviously, your Khan Brother Zia. He may be stubborn as a mule, can't tell up from down, acts like a donkey, but he's a Heshmat Nezami. He gets things done, and he doesn't allow anyone to stick it to him."

It dawned on me that our lives were changing, that there was more here than met the eye. I stammered, "It's eleven years since we've seen a trace of him. We don't know where he is. May God cut my tongue off, cut it off, but what if he's deceased?"

He lowered his head in his hands and reflected. "I've thought of that myself. Some people say he's been executed. Some people say he's at large, has changed his name, is driving a truck in the south. Others say he's still in prison. But I know he's alive. It's been proven to me, and I don't give these rumors the attention I'd give a dog."

I said, "How has it been proven to you?"

He broke into a chuckle and said, "Maybe you won't believe this. I've seen him in my dreams. For two weeks now, I've dreamed about him regularly, every night, Rokni. All my dreams are the same. It's as though once again we've gone on that trip to Nishapur. In front of the house, there's a carriage parked. It's New Year's and the late Homayundokht is straightening your Khan Brother Zia's sailor suit for the traditional visits to relatives. Then there's a knock on the door. When I open it, Big Cousin Mirza Hassibi pokes his head from the carriage. I put your Khan Brother Zia in the carriage. I sense that the late Homayundokht is watching with anxiety. I feel uneasy and I tell myself, Well, she's a mother; she has the right; she can't part with her child. I want to take your Khan Brother Zia off the carriage and give him to her, but the carriage starts moving. Big Cousin Mirza Hassibi motions for us to come aboard. What are we waiting for? I point to the late Homayundokht and shout, 'Mirza, Mirza, we can't, we can't . . .'"

He fell silent. He lowered his head and stared into my eyes. "Do you remember Mirza Hassibi?"

"No."

"It's been a long time since I've seen him. He seldom shows himself. I have no idea where he is. You know, Rokni? It's as if everybody's gone. But there's something in the Heshmat Nezamis that will last forever. It only has to be looked after and protected. Your Khan Brother Zia, with all his obstinacy, would never allow these things to blow away. He'll come back. You must search for him. You must ask this person and that. Masoud was saying that on his trip to the south he saw your Khan Brother Zia. He knows something about him. Recently, Masoud himself has been invisible. That cuckold never keeps his feet in one place. Otherwise, he could find your Khan Brother Zia, even if it meant pulling a few strings. After all, Masoud's a Sardar Azhdari. The Sardar Azhdaris always have their hands in every bowl of henna."

"People say Masoud's in smuggling now," I said. "He goes to Kuwait. He smuggles back American suits, cigarettes, suede vests, and jeans."

My Khan Papa Doctor put on his reading glasses. From behind the lenses his eyes appeared wider and more watery. He stood up and came over to me. He set his hands on my shoulders and looked at me with an expression of discouragement. He shook my shoulders and said, "Now, wake up. You ass, the world is washing away and here you sit with your dreams. From now on, no more playacting. Nothing's going to be helped by those weird masks you put on your face, or those artificial beards. We don't have much time. We can't take our family lightly. It's a pity, Rokni. Listen to me. It's a pity."

He straightened and turned to leave the library.

"Was that all you wanted to talk to me about?" I asked.

He nodded. "That was it."

I said, "What about the story of Homayundokht, God forgive her soul?"

He didn't answer. With shuffling steps, he left the library. I turned my head, and through the window I saw my mother, my Bee Bee, and my half sister Iran following after my Khan Papa Doctor like a pair of pull toys.

I felt tired. The cool, dusty smell of the sugar pouch was still in my nostrils. The furniture in the library looked alive and uncanny. Everything was hunting for an excuse to unlock its tongue and share a confidence with me. But the silence continued, and the only sound was the grinding teeth of a solitary mouse, sawing away at the dark of the night behind the empty bookshelves.

It was clear I had to look for Masoud.

2

After the last few years, facing Masoud didn't much appeal to me. But in spite of all our childhood fights, we couldn't break our ties completely. It seemed to be our destiny that either I search for him or he for me. Even the plays we used to stage were based on that. He always played characters whose underhandedness my own characters relied upon; yet at the same time these characters couldn't get along. If I were the late Shah Sardar Sepah, he was Sardar Sepah's prime minister, Sayed Zia. If I were Shah Anushirvan the Just, he was the Shah's grand vizier, Buzar Jomehr the Wise. Then we got our high school diplomas, went our separate ways, and didn't see each other till the middle of last fall, when his head emerged from the water and, everywhere I went, he grew in front of me in the street like a weed. He wanted to talk, but I didn't give him the chance.

One time in Sarcheshmeh, I exploded, "Masoud, I don't have time to talk! I like to walk in the street alone."

He answered, surprised, "Didn't you promise we'd go south together and find your Khan Brother Zia?"

"That was a few years ago. Now I don't feel like it. Get yourself another traveling companion."

"You Heshmat Nezamis are never in the mood for anyone. You put on a high hat for everyone."

I didn't answer. I ducked into Lazarian's and slugged down beer until the tiredness left me and I felt better and was sure Masoud was gone. Then, through the foggy window, I caught sight of him. He had turned up the collar of his raincoat. He had stuffed his hands in his trouser pockets, and from his half-open mouth the steam of his breath was twisting and knotting in the cold, wet air of autumn. With barely contained hunger, he fixed his sunken eyes on me. I waited till he glanced away. Soundlessly, I slipped through the back door and lost myself in the narrow alleys behind the mosque. I was free of him. When I reached the Curb of Shemiran I saw him again, standing under the lamppost in front of the Women's Hospital. In the dark of the night, he was whistling. He was whistling in the Scale of Shur, and as soon as he saw me he stopped. As I passed, he leaned forward and said, "How are you, Rokni? Are you feeling all right?"

I said, "Not bad. It's getting late. I have to find a cab and go home."

He said, "Never mind about me, but don't you want to come visit my Dear Daddy? He asks about you all the time. He says, 'Where is Rokni?' "

I said, "Give my regards to Uncle Abdolbaghi. Tell him I'll come see him very soon."

Then I set off again in a hurry. From a hundred paces away, I heard his whistling begin once again. He was whistling the Chekavak Corner of the Scale of Homayun. When he reached the Bee-Dad Corner, he started twittering like a nightingale—a constant, massaging twitter that polished the wet street. I felt guilty. Maybe I shouldn't have acted so cold and distant.

It occurred to me that night that much of the split between the children of Heshmat Nezam and the children of Sardar Azhdar was meaningless; it was all a masquerade. There'd been fifty years of bad feeling between Agha Heshmat Nezam and Agha Sardar Azhdar over the late Prime Minister Vosugh el Doleh's concessions to the British. It started at the festival of the thirteenth day of the New Year, when everyone had gathered at the family cemetery. They were busy with chitchat when Agha Heshmat Nezam descended from his carriage in his military uniform and went straight to the late Sardar Azhdar and shouted, "Honorable Brother! I wish our honorable late father could stick his head out of his grave and see that Your Excellency is putting this country in the hands of foreigners for a lousy ten thousand tumans! Agha, what do you feel attached to? What is important to you?"

People say that, because of his deafness, the late Sardar Azhdar didn't hear a word the late Heshmat Nezam said; but then the late Agha Ass Dass Dolah whispered something in the late Sardar Azhdar's ear that split the two brothers forever, as well as the brothers' children. You could see this split in the random photographs Mirza Hassibi had taken of their weddings, their funerals, and the thirteenth days of the New Year. In one corner the two sisters, Great Pride and Superior Venus, the first-ranking grandchildren of the late Sardar Azhdar, sit on openwork metal lawn chairs in the middle of their inherited courtyard. Each of them clutches a nosegay in her fists and gazes so hard at the camera that her eyes are widened. Their late father, Agha Ass Dass Dolah, with an unturbaned head, a Yazdi robe hanging aslant from his shoulders, leans on his cherry cane and admires the two sisters from a distance with a poetic smile. A little farther away, the late Aunt Lady Najafi and her insane husband, Sayed Kazem, the owner of *The Book of Divine Graces,* sit next to the samovar. All around them, Heshmat Nezamis and Sardar Azhdaris and Hamedani Sadats are swarming like ants and grasshoppers. And behind them Homayundokht, God forgive her soul, with her head bare, in her white lace gown, is stretched on the lawn under the walnut tree examining her fingernails. Aunt Lady Badi Zaman, the interpreter of the Koran, employed by Radio Tehran, with her hair cut *à la garçon* and her French cap and broadcloth suit and black tie that make her look like a classroom monitor, has drawn herself up as if to deliver her Friday night sermon. At the left, the Heshmat Nezami ladies are gathered and their gazes, full of pity, fall upon the giddy, coquettish face of Homayundokht, God forgive her soul. It seems they might at any moment move their lips and express their regrets that the daughter of Mirza Yousef had set herself on fire in front of relatives and strangers and her own little daughter Iran, all because of an insignificant quarrel with her obstinate, military husband.

Even now, after some thirty-odd years, they still talked about it as though it had happened yesterday. They had never given any thought to the children of Homayundokht, God forgive her soul, and used to melodramatically describe the onion and garlic of that story in front of my Khan Brother Zia and my sister Iran as though those two were deaf and couldn't hear them. Not only my Khan Brother Zia, who understood a good many things, but even my feeble-minded sister Iran grasped what they were saying. When you looked into Iran's face it would occur to you that still, after some thirty-odd years, she was staring at that scene with the eyes of a three-year-old child. As long as she lived and breathed, her gaze would be branded by that scene. It carved a vacant space around her with an invisible chisel and created in her face a contradiction of childishness and age, of thickheadedness and shrewdness.

But what about my Khan Brother Zia? No matter how well I remembered him, I still couldn't imagine what went on in his mind. In the photo, he looks distant and apologetic. He is sitting on a stool. He has placed one heel on his knee. He leans his elbow against a pillar, tilts his head in the hollow of his palm, and fixes his eyes upon a corner of the sky as though he were about to start singing. The entire background of sky is black except for the corner that my Khan Brother Zia is watching. That corner is yellowed like votive candles, like congealed beads of fat on a bowl of soup. It seems he wants to open his mouth and tell me something but his tongue is tied.

In my heart I said, Oh, God, what's wrong with me? I can get moving and go look for him and ask for clues from this person and that. Eleven years is a long time, but still I have him in mind. A handful of memories and cluttered images rushed into my head. I stood up and left the library.

Since it was late in the evening, I abandoned the idea of calling Masoud. There was no hurry. Maybe tomorrow he would come to the School of Art, or I would run into him in the street. I felt he was loitering somewhere near me. He was passing shadowlike among the trees. I was sure I would find him eventually. Either he would search for me or I for him.

In the courtyard, my Bee Bee sat next to Iran watching television. They were broadcasting news of killings and a bomb explosion in the bazaar. There wasn't a trace of my Khan Papa Doctor. No doubt he'd gone to his office again, or perhaps he was inspecting his crossbred roses in the garden. Then I noticed that Iran's eyes were on me. She was genuinely looking at me. At the same time there spun, behind her pearly and unchanging gaze, a moving pattern of dreams and thoughts and feelings. I bent down and whispered in her ear, "Iran-jun, do you hear my voice?"

I thought she did. From the way she was looking at me, I felt she could see me better than anyone else could. She was screwing questions into me with her drilling gaze. She was asking strange questions I knew the answers to but couldn't explain. My Bee Bee noticed. She turned her head and looked at me curiously. I raised my shoulders, as if confessing to this clumsiness. She poured me a glass of tea and put the sugar bowl in front of me. I said, "Bee Bee-jun."

She said, "Now what?"

"Has my Khan Papa Doctor talked to you too?"

"Of course."

"What did you say?"

"Your Khan Papa Doctor will do what he has to. Maybe you can't see his purpose now, but you will later. There's a time for everything."

"I'm afraid that hunting my Khan Brother Zia won't have a happy ending."

She smiled and said, "Rokni, you with your natural gifts will succeed at whatever you tackle. You're not an ordinary person."

"What if I can't find him?"

"Don't let them discourage you. Don't listen to the Sardar Azhdaris. It's not important to them. They say, 'Shit on the grave of the world.' They say, 'Seize the moment.' But you're not bitter and pushy like them. Go after your brother. It's God you should rely on."

I bent my head and started to drink my tea. A fairy lamp was burning in the vestibule. The servant, Zahra Soltan, was sitting on the bench in front of the kitchen, rubbing her swollen knees with goat lard and sarcocolla. In that old house, everything had the look of something left behind forever, like the cloth bundles in the dressing room of a Turkish bath. Even the walls were longing for movement, and the building seemed about to uproot itself and take off.

I stood up and started walking. I looked at the tiled wall in front of the basement. The late Sardar Azhdar had brought those tiles from Ghom, but after he was removed from office and retired, he couldn't pay for them. The Sardar Azhdaris circulated a rumor that the agha's enemies were jealous of him, that it was they who put the banana peel under his foot and made a scandal of him. As his son-in-law, Agha Ass Dass Dolah, said, "They forced the old man to face the wall."

Anyone could testify that the late Sardar Azhdar's sleight-of-hand and magic shows were much more interesting than those of the most famous magician of his day, Mirza Malkam Khan. The late Sardar Azhdar put a pearl-handled revolver in a sugar pouch and attacked it with a sugar hammer till it was completely shattered. Then, with two of his pen-shaped fingers, he held the sugar pouch in midair and, like Mashd Abbas the bonesetter, he caused the broken pieces to be reassembled in the presence of His Majesty, the Mecca of the Universe himself. He took the revolver from the sugar pouch, whole and untouched, and put it on the blessed palm of His Majesty.

The Mecca of the Universe could not contain his delight. Unexpectedly, he jumped from his seat and embraced the late Sardar Azhdar and kissed his cheeks. He gave him a hat wound around with a scarf, a cashmere cloak, curly-toed shoes, and a robe of honor. The Mecca of the Universe made all the members of the Humanity Society envious. They started ridiculing the late Sardar Azhdar, saying he wasn't worth the smallest fingernail of the stupidest student of Mirza Malkam Khan. Then they invited him to repeat his magic show in a cabinet meeting. The old man was over eighty. He didn't catch the scent of trouble. He didn't know they'd rubbed soap on the soles of his feet and dampened his know-how, his magic skills.

Aping Mirza Malkam Khan, he came one hour later than the

appointed time. All the ministers took their watches from their vest pockets and showed them to the late Sardar Azhdar, asking the reason for his delay. The late Sardar Azhdar, swollen with pride and haughtiness, smiled contemptuously and said that there was no delay. He said it was better for the gentlemen to toss their watches into a toilet and instead buy a Lari rooster to wake them every dawn for morning prayers with its cockle-doodle-doo. To demonstrate his claim, he threw all the hapless watches into the famous sugar pouch and attacked them with the sugar hammer. He hit them without ceasing. When he had finished the job, he used every trick and skill he knew for a full three hours, trying to reassemble the watches. But each time he opened the sugar pouch, sweat covered his forehead as he saw all those broken bits of glass, those bent and crooked gears and loose springs. He was about to collapse when the prime minister, the Lord Amin o Soltan, set His Excellency on his donkey with the help of the footmen. They put the order of removal from office underneath his arm and sent him home.

A few years later, the fall of Vosugh el Doleh's Cabinet added insult to injury, and the late Sardar Azhdar never set foot outside his house again. He also stopped reading the books by Flammarion and summoning the spirits, and he did no work. But four days before his death, he was struck again by the urge to stage his magic shows and jugglery. He took the notorious sugar hammer from under his mattress and went running to the orangery. He found the statue of His Majesty which he had set in front of the rose garden many years before. With his sugar hammer, he broke it to pieces. When he had finished, he threw the sugar hammer in the middle of the rose garden and went straight to his bed. He pulled the edge of the quilt over his nose and until Thursday, which was the day of his passing, he didn't say a word to anyone.

In the dark, I realized that I had arrived in front of my Khan Brother Zia's room. They had sealed it, just as they had sealed the room of Homayundokht, God forgive her soul. In the hundred years since the time of the Martyred Shah, it had become a tradition for our family to seal the rooms of those among us who were unfulfilled prisoners of the earth—those who, to quote Agha Ass Dass Dolah, had "untimely hid their faces behind the veil of dust." The glass panes in the door of my brother's room were dark and opaque. Nothing inside was visible. I put my hand on the door and got a surprise. The door was open. They had broken the seal. Surely this was by order of my Khan Papa Doctor. It was impossible to break the seals of those rooms without his permission. Maybe he wanted to let me know indirectly that he was allowing me inside his private life. Maybe he wanted to make a confidant of me, just for himself.

When I entered the room of my Khan Brother Zia, a strange smell hit my nose—a smell like an old water house, or a pool that has recently been drained. It was as though someone you couldn't see was living there. I turned on the light. The closet door was half open. Inside, my Khan Brother Zia had thumbtacked a picture of himself and Mademoiselle Sonia. Mademoiselle Sonia wore her canary-yellow cloak. My Khan Brother Zia had on his military officer's uniform—no doubt the same uniform whose price he had extracted from my Khan Papa Doctor. What a production he had made over that uniform! No matter how he approached the subject, my Khan Papa Doctor's answer was always the same: "What do you want from me, Zia? Any sane and sensible person would first go through compulsory military service and *then* think of buying an officer's uniform."

My Khan Brother Zia was furious. He ran to the library. He brought Khan Papa Doctor's money box to the veranda, but try as he would, he couldn't open the lock. Then, somehow, he found the sugar hammer of the late Sardar Azhdar, and he flung himself at the box with that. Bronze powder and black enamel flew everywhere, but the lid wouldn't open. He went to the library and came back with the pearl-handled revolver. He held the revolver to my Khan Papa Doctor's belly and forced him to unlock the box. Without a trace of embarrassment or shame, he took a fistful of bills from the box and stuffed them into his pocket. When he was through, he hit the street and didn't even shut the door behind him. My Khan Papa Doctor was so angry that if you'd stuck him with a knife he wouldn't have bled.

The officer's uniform is very becoming to my Khan Brother Zia. It suits his tall body. He rests his elbow on Mademoiselle Sonia's shoulder and holds his officer's hat between his fingers. He is smiling his famous smile at the camera. Behind them, the statue of the Angel of Liberty is stretching toward the sky, and behind that the statue of Baharestan.

As I opened his desk drawer, I saw his old album. Pictures of his favorite movie stars from his high school days were pasted into it—Ingrid Bergman, Greer Garson, Gregory Peck. In the middle of the album was another picture of Mademoiselle Sonia that I hadn't seen before. She is wearing a knitted angora blouse. She turns her head over the curve of her shoulder and smiles a lovely, self-possessed smile. Her face shines with cleanliness, as though she's just come from her bath. Underneath this picture, my Khan Brother Zia had written in his broken handwriting:

> To you who trust and love me,
> To you who are pure and honorable,
> To you, the guest of my empty days.
>   Zia

The pictures on the last four pages had been removed. In their places, dark gray squares were left like a row of vacant windows open to the autumn sky. At the bottom of the final page, my Khan Brother Zia had scrawled a verse from *Rumi:*

> Is there anyone insane enough not to go insane?
> Anyone who sees the head constable and doesn't
>   duck back in his house?

When I first saw my Khan Brother Zia in Mademoiselle Sonia's sports car I couldn't believe it. I said, That's not my Khan Brother Zia. It's some stranger who wants to mold himself in my brother's image. I couldn't believe that, after all the critical and sarcastic remarks the others had made, he would pick up Mademoiselle Sonia and bring her to our house for the New Year's visit. For a full three months my Bee Bee and Khan Papa Doctor had been talking about him every night at dinner. My Bee Bee begged and insisted, but my Khan Papa Doctor stood his ground. He swore he wouldn't let Mademoiselle Sonia enter our house.

"That little Polish slut isn't worthy of us. She's ten years older than that thick-necked boy. A Heshmat Nezami could never get

along with an older wife, especially Zia, who doesn't even kowtow
to God."

My Bee Bee said, "Doctor, all this mischief is just because he's
young and without a wife. He doesn't have anyone to look after
him, to pull him together."

My Khan Papa Doctor said, "Miss Asiah, try to imagine that
this boy is basically not ours, that we never had him to begin with.
Imagine that there is no Zia, that he has perished."

My Bee Bee said, "Doctor, I beg you in the name of my ancestor the Prophet, stop talking this way. It's unlucky."

I was petrified. What had happened? What incident had taken
place? Why didn't Mademoiselle Sonia leave my Khan Brother
Zia alone?

Mademoiselle Sonia was sitting behind the wheel, and it was
she who drove the sports car down the narrow alley. She drove as
slowly as if she were conveying a bride. As they passed me, Mademoiselle Sonia's perfume filled the air and a few men came out of
the grocery store to watch. My Khan Brother Zia was unper-
turbed. Content and in good humor, he puffed on his cigarette.
The sunlight spread everywhere and the gentle spring breeze
sprinkled the fragrance of tulips and hyacinths.

They parked the sports car in front of our house. My Khan
Brother Zia opened the car door for Mademoiselle Sonia. His eyes
fell on me and he raised both arms. I rushed toward him and
threw myself into his embrace. He lifted me from the ground and
spun me around in a full circle. He said, "How're you doing, silly
little Rokni?"

I said, "I'm fine, Khan Brother Zia."

He showed me to Mademoiselle Sonia and said, "This is that
silly little Rokni I told you about."

Mademoiselle Sonia beamed a beautiful smile that made dim-
ples in her cheeks. I knew who she was immediately, but I was too
shy to let on. She herself started the conversation—actually, she
opened her purse and took out a Nestlé's chocolate bar and gave it
to me. I accepted it, and she folded her arms and looked her fill at
me. My Khan Brother Zia cupped a hand under my artificial
beard and asked, "Who are you now?"

I said, "I'm the ex-Prime Minister Sayed Zia. I've struck a deal with the British, and with your permission I also plan to make a small and useful coup d'état."

He didn't say a word. He only grinned. He reached into the back seat of the car and brought forth a musical instrument. "Well, Mr. Sayed Zia, this is for you," he said.

I asked, "What is it?"

"It's a mandolin."

He pretended to play it. I said, "I don't know how to play a mandolin."

He lost patience. He threw up a hand and said, "It's an Italian mandolin; playing it's easy. Practice till you learn."

He gave me the mandolin, and I started running through the courtyard. I reached my Bee Bee, who was on the veranda reciting the shopping list to Zahra Soltan. I said, "Bee Bee, Bee Bee!"

She said, "What is it, dear?"

I said, "Here you sit idle, and my Khan Brother Zia has brought Mademoiselle Sonia for the New Year visit."

My Bee Bee slapped her face and said, "Oh, my dear father! Your Khan Papa Doctor is going to raise havoc. In a moment it will be Resurrection Day."

My Khan Brother Zia stood in front of the vestibule and yelled, "O Allah! O Allah! Where are the inhabitants of this house?"

Fearfully, my Bee Bee pulled her veil over her head. She said, "Agha Zia, we're honored by your visit. May there be a hundred such New Years! What a surprise that you remembered us."

My Khan Brother Zia set a gift box on the ground and hugged my Bee Bee. Then he introduced Mademoiselle Sonia. My Bee Bee stretched an indecisive, clumsy hand from her veil and shook Mademoiselle Sonia's hand. Like the two ends of a seesaw, they gave each other repeated and exaggerated bows.

As we started toward the library, my heart filled with anxiety. I was praying this wouldn't end in scandal.

In the library, my Khan Papa Doctor was offering a box of Yazdi baklava to Mrs. Motlagh and her daughter Farideh. With nervous smiles, they declined. Then Mademoiselle Sonia entered. She unbuttoned her cloak, opened it, and took it off. As my Khan Papa Doctor caught sight of her, he set the box of baklava on the table. He put on his reading glasses and examined her. Then his eyes fell on my Khan Brother Zia, who had just come in. A smile appeared on my Khan Papa Doctor's face. He asked, "Is that you, Zia?"

My Khan Brother Zia put his gift box on the telephone table and approached him. They threw their arms around each other and gave each other long, hearty kisses on both cheeks, as though they'd been awaiting this moment for thirty years without a wink of sleep. Then my Khan Brother Zia turned around and introduced Mademoiselle Sonia. Mademoiselle Sonia gave a sweet, flirtatious smile. She held out her hand for my Khan Papa Doctor. Exactly like a German general, my Khan Papa Doctor clicked his heels, bent, took Mademoiselle Sonia's fingertips, and kissed the back of her hand. Such a European gesture from him was unprecedented; I couldn't remember ever seeing him exhibit so much etiquette. We were all astounded. None of us moved from our places. My Khan Papa Doctor broke the silence and said, in the accent of a Tehran hoodlum, *"Bon jour, mademoiselle!"*

Mademoiselle Sonia tossed her cloak onto the arm of a heavy chair, and with her sweet smile she answered in Persian, "You're very well, Agha. You are honored, Agha. Me wish you a happy New Year."

My Khan Papa Doctor was surprised. He raised his eyebrows with delight, he drew himself up on tiptoe and threw admiring glances at Mademoiselle Sonia and all those present. He sat down next to her and started talking in formal Persian. "This person, both on his own behalf and on behalf of the other members of the respected Heshmat Nezami family, sends you and all your respected Polish relatives good wishes for this auspicious, ancient, traditional celebration. From the time of antiquity, it has been a tradition in our country to pay homage to plants, light, and the health of the body. In other words, just as the Western world grants importance to money and material matters, we the ancient Iranians granted, are granting, and will continue to grant importance to religious principles, ethical values, the love of humanity, the care of foreigners . . ."

He pronounced each word and stretched it out so Mademoiselle Sonia could understand its significance. At the end of every word, he marked time with his hand for emphasis. He went on and on and on, and his speech grew more and more complicated. It grew so complicated that he couldn't even pay attention to Mrs. Motlagh and Farideh. Mrs. Motlagh tried not to show her discomfort. With an artificial smile, she observed the conversation as though listening to an invisible radio. Farideh sat sideways on her chair, her back half turned to my Khan Brother Zia, and with a pouting glance she searched the bookshelves for something.

My Khan Papa Doctor suddenly stood up. He rubbed his hands together like a Park Hotel waiter and said, "How about a drink before lunch, in honor of this auspicious and ancient occasion?"

Without waiting for a reply, he offered his arm to Mademoiselle Sonia. Mademoiselle Sonia tossed her golden hair and burst into high-pitched laughter. She took his arm, and with much pomp and pride both of them went to the dais. My Khan Papa Doctor opened the corner cupboard and brought out the late Heshmat Nezam's special bronze cordial service. He pressed a ramrod in the pitcher, and drink started pouring into crystal glasses from six tiny faucets around the base. He was about to offer one of the glasses to Mademoiselle Sonia when my Khan Brother Zia said, "First let me show you this gift, and then we'll drink to our health."

In a low voice, my Khan Papa Doctor said in my Khan Brother Zia's ear, "I've been to Europe and I'm familiar with European customs. The rule is that first you offer drinks."

In the middle of all this, Mrs. Motlagh and Farideh suddenly stood up and said a hasty good-bye to everyone. My Khan Papa Doctor asked, "Why so early? Stay for lunch."

Mrs. Motlagh answered, "Some other time, God willing, Mr. Doctor. We have to go other places too, to pay our New Year visits."

They left the library in a hurry. With their departure, my Khan Papa Doctor completely forgot about everyone but Mademoiselle Sonia. He lifted two crystal glasses. He gave one to her and kept one for himself. They clinked their glasses and drank to the health of Poland and ancient Iran. Out of joy, he put his hand under Mademoiselle Sonia's elbow and led her on a tour of the bookshelves and told her things that were impossible to hear from a distance. When they arrived in front of the gramophone of Homa-yundokht, God forgive her soul, he cranked it up for Mademoi-selle Sonia and put on Badi Zadeh's "Fall Is Here" and made her listen with silence and attention. Then, to show that he was mind-ful of Mademoiselle Sonia's Western tastes, he changed the disk and put on one of Nelson Eddy and Jeanette MacDonald. As soon as the tremulous, screamlike twitters of Jeanette MacDonald be-gan to rise, he grinned and again lifted his glass to the health of ancient Iran and Poland.

My Khan Brother Zia had already opened the gold wrappings of his gift. Inside was a blue velvet box. He took the box to my Khan Papa Doctor and lifted the lid. The box contained a com-plete set of silver knives, spoons, and forks. My Khan Papa Doc-tor glanced at them in a perfunctory way. He waved his hand and said, "Well, well, God bless you, it's a delight to my eyes. What a service! What a beautiful service! Give it to Miss Asiah so she can hide it in the closet."

Then he put his hand on Mademoiselle Sonia's shoulder. "I myself, before the war, imported a silver service from Germany. You are Polish and have been to Europe, you know better than I. The services they used to make in those days, the days of Ger-many before the war, were very different from what they make now. The one I imported was made by the Schultz factory, which was regrettably bombed by the Allies later. No doubt you know that whatever was worth anything got bombed by the Allies."

My Khan Brother Zia dropped his gift box on the table. He took my hand and pulled me out of the library. He said nothing to me, and I wouldn't have dared ask him anything. Under the warm, dizzying spring sunshine, he sat on the veranda railing and looked out at the flower beds, in which a wide variety of pansies was freshly planted and fertilized. I sat next to him and busied myself with playing the mandolin he had brought me. Through a window I could see my Khan Papa Doctor and Mademoiselle Sonia dancing in the center of the library, and Mademoiselle Sonia's yellow skirt puffed with each whirl like a canary's ruff. I was struck dumb; I couldn't think of a way to start my Khan Brother Zia talking. Finally I took courage and said, "Khan

Brother Zia, it's a long time since I've seen you. I've missed you very, very much."

He threw a sidelong glance at me that made me anxious. He took a cigarette from his silver case and lit a match with a stroke of a thumb and carelessly held it to the cigarette. Suddenly he screamed and jumped up like a firecracker and threw the match to the center of the courtyard. He had burned himself, and he was shaking his fingers with pain. It struck me how much he resembled Homayundokht, God forgive her soul—especially as she appeared in the photo taken during the last year of her life.

She is more mellowed in this photo than in the earlier ones. With her checkered veil spread on her shoulders, with her sleepy, tired eyes, she holds her head high in resignation. Her face is laced with premature lines, like cracked antique china. The lines create a kind of paradoxical mood—not exactly weary and yet not exactly fresh. No longer does she wear the witty, gay expression she used to have in the years before the Third of Pisces Coup d'Etat of 1921. She looks determined and serious, as though she listens to no one and her business is separate from other people's.

My Bee Bee came out to the courtyard and asked my Khan Brother Zia, "What happened, Agha?"

My Khan Brother Zia said, "Nothing much. I burned my thumb."

"Shall I bring cold water and soap to stop the pain?"

"No, thank you. It'll get better on its own."

"Please come in, then. Lunch is ready."

We went to the telephone room. A tablecloth was spread on the carpet. There was vegetable pilaf and fish for lunch. They had seated Iran at one corner of the cloth and placed before her a copper bowl of rice and fish. She picked up handfuls of rice and stuffed them hurriedly into her mouth, as though she couldn't wait. I couldn't understand why my Khan Brother Zia paid no attention to her. He rested his hand on the pillar of a molded plaster niche and stood waiting. My mother looked worried. She opened the door to the veranda and called her husband, "Doctor, Doctor!"

My Khan Papa Doctor's voice rose from the library. "What is it, Miss Asiah?"

"Lunch is ready. Please come."

After a few minutes, I heard Mademoiselle Sonia and my Khan Papa Doctor laughing in the hall. They entered together, tipsy and sweating. My Khan Papa Doctor begged Mademoiselle Sonia to occupy the head place at the table. Then he caught sight of Iran. He pulled himself up and asked my Bee Bee, irritably, "You have brought her here for what purpose? Tell Zahra Soltan to take her to her room and let her eat lunch there."

My Bee Bee said, "Doctor, Iran's not interfering with anything. She doesn't bother anyone. If she sits here with us and eats her lunch, what's the harm?"

"Miss Asiah, don't you see we have a guest—a stranger and a foreigner?"

Suddenly, my Khan Brother Zia stood up and opened the courtyard window wide. Then he came back and gathered the corners of the tablecloth, and with one shake he threw the table-cloth and all that was on it out the window. He gripped the wrist of Mademoiselle Sonia, who looked baffled, and he dragged her out across the courtyard. He heaved her through the street door and slammed it shut behind him.

My Bee Bee had become as pale as chalk and was trembling like a willow. It was obvious that the doggish temper of my Khan Papa Doctor had surfaced. Blood rushed into his face, and anger made his eyelids puffy. He shook his finger at my Bee Bee and said, "Never again let that mule into this house. Don't ever let me see that miserable face of his. If he sets his foot in this house again, I'll make sure that the biggest piece left of him will be his ear."

My Bee Bee caught her breath and said, "Doctor, for heaven's sake."

"Call me Doctor Snake Venom. Call me Doctor Pain and Illness."

"Don't say such things. He's your son, Doctor. He'll do himself some harm. Then you'll be sorry."

"Let him; it's one dog less."

Then, without eating lunch, my Khan Papa Doctor left the telephone room for the library. He locked the door behind him and pulled the shades down.

I hid; I didn't want anyone to notice me. Without deciding to, I went to my Khan Brother Zia's room. They hadn't sealed it yet. Inside the room, I stood in front of his closet mirror and looked at my own face; I don't know why. It seemed to me that my face with its tall and drumlike forehead, the round head, the bladelike nose, was a reminder of an animal violence—the boar claw that suddenly scratches.

I asked myself, now, what I was hunting in that room. On what business had I come? If I were going to find my Khan Brother Zia, I would have to hit the alley outside the old house.

This is the scene that seemed to appear in my mind: A patch of wet, heavy clouds rises before me. Somewhere far away, behind the Elburz Mountains or in the middle of the highway to Chalus, a thunderstorm is wetting the northern forests. In the dust of the storm I see the square black body of a carriage. The carriage driver is bent over, whip in hand, protecting his face from the wind with his sleeve. When he arrives in front of our house, he pulls back on the reins. He glances at my Khan Brother Zia, who is standing at the door in his sailor suit. As soon as my Khan Brother Zia sees the driver, he bursts out crying. The driver says, "Little Agha, this is not the time for crying. Hop up and let's go. Miss Homayundokht, your Bee Bee, has had something happen to her. We're going to take her to the holy shrine in Karbala."

My Khan Brother Zia swallows his tears and asks, "Then where is little Iran?"

"Your sister is feeling upset. We have to bring a doctor for her. When we bring him, he'll write a prescription and make her healthy and fat. Then you can see her, too."

They lift my Khan Brother Zia from the ground and place him in the carriage. The driver's whip snaps and the carriage moves away. As it fades into the dust and the whistling of the wind, the driver keeps turning his head and looking at my Khan Brother Zia with the filmed, malicious eyes of a beggar.

All my family used to say that I was an imagining person, that I believed whatever came to my mind. It was true. Eleven years ago, in fact, I imagined that I saw Homayundokht, God forgive her soul. It was when I was standing in front of the old fig tree. I looked through the dirty, cobwebbed windowpanes into the room of Homayundokht, God forgive her soul. I tried to make out the details of the alarm clock that her Dear Daddy, the late Mirza Yousef, had brought her from Petersburg. In the darkness, I couldn't see very well. I could just discern the vague, borderless outlines of the dolls that she herself had knitted with her own hands and arranged on the mantel with such artistry and good taste. A big copy of *The Queen of Birds* hung on the opposite wall. The Queen of Birds held her palms together and turned her passionate, innocent gaze upon the sky. And what pearl and emerald necklaces she wore on her white crystal neck, and what diamond and topaz rings on her slender hands! A paragon of beauty, popularity, and virtue.

Now, my family says this is just more of my showing off, something to make me seem dramatic—a self-indulgence, like my habit of talking as if I were reading from an ancient tale—but the truth of the matter is, that night eleven years ago I was inspired to take the hurricane lamp from the niche, climb the stairs, and go to the rooftop. In the middle of the stairs, I was overcome by the sensation of a presence. I felt goose bumps and a cold breeze on my skin. A few steps higher stood Homayundokht, God forgive her soul, with a green umbrella in her hand. I couldn't believe it. It knocked the wind out of me. For a twelve-year-old boy to be granted such a privilege? She wore a white lace gown and she raised the umbrella over her head and looked at me intensely. I gathered my voice and asked, "Homayundokht, is that you? Are we asleep? Are we awake? Where are we?"

She didn't answer. Just like a new bride who has painted her face with seven brushes, she went up the stairs and I followed. On the rooftop, we saw the sky decorated with half a million stars, dazzling our eyes. She beckoned to me. When I stepped forward, the smell of her lavender perfume made me giddy. She put her hand inside her glass bead purse, took out the dark mirror of the Master Assar, and held it up so she could watch the world with the eyes of a painter. What a strange mirror! All around it was enamelwork and jewel-studded patterns. And how elegantly Homayundokht, God forgive her soul, held its silver handle with those fingers which, in their satin gloves, looked white as snow! I told myself, Oh, my God, who am I to be in this royal court? She conveyed to me that I must seize the moment, that the nightingale had no more than an instant to sing. I didn't understand. I thought she wanted me to sing a song. I started singing, " 'Portrait maker and painter of china, go and see the face of my beloved . . .' " She listened and didn't shift her gaze from the sky. When I stopped, she smiled regretfully. I sensed that we had lost our chance and would have to endure until our next turn. She spun her green umbrella over her head and disappeared in the dark.

Who knows? Maybe, after eleven years, our next turn had finally arrived.

3

In the hall of the Art School, I looked for Masoud. Two or three
people were sitting on their stools, busy with their work and lost
in their own worlds. Masoud was not among them. But I sensed
he was watching me from some hidden place and would surface in
good time.

I saw Azra Hamedani at the end of the hall, sitting in front of
her locker like a solitary figure in a miniature from the Shah
Abbas period. She was absorbed in the portrait I had painted of
her. I wanted to go talk to her, but I held back. It was better to
wait till a more suitable moment. I looked at my half-finished
statue, and it was as though I'd caught sight of an object from
outer space.

I put on my smock and dipped my hand in a bucket of water
and sprinkled the pieces of canvas that I'd wrapped around my
statue. The wetting of the canvas made it seem thicker. With care,
I lifted off the canvas and examined the statue closely.

In military uniform, the figure was staring at the horizon like a
hero from history. The blade of his gaze sliced evenly to the win-
dowsills. He rested his hands on the curve of his cane and gazed

after a moment that lasted forever. It seemed his sight had been branded by the viewing of some catastrophe—a look similar to Iran's, except that in the statue a cruel, nervous grin was barely suppressed. It was the grin of a fortuneteller, a geomancer, a book diviner whose ominous predictions have finally come true.

Obviously, my Khan Papa Doctor was not yet ready to see that statue. But I wanted very much to show it to him. I would have liked to see his shrewd, yellow-green eyes as they squinted with Heshmat Nezami prankishness, and his calculating fingers as they twisted the tips of his waxed mustache.

When I gave him the news last fall, he chuckled and said, "You want to make my statue? What for?"

I said, "Because your face is dying to be sculptured."

"A Heshmat Nezami face?"

"Yes. Do you remember, in the olden days you used to say I would turn out like the Heshmat Nezamis?"

"Really? I used to say that?"

"Have you forgotten I was your nightingale? Didn't you used to call me the warbling nightingale? Didn't you?"

"I used to call you a nightingale? Maybe you're talking about my cousin, Agha Abdolbaghi. You're beginning to make up strange and improbable stories like the Sardar Azhdaris."

"Don't you remember? The warbling nightingale? The lastborn? The jingle bell at the funeral?"

He burst out laughing and said, "The things you've committed to your memory!"

Then he turned to the mirror on the wall and arranged his hair. When he was satisfied, he stiffened and went straight to his office. There were patients sitting around the waiting room. His office walls, the dirty white color of a camphor candlestick, made me recall Friday afternoons, especially with that smell of alcohol and iodine lingering in the air, and those jaundiced, low-spirited electric lamps.

I wasn't interested in working on my sculpture anymore. My mind was somewhere else, and I avoided looking at the leaden face of the statue. In the wastebasket I saw one of Azra Hamedani's balloon-man sketches. Whenever Azra felt bored and dull she drew hundreds of them, one after another, and threw them in the wastebasket. I wanted to steal one, but she wouldn't let me. She shrugged and said, "Rokni, it's all the same to me. I'll draw a thousand of those sketches in the next ten years, just because I feel like it. But they're not for other people. I don't want to give them to anyone. I like to throw them away."

I said, "Maybe it's all the same to you, but not to me. Your sketches speak to me. They address me."

She said, "That's an illusion. You're imagining it. You're an imagining person."

It was a sketch of a man descending from the sky with three balloons. He held the ends of the strings tightly, and the balloons were slowing his fall. He pressed a strange, upside-down bowl of a hat to his head so the wind wouldn't snatch it away. He spread his legs in midair like the fork of a slingshot, and his face was crumpled with the fear of falling and the pressure of the wind.

I took the sketch from the wastebasket and went to Azra Hamedani, pretending I only wanted to say hello. She was still sitting in front of her portrait and she didn't notice me. It wasn't a bad portrait. I had painted her face from a three-quarters angle. A straw hat's wide brim circled her head and cast a slanted, purple shadow on her forehead. The pale, fluttering shadows of the Judas tree's leaves above her gave her a cloudlike expression, as though her face would scatter and vanish if you touched it. The shaft of her green umbrella rested on her shoulder, and in her other hand she held the dark mirror of the Master Assar. She held the mirror so absent-mindedly that she seemed to be amused by some fleeting, pleasant thought.

As soon as Azra saw me, she rose from her stool, took my arm, and said, "Rokni, how well you've painted this! Do you remember when the two of us walked behind the British Embassy in the rain, and we passed the Catholic church? The church was open, and inside a group of people were singing. Do you remember?"

"Of course. I remember it well."

"This painting reminds me of that night."

She stepped back a few paces from the portrait. She put the end of her brush between her teeth and spoke a few words in a piece-meal fashion that I couldn't understand. I said, "What?"

She took the brush from her mouth and told me, "We have to find a nice place for this painting of yours. It's good for old buildings, somewhere like this hall, with high ceilings and plaster walls, with flower- and bush-carved doors and windows. Your painting doesn't have any special design and pattern of its own. It can appear in any scene, like a background of sky. It can give an impression of vastness to any landscape. You have to hang it somewhere with a lot of surrounding patterns that can hold it together. The night the two of us were walking in the rain, I thought of the same thing. Do you remember how we argued that, for painting, you shouldn't have any particular design?"

I said, "I have to leave. I don't have much time."

She stepped forward and asked, "Do you want to go out and walk for a while?"

I said, "I'm looking for Masoud. My father is talking about my Khan Brother Zia. He thinks Masoud can find him if he pulls a few strings."

Azra wiped her paint-smeared hands with a towel and took off her smock and threw it on the stool. At the window, she grew absorbed in watching the street. Congested black smoke was twirling over the rooftops, and the distant, dragging uproar of the demonstrators was drawing near. I said, "Have you seen Masoud recently?"

She waved her hand and said, "Just a minute. Let me see. This must be Jahangir's car. He's supposed to bring the kids from school, so we can get home as soon as possible. It's not wise to walk in the streets with this angry crowd."

I said, "You yourself said we should go for a walk."

"Rokni, it was only a wish. It's not wise in the middle of this chaos. Let me see. I think this car has to be Jahangir's. Well, what was I saying? Yes, Rokni, you can't live on dreams and wishes all the time. You have to pay attention to the basics, too."

"What basics?"

"Our kids, for instance. You have to pay attention to their homework, their eating and sleeping."

She fell silent and turned her tired, washed-out face to me. I said, "Azra, what's wrong with you?"

"Rokni, we ourselves are kids. Someone has to look after *us.*"

I said, "I have to go find Masoud somehow."

"You'll find him. It's easy to find Masoud. Anywhere you go, it's as though someone conjures him out of thin air. Don't worry about it. You and he will stick together like two ticks and all your thoughts will start revolving around your Khan Brother Zia. Both of you were waiting for this for a long time and you didn't even know it. Look, this must be Jahangir now. He's parking in front of the gate. Rokni, when you cool off a little, come and see us. You know where we live."

"All right."

Azra softened her tone and said, "Rokni."

"What is it?" I asked.

She waved her hand. "Good-bye."

In the street, the crooked, leaning walls piled one on top of the other, and the hush of a silent movie guarded everything. Customers fluttered behind shopwindows with rapid, staccato movements. The pavement at Baharestan Circle was covered with crumpled papers, empty Pepsi-Cola bottles, and burned tires. And up there close to the sky the Baharestan statue rose to heaven like a headless idol. Everything in the circle was waiting for an accident.

On the curve of Safi Ali Shah, I caught sight of Masoud. He leaned against his cherry-colored convertible with his arms folded. His face looked gray and muddy in the twilight. He seemed to have been waiting some time for me, as if we'd had an appointment. We had no more need of formalities than two undercover agents who meet according to plan. As soon as he saw me, he inspected his surroundings with a cool, practiced air and then opened the car door for me. He pretended not to notice me as he watched the aimless traffic on the circle. I, too, played my role. I ducked my head and approached the car swiftly and threw myself on the front seat. Masoud shut the door. Then he took his car keys from his pocket, settled behind the wheel, and started the engine.

The car began to move. The streets were changing their colors; purples and blues first came alive and then faded. From his profile, Masoud appeared remote, bemused and mysterious. If this were old times, he would have slapped his thigh and burst out laughing; he would have shouted, "Rokni, you son of a gun, where've you been?"

The buildings and burning vehicles blazed behind the car windows. I had my ears pricked for what Masoud wanted to say. He started whistling. His dragging, continuous whistle glided through the summer night. As I listened, I started thinking about our house long ago—about the sky that always looked so patchy behind the dusty leaves of the fig tree. I used to wrap my hands around my knees and listen to how Masoud planned to make a submarine from the late Sardar Azhdar's steamer trunk and how he would launch it in the pool at his house so we two could search the bottom of the pool and see what was going on down there.

He said we needed a stovepipe for air. It was possible to close the cracks of the late Agha's trunk with tar and solder. I looked at the sky, and I felt light as a feather. What if we made a pair of cardboard wings and attached them to our shoulders? We could fly over the house, over the city, free and without care, revolving and sightseeing. But Masoud was obsessed with the submarine. He wanted to count the goldfish in his pool. He was convinced that on the bottom of the pool strange, grotesque, prehistoric creatures existed. I went on watching the flock of shadow birds that were circling the sky above our house, and my thoughts were elsewhere.

Now Masoud stopped his whistling and asked, "What did you want me for?"

"I wanted to talk to you about my Khan Brother Zia."

He shrugged dejectedly and was silent. I said, "Wherever you want to drive, you go ahead; I don't mind."

"Now you're satisfied with everything?"

"Not with everything."

His grin broadened and he said, "Are you trying to make me feel sorry for you?"

It was our old, competitive relationship. I didn't answer.

He said, "I was joking. I was kidding you—like the good old days; the days before you cut your ties with us."

He tweaked my cheek and winked at me, and until we reached his house he whistled instead of talking.

I had trapped myself. What business did I have going to the

Sardar Azhdaris'? What could Masoud do that I myself couldn't?
We went up to the rooftop of their house. He poured both of us
smuggled whisky in slender-waisted glasses, and he put a tray
with yogurt and other chasers in front of me and motioned for me
to start. But I didn't touch my lips to the whisky. It wasn't wise to
drink at the Sardar Azhdaris'. You could find yourself in an awkward situation. I wanted to stay alert, in case Masoud planned to
do me in.

He stretched out on a folding cot, puffed on his cigarette, and
said, "Don't worry about your Khan Brother Zia."

I said, "Who says I'm worried?"

"He's driving a truck on the highway between Shiraz and
Bushehr."

"You've seen him yourself?"

"On the road from Lar to Bandar Abbas we ran into each
other."

"You talked to him?"

"There was a flood and the road was blocked and we were
forced to spend the night in a caravanserai of the Shah Abbas
period. I saw him there."

"How did you figure out he was my Khan Brother Zia?"

"From his face, from those eyes of his."

"Do you mean that after eleven years his face hadn't changed?"

"He was a little bit worn-looking. He'd also grown a beard and
mustache. I called him by name and asked if he remembered me.
He didn't answer, not a word. You Heshmat Nezamis suddenly go
deaf when you don't like a question. He turned his head and
started watching the desert. The desert was dark and nothing
could be seen. Your Khan Brother Zia wanted to divert my attention. He played dumb and said, 'Why have you left Tehran and
come all the way to Lar? The roads are not safe. In the desert, if
you blink your eyes, they cut off your head like a bunch of flowers
and place it in the palm of your hand.' I told him that staying in
Tehran makes a person feel useless. He shrugged his shoulders
and said, 'Of course, Tehran is Tehran. You can't view it lightly. It
takes a long time to become a Tehranologist.' "

"Did you ask him about me, too?"

"Yes. I asked, 'Do you remember Rokni?' "

"What did he say?"

"He started laughing and he asked sarcastically, 'Who is Rokni?' I said, 'Rokni? The warbling nightingale? The lastborn? Silly little Rokni?' "

"Then what?"

"Then he shrugged his shoulders, meaning, 'I don't know him.' "

I couldn't believe it. He was telling me things that weren't true. My Khan Brother Zia would grow stubborn now and then, and he would do things no one could understand; but always there was a softness in his manner.

That day when the agents came forward to tie his arms, he rubbed his beard and looked at Iran as though they were merely fanning him with a swan's feather. Iran was standing in front of the kitchen with a handful of fresh, shelled walnuts hidden in her fist, and my Bee Bee stood barefoot next to the pool, biting the edge of her veil. My Khan Brother Zia's face was sliced into parallel pieces by the shadows of the railing. Nevertheless, he bore himself as though he were dancing.

Masoud emptied his glass and said, "Let me go get my suitcase. I've brought you some gifts from the south."

I said, "Wait a minute. These things you said about my Khan Brother Zia don't exactly fit."

He looked surprised and asked, "Are you saying I've made them up? Am I lying?"

"Yes. They've either put him in prison or they've sent him into exile. All that you said is a lie. My Khan Brother Zia isn't the type to drive a truck."

"Rokni, you know what your problem is? Your problem is that you imagine things. I was afraid eleven years ago—when you used to talk to Homayundokht, God forgive her soul—I was afraid eventually you'd go nuts."

"Hereditary insanity belongs to you Sardar Azhdaris. I'm a Heshmat Nezami and I don't give in."

"God bless your moonlike face, it's not written on anyone's forehead whether he's a Sardar Azhdari or a Heshmat Nezami. Listen, wait and see what I've brought you. I'll be right back."

He went downstairs to bring up his suitcase. I wished I could go home without saying good-bye. My Khan Papa Doctor had not yet left for Ghaleh Bagh and already they were breaking the china over my head, as the expression goes.

Masoud reappeared on the rooftop, dragging his suitcase, out of breath. His hair was tossed on his forehead like a horse's mane. As he spoke, his Sardar Azhdari eyebrows moved unevenly, and his glance staggered over my face. He put down the suitcase and said, "What's your heart's desire, Cousin? Whatever you want, take it. Don't worry about a thing, it's dog food."

He opened the suitcase. It was filled with smuggled American goods—a row of ties, two bottles of whisky, four Kodak cameras, a net bag of Colgate toothpaste, ITT batteries, girlie magazines, and a handful of other odds and ends. I said, "Where did you steal all these?"

"Never mind. Whatever you see, if you want it, take it."

"What would I want these for?"

"By my soul, may I die if you don't take something! Do you want an American suit? You young goat, you never wear suits. You don't do anything like a normal person. Bless you, if you want so much to be free and informal, how come on a hot summer night like this you're wearing a pair of boots?"

I stood up and said, "I have to get to the bus stop. How about meeting again tomorrow in the Art School?"

"Rokni, do you know why I like you so much? Because you're a donkey—a thick-skulled donkey. Your head's in the clouds and you don't have any idea what's going on around you. This city is in chaos, my dear Agha. On every one of its intersections a soldier is standing. And at this hour of the night you want to find a bus and go home? God bless you, is this our genius?"

He tweaked my cheek and burst out laughing.

"Now, why have you got your hooks in Azra?" he asked. "My dear cousin, Azra has a husband and family. If you want to hook someone, there are a lot of other girls."

He took one of his magazines from the suitcase and held it in front of me so I could see the nude woman on the cover. I was furious. I started to leave, but he grabbed my wrist and stopped me. He put his hand in his pocket and took out a folded paper. I knew it was the sketch of the balloon man. I said, "Where did you find this?"

"Never mind."

I snatched the sketch from his hand and started to leave. He shouted, "You're upsetting yourself for nothing! All right. You say your Khan Brother Zia's in prison? He's in exile? Very well. I won't argue. Tomorrow we'll go to the Security Organization and investigate, tomorrow afternoon at two o'clock, remember, in front of the Safi Ali Shah cleaners."

I grew so lighthearted, they could send me to the sky like a dandelion with one puff. Still, I could hear Masoud: "Forget your childhood. The days of summoning spirits and talking with Homayundokht, God forgive her soul, are past."

Street after street I traveled aimlessly. The night-walking people drew closer and went away. Traffic lights—green, yellow, and red—winked until finally our frowning, sleepy house appeared. Everything seemed large, unchanging, and eternal. In the courtyard I sat wearily on the edge of the pool and splashed a few handfuls of water on my face. The Big Dipper dragged behind the moon like the tail of a kite.

I set my palms in the wet dirt of the rose bed behind me and listened to the easy, flowing silence of our old house. A large rose hung over my face. I had spent a strange day, and in the hollow of the sky, Orion's Belt and Gemini had ceased moving. A gentle breeze was swinging the curtain of the night. Impulsively, I called, "Homayundokht, Homayundokht, is that you?"

No answer came. Even so, I clearly sensed a presence. She was around me. She was walking among the boxwood and the pearlflower bushes. I climbed the stairs. The closer I came to the rooftop the faster my heart beat. The wide, starry night rose above the roof, and a druglike sleep came over me.

BOOK TWO

The Fortuneteller's Lot

1

I wanted to go see Iran, but my Bee Bee took hold of my wrist and stared into my eyes. I knew that stare well. She was telling me to be careful, but she didn't like to say it. I asked, "What do you want?"

She said, "Rokni, you were asleep and we didn't like to wake you. Your Khan Papa Doctor left without saying good-bye. It upset your sister. I think she wanted to cry, and she locked herself in the bathroom. She stood stark naked in the middle of the basin and ran hot water onto her foot and then she started screaming and embarrassing us. We sent Uncle Aziz to the drugstore for gauze and we bandaged her foot ourselves."

"How's she feeling now? Can I talk with her?"

"Yes, dear. She's fine, and she's not complaining anymore. But you mustn't touch her. If even a finger touches her, she'll scream to high heaven."

We entered the library. From the windowpanes, ingots of sunlight stretched across the library floor. The photos of the late Sardar Azhdar and the late Heshmat Nezam, and the full-length photo of my Khan Papa Doctor, still hung on the walls. The only difference was in the atmosphere of the library, which seemed slightly looser and more open than it had the week before. It reminded me of an empty, rugless mosque.

Iran was sitting all alone on my Khan Papa Doctor's desk. Her bare feet hung over the edge, one of them thickly bandaged, and she swung them with a sort of childish carelessness. In her thin slip with the lace hem pulled up to her thighs, her unbraided hair frizzing around her shoulders, she looked like a creature who lived in a cave and didn't glimpse the sunlight from decade to decade. When we walked in, she turned her face aside. As my Bee Bee had asked, I tiptoed up cautiously, as though I wished to surprise a pigeon. With every step I took, Iran drew farther away on my Khan Papa Doctor's desk. When I came within two paces of her, she folded her arms tightly. I said, "Iran-jun, what's all this about?"

She pulled herself together nervously and prepared to fly. I stopped and went no farther, hoping she would calm down. I gave a foolish laugh to show I was only playing. My Bee Bee lost her patience and left the library. Outside on the veranda, she covered her face with her veil. She put her nose to the window and watched us. I thought if she had stayed in the library any longer her heart would have failed her and, just as in the ten days of religious mourning during Ashura, she would have passed out; my Khan Papa Doctor would have had to percolate cow-tongue flowers and valerian and make her drink it until she felt better again and stopped talking in the Kangavari dialect. Any time she got upset, she talked yakkety-yak in Kangavari, as if she were back in her childhood home.

I said to Iran, "Iran-jun, what are you afraid of? I'm not a stranger. I'm Rokni—little Rokni, Wee Billy Goat Gruff, the lastborn."

For lack of anything better to do, I took another step toward her. As soon as she noticed, she narrowed her eyes. I said, "Iran, Iran-jun, do you hear me? If it's the burn, that's not important. It will get better, it will heal. Khan Papa Doctor has a medicine for burns—the seven-sectioned plant and lard and dates pounded together, scorpion ointment."

Without motion or passion, she watched me. My words had no

effect on her, not so much as a pinprick. Now I couldn't hold back
any longer. I had to say something that would break that frozen
expression of hers. "Iran, I know you hear my voice, but you
don't want to let anyone in. I won't tell anyone. Whatever you say
will stay with me alone. Iran-jun, my chest is a graveyard of
secrets. If you want to talk, do it softly in the ear of this crazy
brother of yours. I know you miss my Khan Papa Doctor. You're
cross because he's gone to Ghaleh Bagh without saying good-bye,
isn't that it? Instead of answering, you can give me a sign. For
instance, you can raise your eyebrows, squeeze my hand. Only a
small, simple sign."

Almost imperceptibly, I set my fingertips on her arm. As soon
as I touched her, she started screaming. She jumped up and went
to the dais. She went so hurriedly that the bandage fell off her foot
and her red, swollen sole grew white from the limestone floor of
the library. Her shoulder hit a bookshelf. She lost her balance and
fell to the floor. I ran toward her, and before she could escape I
grabbed her lace hem. She hit me in the head with her fists, but I
told myself not to give in. Now that my Khan Papa Doctor had
gone to Ghaleh Bagh everyone's hopes were on me; they all expected me to behave like a Heshmat Nezami and not some sort of
willow that trembles in the wind.

When Iran calmed down, she slowly lifted her head. From a
tilted angle, almost birdlike, she looked at me. She put her nose to
my shoulder and sniffed at me, and she listened to ambiguous
sounds and mysterious rustlings in the side rooms. Finally, she
laid her head on my chest.

I said, "Iran-jun, at last you recognize crazy Rokni."

She didn't answer. She only nestled into my chest, as though
she lay on a swan's-feather pillow preparing for a long, deep sleep.
I said, "Iran-jun, when are you going to want to speak? Do you
remember how you used to sing songs for us?

"Ali Baba, the son of the rogue, hoo?
The lid of the lighter in the box, hoo?"

"Do you remember, Iran?"

It was years since she had stopped talking. They used to say she
would only talk with my Khan Brother Zia. My Khan Brother

Zia said the trick was to put her hand on your heart. Then you had to kiss her face and squeeze her arm twice. I did all he said, but with no result.

I think I was nine years old. I was coming back from school. I saw my Khan Brother Zia standing in front of our gatehouse. He was spinning a key chain around his finger and whistling a rhythmic tune. He had on his Army uniform and his hair was cut very short—was shaved off. He looked fresh and clean and he smelled of barbershop perfume. As soon as he saw me, he laughed and winked at me. I threw my books in the gatehouse and yelled, "Khan Brother Zia!"

He said, "How are you, Rokni?"

"I'm fine, Khan Brother Zia."

"Why are you limping like that? Is your foot hurt?"

"It's nothing. We were practicing *Tamerlane.*"

"Aren't you tired of playacting yet?"

"We don't bother anyone. How are you? Where've you been? It's a long time since I've seen you."

He put a hand at his waist, and he drummed a shiny boot tip on the cobblestones. Maybe I'd made him uncomfortable with my questions. He said, "Where did you think I was, stupid? I was away on compulsory duty."

"Please come in the house. I have to tell Khan Papa Doctor and my Bee Bee."

"Here's all right. I don't want to create a commotion. Now, can you show me how cunning you can be? Can you go quietly into the courtyard and take your sister's hand and bring her to me with no one hearing? Say that someone's come and wants to see her."

"How can I make her understand all that? She doesn't understand things."

"It's simple, little donkey. When you want to talk to her, you have to speak her language. Put her hand on your heart. Kiss her face and squeeze her arm twice a little below the shoulder. She'll understand."

I collected my books from the floor of the gatehouse and went running into the courtyard. My Khan Papa Doctor was busy smelting red sulphur and golden-flower beneath the trellis. He had his sleeves rolled up and he was stirring the embers with steel tongs, searching for something. The smell of coal recalled the blacksmith shops of Gas Lamp Street. I said a hello that he didn't hear. He wiped the sweat from his face and glanced sideways at his alchemy book, *The Deleted Beginning*. Again he poked at the smelting furnace with the tongs. I went straight to the kitchen. Iran sat cross-legged by the kitchen sink, like a bride at a decorated wedding tray, and bowed her head so Zahra Soltan could comb her hair. I said to Zahra Soltan, "If I tell you something, do you promise not to tell anyone else?"

She stopped combing and said, "Yes, dear Agha. Whatever you say, my tongue will be dumb. It will stay only with me."

"Swear to it."

"Swear by what?"

"By the soul of your father."

"All right, by the soul of my father, let whoever tells a stranger your words die speechless."

"My Khan Brother Zia's come back from compulsory duty and wants to see my sister."

She screamed, "God kill me! Oh, dear God, Agha Zia is back from compulsory duty and no one's gone to welcome him?"

"Shut up. Didn't you swear by your father's soul that you wouldn't make a noise? He's asked us not to let anyone scent his presence. He only wants us to take my sister secretly to the gatehouse so they can see each other."

"Dear Agha, I beg by the cut-off hands of the martyred saint, the Moon of Bani Hashem, let me just glimpse him too. After my precious mistress, Homayundokht, God forgive her soul, passed away, who nursed him? Who sang lullabies in his ear every night and soothed him till he went to sleep? Agha-jun, I raised him on these knees of mine. You'll be rewarded, I pray you'll be rewarded. Don't withhold this from a white-haired old woman."

"But you mustn't make any noise about it."

"Very well. I pray God will reward you. I hope you reach old age, Agha-jun."

With the corner of her flour-sack veil, she wiped her tears. Then I put Iran's hand on my heart, kissed her face, and squeezed her arm as my Khan Brother Zia had ordered. She turned her head toward me. I started to squeeze her arm again. She thought I was tickling her. She giggled and grew silly, but she didn't move. I told Zahra Soltan, "She doesn't make any sense of what I say. Can you bring her to the gatehouse without a sound, and not let anyone guess?"

She said, "Of course I can, Agha-jun. You go to the gatehouse and tell Agha Zia I'll bring her in two minutes."

Hastily, without looking at my Khan Papa Doctor, I returned to the gatehouse. My Khan Brother Zia had set one foot on the stone bench. He was still spinning his key chain and whistling. When he saw me, he stopped whistling and asked, "Where's your sister?"

"Zahra Soltan is bringing her right away."

He grew angry and shouted, "Didn't I say not to tell anyone, donkey?"

"I did what you said. But she couldn't understand. She didn't come when I told her. She won't listen to anyone but Zahra Soltan."

"You can't tackle even so simple a job?"

"Why, Khan Brother Zia, I can tackle the job."

The gatehouse curtain lifted and from behind it Zahra Soltan appeared. She had covered her face and she was dragging Iran behind her. As soon as she caught sight of my Khan Brother Zia, she bowed and said, "Little Agha, our eyes brighten. I bid you greetings."

She let go of Iran and stepped forward to kiss his hand. My Khan Brother Zia looked nervous. He spoke to Zahra Soltan as if to a child. "Zahra Soltan, how are you?"

"Praise God, under your shadow . . ."

She burst into tears. My Khan Brother Zia grew even more nervous. He patted her shoulder and said, "Zahra Soltan, what's all this for? Has someone brought news of my death?"

Zahra Soltan wiped her face with her veil and released her trapped breath with a sigh. My Khan Brother Zia turned to Iran and looked her over thoroughly, as though she were a sports car he wanted to tinker with but he didn't know how to start. Iran was mumbling to herself. From time to time she took a deep breath, like someone swimming in a cold stream. My Khan

Brother Zia put his key chain in his pocket and took her face between his hands. She didn't pay any attention. He bent and kissed her cheek, and with his palm he pressed her face against his own. Just this small and simple act awakened her. She threw her arms around his neck.

My Khan Papa Doctor's voice came from the courtyard. "Zahra Soltan, why is Iran screaming like that?"

Fearfully, Zahra Soltan lifted a corner of the curtain and answered, "Agha Doctor, it's nothing. She has a yen for milk and rice pudding. She wants us to cook her milk and rice pudding."

My Khan Brother Zia, indifferent to the others, rocked Iran in his arms like a baby in a cradle. My Khan Papa Doctor could be heard speaking to my Bee Bee. "If it's not possible to transform red sulphur into gold, we can still cure syphilis with it. The meaning of the elixir of life is just that: it means healing, eternal life, the absolute cure."

My Khan Brother Zia put his hand in his pocket and took out the medals he'd won in the championship wrestling contest. He laid all of them in Iran's hand. Now Iran's attention was genuinely fixed on him. From her response, it was obvious that her mind was clear and she was aware of events.

My Khan Brother Zia turned to me and said, "Rokni, you must excuse me."

"Why, Khan Brother Zia? Excuse you for what?"

He said, "I have to sing my good-bye song. I have to tear my heart away and go. Take your sister to the house."

"In God's name, stay a little longer. We haven't had our conversation yet."

"Rokni-jun, in the Army you don't make decisions on your own. It's not for nothing they call it compulsory duty. If I don't go, they'll come down on me hard."

"When will they let you back?"

"When the bamboo flowers. It's not up to me. But I'll try to come as soon as possible. Then we'll sit and have our conversation. I have a lot to tell you. Your breath still smells of milk and you don't know much."

I wanted to answer, but he turned away. With his face averted, he took a brand-new five-tuman bill from his pocket and gave it to me, and he went into the street without saying good-bye.

Now I closed my eyes and conjured up my Khan Brother Zia. I put Iran's hand on my heart, the way he'd said to do so long ago. I kissed her face and squeezed her arm twice. I waited to see if finally she would say something. She didn't. It was odd; tears filled her eyes. I was taken aback. I didn't expect that. I turned toward my Bee Bee. She was still bent behind the veranda window, watching us. The pale, weightless sunlight passed through the grape leaves and, like thousands of gold paper coins, it scattered across her veil and turned it into a leopard skin. She could see us, but it was obvious she couldn't tell how we were feeling. Iran stood up. She took my little finger and pulled me toward the dais. I was so happy I didn't know what to do. I turned around and threw meaningful and excited glances at my Bee Bee. My Bee Bee was wiping the fog from the windowpane with a corner of her veil. She didn't understand my glances. She frowned and shook her head inquiringly.

When we reached the dais, Iran dropped to the floor and opened my Khan Papa Doctor's cupboard. First, she took out Meghdadi's *Secrets of Numbers* and tossed it aside. The smell of herbs hit my nose—smells that created a clear pattern in my mind. Though mixed together, they didn't lose their individual characteristics. It was as if, suddenly, I'd been thrown into one of the old perfumeries in Sabzeh Square, full of strange, shy scents that had been kept from human reach for years, or for centuries— smells that belonged to the velvet boxes of a new bride, to the cool corners of old pool houses, and to the fresh, clean gift bundles that people hide in their closets for their grandchildren and their great-grandchildren. Iran wanted to take out the sugar pouches of herbs, but I held her wrist and stopped her. She tugged herself free. I let her go. This time, she took out only the perfume vial and the chiffon kerchiefs my Khan Papa Doctor had brought her from his trip to Germany. She smelled them and showed them to me. I lost my balance; I wanted to kiss her hands for the favor she had granted me. It was proof she would eventually talk to me and tell me all that she'd kept hidden from everyone up to that time. I too smelled the perfume and the kerchiefs. I told myself, Oh,

Lord, how long does she want to keep her secrets? When you
looked at her you knew those impassive and indifferent eyes had
seen the hapless Homayundokht, God forgive her soul, in the
middle of the flames, and they didn't want to let anything else in,
and they were silent.

My Bee Bee tapped the window for me to go out and talk to
her. When I emerged from the library, I saw that she held a bowl
of ice water and was looking at me with indignation. She asked,
"What's the matter with you, Rokni?"

"Bee Bee-jun, you don't know. I think my sister wants to talk."

"Well, of course she wants to talk. But I'm afraid she's going to
break down. If she breaks down, we have to take her to your
Khan Papa Doctor. I can't do anything myself—a woman on my
own."

"Yes, we have to take her to him."

"You say we should, too. But wouldn't it make him cross?
Wouldn't he shout, ask why we didn't let him alone?"

"Bee Bee-jun, I don't know what will happen. But you're right,
you can tell what's behind her behavior. She has to see my Khan
Papa Doctor. What if you call my Uncle Aziz and ask him to
bring his car and take us to Ghaleh Bagh?"

"You mean right this minute?"

"Right this minute."

"Masoud phoned before noon and left a message not to forget,
tomorrow at 2 P.M. He said it's very important and you should
wear a suit and tie."

"All right, how about the day after tomorrow? Let's go to
Ghaleh Bagh day after tomorrow."

My Bee Bee handed me the bowl of ice water. She grew reflective and said, "Let me think about it."

She leaned her forehead against the windowpane and looked at
Iran. I returned to the library and offered Iran the bowl of ice
water. She had in her lap the late Sardar Azhdar's pearl-handled
revolver, my Khan Brother Zia's wrestling medals, and a few
black and white photographs. She gave them all to me. She took
the water and gulped it down.

My Khan Brother Zia had taken those photographs a year and
a half before leaving for compulsory military duty. He set Cousin

Batul on his shoulders in front of the automatic camera. He flexed his biceps and bent his elbows up like a wooden hanger. Then he placed the table in front of the camera and on it he set our cousins Mrs. Motlagh and her daughter Farideh. He raised the table from the ground with his teeth, and wobbling and staggering, he waited for the click of the camera. After that, he hid Farideh and Batul behind him in the telephone room. With clenched fists, he prepared to defend them. The automatic camera clicked and took their picture. My Khan Brother Zia laughed.

Iran gave me the bowl and she took back the pearl-handled revolver, the wrestling medals, and the photographs. She carefully placed them in the cupboard, and she locked the door. I said, "Iran-jun, I'll bring him back for you. It won't take a long time, either."

She nodded her head.

"Let's go, then. You have to rest a little. Too much walking isn't good for you."

She stood up simply and without much trouble. She took her bandage from the floor and left the library. On the veranda, my Bee Bee was waiting for us with a cup of cow-tongue flower tea. She held the cup to Iran's mouth. Iran obligingly drank the tea to the last drop, then she went straight to the telephone room and stretched out on a corner of the rug where my Khan Papa Doctor liked to sit alone every evening and read the paper. She was asleep in the blink of an eye.

My Bee Bee and I, together, were thinking of my Khan Papa Doctor. I broke the silence and said, "Obviously, she misses him."

My Bee Bee said, "What about you, dear? Do you miss him too?"

"For me it's different."

"For me too. How about your Khan Brother Zia? Do you miss him?"

"Yes."

My Bee Bee sighed and sank into her thoughts.

2

Masoud parked his car in front of the police station. In the yard, he straightened my jacket. He tightened the knot of my tie. Plainly he was dissatisfied with the poor fit of my suit, but he couldn't do anything about that. He took his comb from his pocket and combed his hair in the window of the front door. He patted his clothes and told me confidentially, "There's no need for you to talk. Sit quiet. Don't open your mouth till they ask you a question. You understand?"

I said, "All right."

We started walking again. In front of Mr. Farzaneh's office, Masoud stopped again and said in my ear, "If they ask you a question tell the truth, you understand? You can't pull the wool over these people's eyes. They know everything."

Masoud knocked. The attendant opened the door for us and we entered. No one was sitting behind the desk, and I thought the room was empty. I asked Masoud, "Where's Farzaneh?"

He pointed behind us and laid a finger to his lips. As I fell silent, I heard the wheezing breath of Mr. Farzaneh. From my very first glance, he struck me as an unpleasant person. He seemed more like a registrar of documents than a security agent. He was sitting on the floor in the corner of the room, reading a few dossiers. He licked his thumb and leafed through the dossiers, meanwhile taking deep, broken breaths. He had a neck so short that you'd think his head had been fixed to his humped chest with nuts and bolts. He could hardly turn his head on his shoulders.

Eventually, he raised his chin with an effort. His dark, cast-iron face emerged from his chest like a turtle's head, and he looked at us with his froglike eyes. He asked wheezily, "How are the gentlemen feeling? Please take a seat. Would you care for a cup of tea?"

Masoud answered, "Thank you, we just had one."

Mr. Farzaneh turned to me, and the skin beneath his chin folded like a prehistoric animal's hide. With a crumpled, sickly smile he asked, "What about you, Agha?"

I said, "I don't feel like one."

He stood up and came over to me. He said, "You don't feel like one?"

"No, I just had one. Thank you very much."

"A Heshmat Nezami, very well fed."

He studied me as if an old idea had reawakened in his mind. Without looking at his dossiers, he put them on the desk. Nothing else lay there except an enameled Ghom vase, a little Iranian flag, and a calendar, at the top of which the Shah of Shahs held his military hat beneath his arm and laughed without apparent reason. Really, everything in that room looked dusty and unused, as though Mr. Farzaneh only sat there out of habit. Indifferent and untidy, he walked around. His café-au-lait suit had not seen pressing for years. The collar of his shirt was as dirty and rumpled as a dishcloth, and the loose knot of his tie swung in the middle of his chest. He pulled a Yazdi handkerchief from his pocket and spat into it. Then he asked Masoud, "What is it you want?"

Masoud shifted his feet. He pointed to me and said, "This is Rokni, Dr. Heshmat Nezami's youngest son. I've brought him here so you can examine this matter yourself. We're not asking for your pity and we don't expect any special consideration."

"All right. What's the issue, then?"

"Dr. Heshmat Nezami and my Dear Daddy send their greet-

ings, saying they haven't seen you for a long time and they miss
you."

"Fine. All this aside, what is it they want from me?"

"They thought perhaps Your Excellency would be kind enough
to look into the records of Agha Zia's case."

He threw his hands up, but began to cough. "Ohoo, ohoo, what
can I do? I don't have radar to figure out who's running things,
who's alive and who's dead. I'm not the top of the onion, nor am I
the roots. I'm only an old agent of the Security Organization,
Agha-jun."

Masoud grew bold and said, "You're too modest. In the government, they all listen to Your Excellency. Just yesterday, when the
reporters asked about conditions for political prisoners, the Shah
of Shahs said that he was not informed, and they must ask Mr.
Farzaneh. He said Mr. Farzaneh was the one who turns the
wheels of the country."

Mr. Farzaneh threw his hands in the air again and said, "The
Shah of Shahs has made many of these utterances. It's easy for
him to talk. The problem is that nobody knows who turns the
wheels of this country. Ohoo, ohoo, ohoo . . ."

He gestured for us to leave his office. Masoud didn't say anything. Dejected and embarrassed, he backed out and I followed
him. Again the wheezing voice rose: "Rokni Heshmat Nezami."

I said, "Yes."

"*Bon voyage.* Where are you going?"

"You excused us."

"I meant the son of Abdolbaghi, not you. No one has the right
to leave this office without my clear permission."

With wide, worried eyes, Masoud disappeared behind the door.
I was speechless with fear. I stood in my place and stared at Mr.
Farzaneh, trying to figure out his intentions. He didn't say a word.
He was in his own world and slowly perused the dossiers for a
long, long time. Now and then he took the Yazdi handkerchief
from his pocket, wiped his nose, and put the handkerchief away.
Finally he looked up at me. He was surprised to see me there. He
seemed not to remember why he had kept me in his office. Lines
deepened in his forehead. He searched for a thought. Suddenly he

grinned. With difficulty, he stood up and beckoned for me to follow him.

Out in the streets it was already twilight. We walked shoulder to shoulder. He seemed secretive. Because of this, it was hard to start a conversation with him. Without any introduction, he began murmuring:

"Yes, one should not run away from Providence.
No matter how little the cupbearer pours, it
is the essence of kindness."

Then he turned his face to me and said apologetically, "Shortness of breath . . . one's voice . . . anymore . . ."

He couldn't finish his sentence. I had no idea where we were heading or what was the purpose of this mysterious behavior. He said, "Sayed Bagher, the elegist of the martyred saints, used to come to the late Sardar Azhdar and tell him the story of the Prophet's robe. You weren't born yet. Sayed Bagher always finished his elegies with the same verse:

"Yes, one should not run away from Providence.
No matter how little the cupbearer pours, it
is the essence of kindness."

Darkness circled the rusty gables and filled the squares. We passed the bazaar and turned down a narrow alley. In the middle of the alley, he blocked me. He put his hands behind his back and looked into my face. I said, "Mr. Farzaneh, what's your plan? What are you going to do?"

"Mr. Heshmat Nezami, for every task there's a way. Isn't that so?"

Maybe he was baiting a trap for me. He frowned and continued, "In my humble opinion, you're very naive. You understand? If I didn't want to help you, I wouldn't tell you these things. Ohoo, ohoo, ohoo. You have to find your brother Zia among your own relatives, not among strangers. You must know your own family first, and then start attacking this one and that one's leg. My plan is to take you tonight to the house of your father's cousin, Mirza Hassibi. Have you heard his name?"

I shook my head. He pulled the Yazdi handkerchief from his pocket, blew his nose, and resumed walking.

Gradually, I began to worry. I wondered if he planned to harm me. A lot of people were disappearing. They would leave their houses whole and hearty and no one ever found them again. But, hard as I tried, I couldn't think of any crime I'd committed. I hadn't shouted any slogans, even against Shemr, the killer of the saint Hosein. I hadn't insulted even a policeman. Maybe Mr. Farzaneh thought I knew something and wasn't letting on. I wanted to ask him, but it occurred to me that if I did he'd grow more suspicious. Then he would really go for my throat. Meanwhile, he was looking back at me like a whale with those fatty, half-drunk, languid eyes. Because the alley was so narrow, we couldn't walk side by side. Mr. Farzaneh led the way. We walked silently, and our silence was our conversation. A complicated, inexpressible communication flowed between us—the connection that exists between two night-traveling tigers.

In front of Mirza Hassibi's, he paused and said, "No one who judges things only by their looks should set foot in Mirza Hassibi's house. Whatever shabbiness you see, don't forget your manners. That's an old tradition of the Sardar Azhdaris."

Then he held out his hand and asked, "How much money do you have in your pocket?"

Surprised, I answered, "Two or three hundred tumans."

"If it's no trouble, cough up fifty tumans. Don't waste time. I'm in need of a fix."

I counted out fifty tumans and put them on his palm. Without looking, he stuffed the bills in his pocket. He rubbed his face and arranged himself. When he noticed me watching, he charged at me and said, "What now? Are you in a zoo, that you stare at me like that?"

"I'm just trying to find my brother."

He knocked on the door and said, "Ask Mirza, he knows all the skeletons in the Heshmat Nezami closet. He's the one who can make you understand. Who am I to tell you? What am I? I'm only an agent, that's all."

The door opened. In the dark of the hall, Mirza Hassibi's face wasn't visible. We could only hear his low, distinguished voice.

The clarity of his words contrasted with the aged and worn-out look of the house. He asked, "Farzaneh, is that you?"

"Yes, Mirza. Are we bothering you?"

"Come on in and lock the door behind you."

"Very well."

Mirza Hassibi went down the hall. Like most of the Sardar Azhdaris, he seemed to see no difference between strangers and relatives. From that one brief encounter, his patient movements lent a feeling of belonging and informality. I felt I could enter any room in that house and open any curtain without permission. Nevertheless, I detected a sort of cold and demanding air underneath it all. I was sure that if I had wanted to stay in his house he would have welcomed me, and he wouldn't have let me lift a finger. At the same time, he would also have coolly possessed me, like an antique object.

I asked Mr. Farzaneh, "How long will it take you to finish your business?"

"Don't hurry, Agha. Hurry is the work of the Devil. Ha, ha. . . ."

"How dark this house is!"

"They've confiscated his property. Of all his worldly possessions, only this little house is left. That's why he spins the wheels of his life with an opium brazier. Do you believe it, Agha—that the grandson of Sardar Azhdar makes his living this way?"

The smell of opium and burnt rock candy rose from Mirza Hassibi's room. Mr. Farzaneh pushed aside the paisley curtain. Now I sensed I was facing an unusual person. Mirza Hassibi reclined against a pillow on a small mattress. He was reading a *Kayhan* newspaper. The room was not rich and splendid, as I'd imagined it would be. A piece of thick-napped carpet was flung in the middle of it. Scattered around Mirza were a charcoal brazier, a primus stove, a brass tray, and teacups. Mr. Farzaneh bowed and stepped forward humbly and said, "Greetings, Mirza. Are we bothering you?"

Mirza raised his eyes from the newspaper and with exaggerated politeness said, "Please, you're welcome."

He was seventy or seventy-five years old, roughly the age of my Khan Papa Doctor, with a bald head and wide, flat birthmarks that made his face look like tannery leather. Fiddling with charcoal and opium and opium paste had not affected the extreme cleanliness of his hands. Really, he didn't belong in these surroundings. He was sewn to that room like an ill-matched patch—an aristocrat among rags. Mr. Farzaneh bowed again and laid the money in front of Mirza. Mirza said, "What are you doing this for? You're embarrassing me."

"It's not worthy of mention, Mirza."

On the surface, Mirza's attention seemed to be on Mr. Farzaneh. But secretly, he was watching me from the corner of his eye. He expected an explanation. Mr. Farzaneh said, "Mirza, this is Agha Roknideen. He too has an interest in painting. Well, now you can talk together all you want. We ourselves will sit in this corner and with your permission we'll smoke two portions of opium and make ourselves feel good."

For no reason, he burst into laughter. Mirza half rose and made a welcoming gesture to me. "O Allah, welcome. I'm very pleased."

Then a thought occurred to him. He looked directly into my eyes and said, "Your Excellency, you're the son of Mirza Sadegh."

I said, "Yes."

"It's a long time since I've been in his presence."

Once again he assumed an expression of impassivity and vagueness. He turned the rose- and bird-figured china bowl of his opium pipe over the burning brazier. He motioned for me to sit next to him on the mattress, and I did. He stuck a portion of opium to the pipe and offered it to me. I excused myself. He passed the pipe to Mr. Farzaneh. Mr. Farzaneh began puffing without hesitation, and the room became hazy with opium smoke.

Mirza seemed uneasy. He wasn't looking at me. He was pinching the mound of ashes in the brazier with his tongs. Finally, he embraced his knees, looked at the ceiling, and with no introduction said, "We both used to go to the Polytechnic. He was one year behind me."

I said, "Who do you mean?"

"Your father."

"My Khan Papa Doctor?"

"Is that what you call him?"

"Yes."

"Yes, of course. I'd forgotten. How is he?"

"He's gone to Ghaleh Bagh. He wants to stay there."

Mirza fell silent again. I didn't know what to do. I took paper and pencil from my pocket and drew a loose sketch of him that didn't resemble anything, especially Mirza. I grew bored and stopped drawing. He said, "Why don't you go on with your work?"

"What work, Mirza?"

"You were facemaking."

I hadn't expected to hear that archaic word. I liked the way he caught me by surprise. When I answered, I too used the word. I said, "Because I'm a facemaker. Facemakers have different temperaments from ordinary people. Sometimes they're compelled to follow their instincts."

He smiled. He said, "How . . . how long have you been facemaking?"

He was mumbling and drawing out his sentences, as if to give himself time to think. I said, "I don't know exactly how long. The idea doesn't hit your mind at a certain day and time."

He fixed his eyes on my face with unintrusive attention and said, "Why do you want to do a facemaking of me?"

Mr. Farzaneh had smoked his opium, and now he was slurping his tea. He said, "Ah, ah, how light a man gets, Mirza!"

He gave a full, congested cough. Mirza took the pipe from him and busied himself sticking a new portion of opium on it. He said, "Facemaking tells lies to people."

"How?"

"It double-crosses them."

Then he turned the pipe toward me and said, "This is for you." He had stuck to the bowl of the pipe something like a black wart or a meaty mole. I wanted to excuse myself and pass it on, but I couldn't bring myself to do it. He emphasized, "This is especially for you."

Mr. Farzaneh watched us from the other side of the brazier with an elated, diabolical smile. He had hooked his hands around his knees and was wiggling his toes inside his mended socks. He said, "Mirza, be careful with your cousin. He's inexperienced."

Mirza leaned on one elbow and put the opium pipe in my mouth. He said, "In the name of God, slowly and cautiously, with the help of the saint Ali."

Unresisting, I began to puff. Mirza's voice came to me through the thick of the smoke. "Facemaking . . . facemaking lures a person into swindling. The person becomes a fake."

I opened my eyes. Mirza's round, bald head was floating in the dense gray smoke like a big amber stone. Little by little I grew lighter, and the lightness lifted me. Space became hollow. The distance stretched between the brazier and the primus stove, between the brass tray and Mirza, and that made everything seem deeper. Looking at the room was like standing on the edge of a cliff; it tempted me to jump off and fly. I felt expanded. I said, "What's your point?"

He passed the opium pipe to Mr. Farzaneh. He stood up and beckoned me to follow him. He pushed aside a curtain and we entered a storeroom.

The storeroom was dark and moldy-smelling. He turned on a light. Fat, pregnant crocks of lard and pickles stood next to each other around the room. In the corner was a giant earthenware jar. He pointed to it and said, "That's the wheat-flour jar we brought from Varamin for the food shortage during the war."

On the opposite side, in front of vinegar flasks and jam jars, hung a piece of linen with a face charcoaled on it. It resembled a water-shrine icon with its almond eyes, arched brows, and empty gaze. The cheeks and lips were reddened with Mercurochrome. The tongue-tied little mask was shouting in the dusk of the storeroom. Mirza said, "Zobaydeh, our servant, hung this here so her grandchildren would be afraid to snitch the food."

He looked for something in the storeroom's nooks and crannies. He apologized: "I haven't been in here in a long time. After the confiscation of our lands, there was no need to search. Nothing was left for us to search for."

He smiled faintly. From one wall he lifted a big frame wrapped in a few old, yellowed newspapers. Under the electric light bulb he carefully took the frame from the newspapers' folds. He set it in front of me so I could look at it. It held a tableau. When I studied it closely, it seemed to me that I'd seen the landscape of the

painting before. A brass plaque at the bottom of the frame read
THE FORTUNETELLER.

The fortuneteller is squatting in front of a veiled woman at the
edge of a field, looking at her sideways. He is a middle-aged man
with a pulled-down mouth, a goatee, an egg-shaped hat, a buck-
ram robe, and Kermanshah slippers. At his feet, the fortunetelling
kerchief lies spread with its seal and rosary. The fortuneteller has
brought his nearsighted eyes a finger's distance from the woman's
palm, and he shows astonishment—a sort of dispassionate, profes-
sional astonishment. Behind him, far away, the surface of the field
shimmers under the spangled sunlight. Farther than that, on the
edge of the horizon, the dim color of the crowded trees has transformed the sky's blue to purple, and the purple lends the field an
edgeless vastness that gives the viewer a fear of falling. The dead
eyes of the woman gaze at a scene beyond the field, and her ear is
attentive to the voice of the fortuneteller. In the spiral of her
pupils the artist's purple paste forms a clot, a clot which in drying
has lost its glistening freshness. Between the astonished expression
of the fortuneteller and the worried and helpless expression of the
woman, the painter has created such a visual tension that looking
at the painting hurt my eyes.

Mirza asked, "What do you think of it?"

I lifted my head and said, with awe, "It's a fascinating piece."

"Your taste is good, Agha Rokni."

"Why is that?"

"This painting is one of the most important works of the Master Assar. He finished it a few months after the Hoseinabad incident."

"How strange."

Mirza seemed very pleased with himself. He folded his arms
across his chest and looked at me with a lofty head and a smile
full of pride. I pressed him: "What is this Hoseinabad incident?"

"Ask your father, I mean your Khan Papa Doctor. We didn't
used to call him Khan Papa Doctor. In those days, he was Major
Sadegh Khan. You understand? Major Sadegh Khan."

He bent to study the painting and said, "The art of the Master
Assar lay in the fact that he never depicted the real subject in his
paintings. You had to guess what it was he wanted to show you,

what he wanted to say, what his concern was. For instance, pay attention to this field, Agha Rokni. This is the place where the Hoseinabad incident occurred. I have photographs of that incident. I can show you, so you'll see what a difference there is between photography and facemaking."

He opened the lid of a steamer trunk and searched for the photos. My mind was on the painting. It seemed a breeze was passing over the mud houses, the trees, and the field, and in passing had snatched up and borne away the scattered voices and the signs of the animals' movements. A leftover vestige of the Hoseinabad incident, like the smell of a dirt road newly sprinkled with water, lingered in the air.

From a yellow envelope, Mirza took a few old photos and gave them to me. These black and white photos showed the field from several different angles with a vulgar bluntness, a sort of dumb crudeness.

Peasants' dead bodies lie littered here and there as though tossed around by a tornado. In one photo, the peasant in the foreground has pulled his hands up to his armpits. His loose, open legs point to opposite corners of the field. His head is bent back and his eyes are rolled up into their sockets. His frozen claws of fingers reach toward his throat. The arms of the second peasant are raised above his head, and the lines of his face are pressed together like those of a person who has swallowed a purging cassia. The third peasant is curled around the trunk of a walnut tree, and his legs are folded at the knee as if he were prostrate in prayer, though on his side. At the edge of the horizon, frightened little peasants scurry away. Their escape gives the photo a sense of illogical haste—like a movement that is halted abruptly, a struggle that is rendered motionless with one stroke.

Mirza said, "Agha Rokni, if the Master Assar's painting was not in front of you, would you be able to find anything interesting in these photos at all? You would have given them a passing glance and said there were plenty of these old photos. If you look at any books and newspapers printed during the Coup d'Etat of the Third of Pisces, 1921, you can see thousands like them."

Expecting an answer, he looked at me. But I was busy examining the photos. He rested his chin on his fist and said, "Looking at a painting is very different from understanding it. Most people, when they look at a painting, search their minds for something that bears a resemblance, even a farfetched resemblance, to the patterns of that painting."

"They search for something that explains the real world to them," I said.

A smile widened his brown birthmarks. He lowered his voice, and confidentially he said, "God bless you, Agha Rokni. It's obvious you're a genuine Heshmat Nezami. God willing, you'll also become a good facemaker."

He pointed to the painting and continued, "Many search only for their peace of mind. They search for something that reassures them, that promises them everything is safe and secure. For these people, everything is a means of rescue. But now, look carefully at this painting."

"Yes."

"There! The person who doesn't let his security be disturbed would look at that field and his heart would be delighted by the sight of the greenery and the wheat. You see what I'm saying."

"Yes, Mirza, I see very well."

He narrowed his eyes and said, "If you see, tell me what it is."

"When someone who wants only security looks at your photos, the Master Assar's painting comes to his mind and not the Hoseinabad incident."

Mirza laughed. He looked at me admiringly and said, "What you say is right, I mean it's both right and wrong. Wrong because the Master Assar's tableau is not so simple. People who talk about the Master Assar are generally Pollyannas, comfortably well off and inexperienced. Look at this painting. See how the Master addresses both the comfortable group and the anxious group? For the comfortable he has painted the field, the green crops and pastures, so they'll feel better just looking at them, so they'll feel delighted. But the anxious will worry about the feigned astonishment in the fortuneteller's eyes; you could even say they'll feel horrified. Am I right, Agha Rokni? Don't you feel horrified?"

At that moment, I was looking at a person in one of the photographs. He stood next to a faraway tree, a woolen Cossack hat on his head. He held a Hassan-Musa rifle and he chased the scurrying peasants with his eyes. I set a finger on the photo and said, "This man looks familiar to me. Do you know him?"

He stared at me and said, "Do you mean that officer?"

"Yes."

"That's Major Sadegh Khan."

He drew back, as if expecting an attack. I said, "My Khan Papa Doctor?"

"Yes, your honorable father. We used to call him Major Sadegh Khan."

"Why show me these photos? What's your point?"

Mirza assumed a distinguished, starchy posture and said, "Don't get upset over nothing. I didn't mean any harm. I thought, well, you're a facemaker and you have to have the heart to look at anything. Whatever you look at, you have to disbelieve. Ordinary, trivial things should surprise you, and you should grow horns just looking at them. Because, Agha Rokni, we live in a strange world. Whatever shouldn't happen is happening. Our world is a strange and unbelievable world."

"I still don't understand why you've shown me these photos. What do you want to prove by showing me my father in a Cossack uniform, among a handful of slain peasants?"

"I know I've upset you. The Heshmat Nezamis get offended very easily. But I'm hopeful that years from now, when you're older and you've tasted the cold and the warm of life and become a little more seasoned, you'll recall this lowly cousin and you'll recite the prayer of the dead for me and please my soul. I am absolutely sure that in the years to come you will please the soul of your big cousin. You'll say, 'God forgive the soul of Mirza Hassibi, let light be on his grave, because he rescued me from confusion.' You'll look at your sketches and understand that confusion is the true meaning of your life. Whatever you don't see is in front of your eyes. I have angered you tonight, Agha Rokni, but I'm not talking about tonight. My conversation is a conversation for the future. In a way, I am telling your fortune."

He rewrapped the Master Assar's painting in the old newspapers. I said, "Still you haven't told me why my Khan Papa Doctor was in Hoseinabad."

He leaned the painting against a pillar. He scratched his head and sank into thought. I asked, "Don't you want to answer me?"

"The story dates back to thirty or forty years ago. His late Royal Majesty had sent the Army to put down the uprising of Mirza Kazem Feshangchi. Mirza Kazem had got himself to Nishapur with ten or fifteen people. He'd put them into peasant outfits and was causing trouble for the landowners. If you examine the photos carefully, you will see they're not real peasants because of their boots. Peasants don't wear boots, especially Russian boots."

"You mean that His Majesty commissioned my Khan Papa Doctor?"

Mirza replaced the photos in their yellow envelope and laid the envelope in the steamer trunk. He was leaving the storeroom when I said, "Mirza, aren't you going to answer me?"

He turned and put a hand on my shoulder. He looked into my eyes in such a way that my breath became locked in my chest.

I was back in the time when they took away my Khan Brother Zia. Iran was absorbed in her handful of fresh walnuts, and she paid no attention to Zahra Soltan. Zahra Soltan was still wiping her eyes. At the side of the pool, my Bee Bee rose on tiptoe, turned her head, and watched my Khan Brother Zia as long as possible. Then suddenly she took off and ran after him. When she'd come within a few steps of him, she paused. Shyness halted her. She slowed her pace. She pulled the veil over her hair and with one finger she tapped his shoulder gently, as though tapping the windowpane to say lunch was ready. My Khan Brother Zia turned back and his eyes fell on her. He motioned for her not to worry. He assured her he would soon be home. In front of the agents, my Bee Bee covered her face with the veil, collecting herself and trying to keep up appearances. It was painful to see the mixture of suffering and patience expressed by her movements. My Khan Brother Zia soothed her with his embarrassed smile and said, "It's nothing. It's not important. A misunderstanding's occurred, it'll soon be cleared up. Don't feel bad."

My Bee Bee shook her head. Then she couldn't contain herself. She threw out both arms. Her veil fell to the ground. She reached for my Khan Brother Zia and pulled his head to her bosom and kissed his hair. She whispered something in his ear that I couldn't hear from the balcony. I could only see her lips moving as if reciting prayers.

I didn't want to ask Mirza Hassibi anything more. I wanted to say something to convey my appreciation and gratitude. Maybe he knew what was in my head. He was looking at me in a fatherly way, without speaking. I said, "Mirza, you must have seen many things in your life."

"More than you can imagine. But the length of a life doesn't matter. What matters is that a person wants to see and is able to see. Some people come into this world only to watch. For them, the world is a giant movie house, showing them a film without end. Whatever comes on the screen of this movie house is interesting and worthwhile. Your ancestors, the great thinkers of this country who prided themselves to the heavens and condescended to the stars, were good watchers, Agha Rokni. When they looked at the sky, they saw the sky they'd created within them, and all the troubles of the world couldn't affect that. The gaze of your ancestors was not the gaze of comfortable people. Their gaze was filled with fear and hope."

He lifted his hand from my shoulder and turned away impatiently, indicating that it was late and I must go. He drew aside the storeroom curtain and we both entered the room.

Mr. Farzaneh had spread the *Kayhan* newspaper on the rug in the middle of the room, and he was reading the news. Mirza, with that polite, fixed smile of his, was implying we should leave his house as soon as possible. I said, "I want very much to talk to you. I'm grateful for your conversation with me tonight."

He lowered his head and said, "Please brighten our eyes with your presence whenever you find time. The door of this house is open to you. The sight of you gladdens the heart."

Everything he said had a good-bye flavor to it. When we passed through the room, Mr. Farzaneh silently interrogated me with his bulging eyes and half-open mouth. I left him there without explanation and hurried from the room. I ran to the alley, sat down on the curb, and burst into tears.

3

At last Mr. Farzaneh's shadow appeared in the dark. Humming and holding a cigarette between his fingers, he came close like a flowing denseness. He bent over me and said, "How are you, Agha Rokni?"

I shook my head. He said, "So, that was Mirza Hassibi, the grandson of the late Sardar Azhdar. If you had seen him in the street, no doubt you wouldn't have recognized him. You'd have thought he was a lower-echelon civil servant, that he didn't own so much as a sigh, that his eight was pawned to his nine."

He raised his chin with difficulty and looked at the sky. He threw away his cigarette and said, "Such is life, Agha. It has its ups and downs. It has its good and bad. It has its right and wrong. Somehow you have to live it through. With a friend and companion, a bottle of booze, a brazier and an opium pipe, the moan of a fiddle, a skewer of kebab—what more do you want from life, Agha?"

He hitched up his trousers. He hooked his thumb in his belt and pointed to the sky.

"Do you see those stars, Agha? Mirza Nasrolah Khan, the

Scholar of Gorgon, the half brother of the late Heshmat Nezam
and the special royal astrologer, said himself that when you pon-
der on the world in depth you will see it's not a mishmash. It has
law and order. In any of its rotations, it moves according to a
formula. You don't know how scholarly and scientific Mirza Nasrolah Khan was. On Mirza Hassibi's rooftop he installed a telescope. Every Ramadan, each midnight, he would sit behind the
telescope and dive into the sea of stars. What a prodigy he was!
He made an ointment for Superior Venus's scrofula; in two hours
it would heal anything you put it on, even a phagedenic ulcer or
leprosy. God forgive his soul. He used to sit in front of his door
and hold his beard in his hand and say that the world has order, it
has formulas and laws. If you understand its formulas and laws,
nothing is impossible."

I said, "I can't make sense of anything you're saying. I don't
understand what your point is."

"My point is that you're wasting your time, Agha. Here you
stand, all happy that you're searching for your brother. As the
children used to say during the war, it's a lie like Ghasem the
Blind. It's a sort of masquerade, like everything else the Heshmat
Nezamis do. These differences they've created among themselves
are so much ass-branding. Among your people, there are all sorts
of characters, from militarists and monarchists to Tudeh Communists and National Frontists. You have rightists and also leftists.
You have progressive revolutionaries and also conservative reac-
tionaries. Whatever happens in this country, it's all the same to
you; in any faction you have someone to protect you on a rainy
day. If your brother's a revolutionary, your Uncle Agha
Abdolbaghi's an appointed senator. What I want to say is this. No
matter how you look at me and think in your heart that I'm no
good even as a registrar of documents, you shouldn't judge people
by appearances alone. Under this one-cent robe, there's a handful
of flesh and tendons and bones that have seen everything, and I
am the last of the world and no one has yet been able to shove it
to me. Do you understand, Agha? It's you who's the donkey. Go
and give your honorable father Sohrab Farzaneh's message: you
may have stuck it to everyone else, but you can't stick it to me."

He shook his finger in my face and looked at me with his buggy eyes. Then, loose and staggering, he went off in the direction of College Square. He wasn't yet dissolved in the dark of the street when he began to mumble:

"Yes, one should not run away from Providence.
No matter how little the cupbearer pours, it
is the essence of kindness."

I didn't know what to do. I couldn't form a plan. I walked one street after another and looked at the surfaces of things. In Mokhber al Dolah Square, some people in black clothing walked in two parallel lines, carrying something on their shoulders. Like an ethereal centipede, with the softness and silence of dust trails, they passed in front of the Nil Bookstore. A light was still burning in the bookstore and a man was hunched behind the desk, reading a book. Suddenly, an image of a man with a drawn sword appeared to me, passing behind the constellations and traveling toward the Pleiades and Capella. I wondered on whose shoulders I myself would be carried, who would wash me and who would pray for me. A passerby asked me how to get to Khaniabad. I answered, "It's not possible to get to Khaniabad from here."

He was surprised and went away.

When I reached the vicinity of Yousefabad, the traffic had thinned in the streets. The uproar, the cars in flames, and the burned tires were far away. It was late at night, and the back of the heat was broken. A cool, gentle breeze circled my neck and poured down my chest through the opening of my vest.

I decided, as I walked, to visit Azra and her husband, Jahangir. I hoped they weren't having a party so they couldn't invite me in. Jahangir frequently had to go to foreign embassies or entertain foreign diplomats. But in Mohsenin Street all I heard was the distant, weak voice of a radio announcer whispering the news behind the dark windows of a house, and the hissing of a sprinkler watering an invisible lawn. I stood in front of their house and rang the doorbell. The bell croaked, but nobody answered and I rang again. A footstep sounded on the second floor. Someone opened a window, paused, and closed the window. Everything fell silent and I rang the bell again. Now I was ringing with passion, and I imagined that if I pressed harder the bell would ring louder.

I sensed that someone was descending the stairs. Suddenly the courtyard lit up and Jahangir opened the door. He wore only his T-shirt and underpants. He rubbed his eyes and focused on me sleepily. He asked, "Who is it? It's late, Agha. People are asleep."

I froze. It occurred to me that I didn't know why I'd disturbed them at this hour of the night. Jahangir was still examining me with a dazed and impatient expression. When he recognized me, he pulled himself together, smiled, and said, "I didn't know you. Has something happened?"

I smiled, too, and said, "Hi! How are you? You're not around much nowadays."

He stepped back and I came in. In the courtyard, I put my hands behind me and pivoted on my boot heels. I looked at the sky and said, "What a sky! Full of stars."

Jahangir put a finger to his lips and said, "Ssh . . . the kids are asleep. You'll wake them up." The hall light came on and I saw Azra at the top of the stairs, wrapped in a red bathrobe. Impulsively, I asked, "How do you get to Khaniabad from here?"

With a shake of her head, she tossed her mussed hair back. She clutched her bathrobe to her bosom and waited for an explanation. I didn't have any explanation. We went to the living room and sat on chairs around a big table. Azra clutched her robe more tightly. She peered at me. She asked, in a concerned and sympathetic tone, "How are you, Rokni?"

"Not bad. If I've disturbed you, I apologize. I could go if you like and come back again tomorrow."

Azra and Jahangir exchanged glances. I tried to keep myself occupied. I put my hands in my pockets and searched for something aimlessly. My hand touched the folded balloon-man sketch. I took it out and put it on the table and waited for their reaction. Azra brought her head close and asked, "What is this, Rokni?"

"It's one of your balloon-man sketches. I want to apologize for taking it without your permission. Now I've brought it back. Well, with friends, this kind of misunderstanding often happens. It shouldn't be taken seriously."

Azra looked back and forth between me and Jahangir. Then she drew her chair a little closer. She pulled me to her and said, "Oh, Rokni."

"When I like something, the Devil gets under my skin. Then it's no longer within my power. I habitually pilfer."

She laughed. She showed the sketch to Jahangir and said, "Look at this. Do you like it?"

Jahangir examined the sketch and smiled with a forced expression of approval. Then he laid the sketch on the table and rested his head in his hand. A cigarette burned between two of his fingers, next to his temples, and his eyes were sunken with sleeplessness. It seemed he was waiting to find out what he had to do. Azra asked, "Well, Rokni, how'd you get here?"

"To tell the truth, I don't know myself. On foot."

"On foot?"

"Yes, I went to someone's house who's a distant relative. He's a strange person. You have to meet him. He owns one of the Master Assar's best works. Have you seen *The Fortuneteller?*"

"No."

"When you look at the painting, you somehow lose your orientation. As you study the fortuneteller's face, you imagine that two images are superimposed. Those eye cups, those shadows under the cheekbones, those rounded lips—it's as though the fortuneteller's head is hollow, as though they'd put a mask on an empty cave and the wind was passing through it, howling. Especially that mouth, I don't know how to describe it for you. It seemed to be whistling, like the leftovers of a gasp of disbelief."

She said, "Maybe you're tired."

"Azra, Mirza Hassibi knows things you can't believe. He showed me a photo I hadn't seen before of my Khan Papa Doctor in a Cossack uniform . . . To tell the truth, I don't know why I'm saying all this. I only know that I was provoked by what Mirza Hassibi said. I wanted to figure something out. I asked myself how to push the right button, how to pull the right string."

"I think you're tired. Would you like to spend the night with us? We'll spread a mattress for you on the balcony."

"Thank you, I have to go home."

Jahangir said, "Don't worry, I'll see you safely home."

"There's no need. I know the way."

He put out his cigarette in the ashtray and ran upstairs to the second floor. Azra drew closer and asked me, "What's the news of your Khan Brother Zia? Have you found any trace, a footprint, anything about him?"

I shook my head. Her eyes flickered and she said, "I gave your message to Masoud. He says finding your Khan Brother Zia is easy."

"He's talking nonsense."

"What a negative person you are. It's easy. First you have to make contact with him somehow. Print an ad in the newspaper: *Mr. Zia Heshmat Nezami: Your late mother, Miss Homayundokht, God forgive her soul, is worried because of your absence. Please get in touch with her as soon as possible.* How do you like that? Or put an ad on the radio: *Your Excellency, Mr. Ziadeen Heshmat Nezami: If no news of you reaches your sister, Iran, we will see you on Resurrection Day.* Rent a Blue Angel jet to write his name in the sky for three days at noon and sign it 'Mademoiselle Sonia.'"

I looked away, toward the folded sketch of the balloon man. I said, "Azra, don't you wish you had wings and could fly, you could circle the sky over the city?"

Azra sighed and said, "I don't know, Rokni."

I was avoiding looking at her. I saw only the flowing, sloping lines of her head and her neck that bent like a willow branch. At the same time, my chest was filled with a sort of deadness, a heaviness, an indefinable pressure. I started to scratch the varnish of the table with my fingernails. It wasn't scratching; it was more like digging. Again Azra's voice came: "Always thinking of flying, always among the clouds . . ."

My mind was on my nails digging at the table. It was like the sixth grade in primary school, when I used to dig a hole in the crossbred rose garden, hoping to discover a body under the dirt.

Jahangir ran down the stairs. When Azra saw him, she reached for the balloon-man sketch and took it away from me. Jahangir told me, "Agha Rokni, good night."

I knew I had to get going. I said, "Good night to everyone. I want to apologize again. Please forgive me."

Azra rested her elbows on the table and held her head between her hands. She didn't move. She said, "Rokni, don't forget to keep me informed. Maybe we won't see each other for a while, but we can talk by phone."

Jahangir followed me through the courtyard. He shifted his feet a little at the door and said, "There's nothing to be afraid of."

I said, "I know."

I stepped out into the street. When the door closed behind me, the light at my feet narrowed to a thread. I was alone in the dark and silence. I told myself, Never mind. I had to think of my family. I had to go back home.

At the head of the street, Masoud had already opened the door of his cherry-colored convertible. He was leaning against it with his arms folded, drilling questions into me with his damning eyes. I went to the car and took a seat, and till we started moving I didn't even chirp.

It was very late. Not a bird was flying in the streets. Spot by spot, the neon lights were melting the wax of the dark. The sharp, harsh lines in Masoud's face relaxed. Now his expression had some softness to it that made me feel he was sad. I said, "Do you have an order to take me someplace specific?"

He lost control and screamed, "What is this business you've created for us? Why do you bother people in the middle of the night? What is this business, hah?"

"What's eating you?"

"In which grave were you lost since this afternoon?"

"You know yourself that my leash was in Farzaneh's hands. He took me to Mirza Hassibi's house. You must know Mirza. He's a Sardar Azhdari."

He shook his head angrily and said, "It's my own fault that I troubled myself. Like a dog, I'm running in the streets for your sake, your Khan Papa Doctor's sake, your Khan Brother Zia's sake."

As he talked, the stink of arrack filled the car. I thought, What's the use of arguing with a drunk? I said, "Don't get upset over nothing. I don't want your favors. I can find my Khan Brother Zia myself. But I want to go to Ghaleh Bagh. I want to go see my Khan Papa Doctor. He's the one who knows everything."

"Why didn't you tell me this earlier?"

"What do you mean, tell you earlier?"

"Searching for this and that takes time, it's not easy."

In front of Lazarian's Café, he slammed on the brakes. We were both jerked forward by the car's sudden stop. He jumped out immediately, opened the door on my side, and yelled, "Hurry, for heaven's sake. I have to catch up with my friends."

"Go ahead and catch up with your friends."

"I have to introduce you to someone, too."

He spat on the pavement. Inside Lazarian's, his friends were sitting around a big table, and the table was covered with half-filled vodka bottles and Pepsi bottles and pieces of sandwiches. Masoud took hold of my wrist and bent toward the display window. He whispered, "Look. I thought you might want to meet this lady."

I looked. Baharestan Circle's purple sky was leaning against the windowpanes. A fat, middle-aged woman walked slowly toward us. Her short white socks were unbecoming to someone her age. She had a wire basket on her arm as though she were returning from grocery shopping. When she reached the display window, she tapped the glass with her finger. Masoud said, "Do you recognize her?"

I said, "No."

"That's Madame Sonia."

He opened the door for her and said, "Madame, come in. As usual, it took you a long time."

Madame Sonia said wearily, "Darling, thank you. She is tired, darling."

She had in her basket two bottles of vodka, a few loaves of French bread, packages of salami, dill pickles, and pickled vegetables. She put the basket on the next table and wiped the sweat off her forehead with the back of her hand. She looked around and asked Masoud, "How are you? Your feeling is good? Your nose is healthy and fat?"

Masoud said, "I'm fine, madame. I have to catch up with my friends."

He pointed to his friends. Madame took a pack of cigarettes from between her breasts and lit a cigarette for herself. Then she set a fist on her hip and, blowing circles of concentrated smoke toward the ceiling, she said, "Go ahead, darling. Catch up with your friends. Madame walks alone in the streets and the soldiers can't touch Madame. If they touch her, Madame will pick up the soldier with her fingertip and throw him in the trash can like a dead rat."

She burst into sudden, scratchy laughter. Then she raised her fist to her mouth and started coughing.

Everything about her had changed. The opening of her short-sleeved jersey dress was stretched below her large, braless breasts. With any movement, the beefy flesh of her arms floated in the air. Her blond hair had lost its smoothness and liveliness and it spun around her face, uncombed. Only the honey color of her eyes remained the same, looking at the world with the clarity of a still spring.

She turned and saw me. She took the cigarette from her lips and said, "Have I seen you before? Do I know you?"

Masoud said, "Can't you tell who this is?"

"Who is he, darling?"

"Zia's little brother, Rokni."

Madame smiled and said, "I am thankful to see you, you are very dear, I am very much honored."

She patted her crumpled hair with the shyness of a young girl. Under her breath she said, "Zia's little brother! You were so little and now you're so tall. How big are you! You've become like a desert monster, God willing."

She held her hand first low and then high, indicating how I'd grown. She rounded her eyes with happiness. I said, "Madame, you've changed too."

She put on a pouting expression. I asked, "What's new with my Khan Brother?"

She twisted her lips and said, "Nothing new about Brother."

"Have you forgotten all about him?"

"Madame never forgets. Life is difficult. Madame has to work and make money for supper, but she doesn't forget."

Then she flung out her hands, as if giving up. She sat down at the next table and said, "Madame doesn't like talking."

She took one of the vodka bottles from her basket and opened it. Masoud waved to us and said, "I'm going to sit with my friends now. Rokni, I'll get in touch with you tomorrow."

He went off to his friends' table. Madame took a gulp from the

vodka bottle. She shouted, "Madame doesn't wish to talk. This is
the only wish that Madame expects the world to grant. Madame
doesn't wish to talk."

I said, "Madame, I just wanted to ask you one thing. If you
know the answer, don't withhold it. Is my Khan Brother Zia
alive? Is he?"

She banged her fist on the table and said, "Your brother will
never die. Do you understand? The man whose heart comes alive
with love will never die. He may be tortured, he may be hurt, but
he'll never die."

Her face had grown red, and sweat was dripping from her temples. She relaxed on her chair. She let her legs spread apart, and I
could see the elastic bands that encircled her fat white thighs.
With one hand she groped on the table for her cigarettes and
matches. When she found them, she shoved them between her
breasts. She rose and said, "Madame has to go. Madame is very
tired."

She left the café in a hurry. I, too, left. I found her sitting in a
rickety car, a Stone Age model, which she was turning around in
the street when I reached her. I hooked my fingers on the window
ledge. I smelled the bitter smoke of the cigarette that hung from a
corner of her mouth. I didn't retreat. I said, "Madame, madame."

She answered me with tight lips. "It's getting late, Agha."

I begged, "Madame, I won't take long. I only wanted to talk to
you for a few minutes. It's important."

She got the car moving, and as I hung on the door, I was
dragged along the pavement. Madame said, "Agha, let Madame
go home. She will talk some other night."

I gave up. I let go of the door. Madame put her foot on the gas
and drove away. I hadn't taken more than a few steps when I saw
her stop at the intersection and back up. When she reached me,
she set her fat elbow on the window ledge and said, "Get in,
darling. You've twisted my arm."

I got in. The car was filled with old newspapers and wooden
crates. The smell of onion, garlic, and pickles burned my nose.
After riding awhile, I said, "Look, madame. I want to ask how
long it's been since you've heard from my brother."

"Ten years, darling. A little more, a little less, perhaps ten years."

She started coughing. She put her hand between her breasts and took out her pack of cigarettes, as though the cure for her cough was to chain-smoke, puff-puff. We entered Naderi Street and went toward Shah's Three Points. She wanted to light her cigarette but had lost her matches. At the same time she continued: "I'll tell you one thing. Your brother is not a chicken. Whatever he is, he's not a chicken."

She stopped the car beside an Army truck. Two soldiers stood there, each with a foot on the running board. They were joking with each other, and their laughter rang out in the empty street. Madame yelled, "You soldiers!"

They stopped laughing and looked over at us. Madame Sonia waved and said, "Do you have a match for Madame's cigarette?"

The younger one, who had the face of a country boy, came close to the car. He still showed traces of laughter. He set his hands on the car roof and asked, "What are you doing in the streets at this hour?"

"Madame has business. She has to go to the hospital and give birth."

The soldier tried not to laugh at Madame's accent. He said, "Now, what is it you want?"

"I want you to light Madame's cigarette."

The soldier took a lighter from his pocket and lit Madame Sonia's cigarette. She blew smoke in his face, and he pulled his head back. Madame said, with a sigh, "Madame is very thankful. Madame expects that someday she will light *your* cigarette."

The soldier saluted and we started off. As we grew distant, the soldiers' laughter faded behind us. Then Madame Sonia's expression changed. The complimentary smile was washed from her face. She hit her hand on the wheel and said, "May their fathers burn in hell! One day they should be choked. They should be punished. Darling, if they shut your mouth, if they don't let you talk, you're not alive. You're worse than dead. A dead man doesn't have feelings, but a suffocated man feels and can't say so."

She grew thoughtful, and her silence forced me into silence

also. At Shah's Three Points, she sighed and asked, "What time is it, darling?"

I didn't have a watch. I said, "It must be past midnight."

"Want to drink vodka and talk?"

"All right."

"Whatever Madame says, you do? Because you want Madame to tell you things?"

She parked in front of her apartment and climbed out. She opened the back door of her car and said, "Help Madame carry her load to the house. Then Madame will talk for you. She'll entertain you so you won't get bored."

I carried the crates to her apartment. The apartment, too, smelled of salami, garlic, onions, and pickles. She turned on the lights and we took the crates to the basement and stacked them against the wall. Madame Sonia drew a half-empty vodka bottle from a cardboard box and poured each of us a glass. She also chose a few pickles, put them on a china plate, and set everything on a wobbly table. She said, "Darling, this basement is Madame's real home. Here you can say whatever you want. Here you're free. Nobody will bother you."

She threw herself onto a chair. She pushed back her hair, which had fallen over her face, and said, "To your health. To your brother's health. To the health of Iran."

She emptied the glass and set it down. She put her hands on her knees. She leaned forward and asked, "Well, darling, so you're searching for Brother?"

"Yes."

"No use, darling. Brother won't be found."

"How do you know?"

"Ten years ago, Brother goes underground. He doesn't want to see anyone. He doesn't want to talk to anyone. Brother says a revolutionary has to cut his ties. It's ten years ago that Brother was imprisoned, and then he escapes. Again he's imprisoned and again he escapes. But he won't come to Sonia. He won't go to his father. Sonia says, let it be. Sonia doesn't want to see Brother. She doesn't want to go to the prison in the middle of the night and see Brother getting beaten but not talking."

She wagged her finger like a pendulum and continued. "Tsk,

tsk, tsk. Brother bit his tongue but didn't talk. Ten years have passed since that night Sonia saw Brother in the prison. Sonia encouraged Brother. She begged Brother, 'Don't think of Sonia, Zia. Sonia is all right.' Sonia knew that if Brother opened his mouth and betrayed himself he would die. What a brother, how courageous! In front of the police, he yelled, 'Sonia, Sonia, go and get lost!' But those mother-fucking police did bad things to Sonia in front of Brother. They tore Sonia to pieces."

She put her glass on the table and wiped the tears from her face with her fat fingers. She slammed her hands hard on her knees and said, "Madame became helpless. She became a dishrag. You can blow your nose in it and throw it in the toilet. Every Friday I went to prison to see Zia. But then Brother escaped from prison and hasn't come to Sonia for ten years. Look, darling. To tell the truth, Madame doesn't want to see Brother ever again. Sonia is tired. Sonia likes to live alone and comfortable and never see Brother again."

"What happened then to all that love? You two cared about each other so much!"

She answered with exasperation. "Go and ask your crazy brother, darling. Sonia was happy to do whatever Brother wanted. But woe to that crazy brother, that Heshmat Nezami brother. Any time Sonia begged, 'Zia, come and get married,' Brother said he wouldn't marry, he doesn't like marriage."

"Why not?"

"Because of jealousy. Your brother was jealous. You know before going to prison he hit Sonia, asking why she talks to gentlemen in the Maxim Bar, why she dances with gentlemen. Your brother came down the stairs and bang, slapped Sonia in the face and cursed her, said, 'Sonia's a whore. Sonia shouldn't drink whisky with American soldiers.' Sonia said, 'Dear Zia, come and kiss me.' Your brother sat at the table and peeled a cucumber. He was angry at Sonia and wouldn't talk. He spat at the wall."

"Just think, I imagined you would swoon and die for each other."

She laughed. She wiped her tears and said, "To the health of little Rokni. Oh, Rokni, you were so little, and now you're so big."

"Madame, you, too, have changed."

With both hands, she lifted the bulge of her abdomen. "Madame became fat, she became like a wineskin."

"You're still beautiful."

"What beautiful? She became like a wineskin, she got wrinkled, her teeth got yellow and rotten."

"Do you remember that day you came to our house?"

She bit her lip with pretended shyness and looked at me mischievously from the corner of her eye. "It was a scandal. Remember? God kill me."

She stood up. She smoothed her dress. She put her hands on her hips and turned this way and that, as though admiring herself in a mirror. She said, "Rokni, really, is Madame still young and beautiful?"

"Yes."

"Madame has to go on a diet and get thin, wear fashionable clothes and put on makeup. Woe to your crazy brother. Bad brother. Your brother didn't appreciate Sonia. A year before going to prison, he grew a beard. He shaved his head. He became a Moslem and a fanatic. He prayed in the morning. He prayed in the evening. He prayed in the middle of the night. He coughed and prayed. He got headaches and prayed. From morning till evening he prayed like a seesaw. He told Sonia she's a Moslem, she has to pray. She has to wear a veil. Sonia said, 'Very well, darling. But let Sonia be free. Sonia's a little sparrow and she withers in a cage, her heart will crumble.' But woe to that crazy brother of yours. He didn't listen to Sonia. He grew stonyhearted. He took Sonia to the shrine of Shadoolazi."

"To what?'

"St. Shadoolazi."

"St. Shab dol Azim."

"Yes, of course, darling. He took Sonia to Shadoolazi. He poured the water of repentance on her head. He made Sonia a Moslem."

She refilled her glass and continued. "Well, Sonia liked your brother. She was in love. She wanted to melt his stony heart. She was crazy about your brother. What a brother! Sonia sleeps at night and in her sleep she dreams about your brother, who looks at her with those eyes of his. His eyes scratch Sonia like a kitten's paw, and burn her heart."

She stood up. She searched around and muttered, "It's enough, Rokni. Madame's tired, she wants to sleep."

I said, "Madame, I'm afraid."

"Of what, darling?"

"I don't know of what."

"If your brother doesn't return, you still have to live."

"Madame, do you want to go with me and search for him? I know he's alive, and in the end they'll set him free."

She smoothed her hair nervously. She arranged her hem over her bare knees. She examined her fingernails from beneath her lowered eyelids. There were still traces of red polish on her bitten nails. Carelessly and sleepily, she spread an old blanket on a bench and said, "Darling, Madame's tired. In her life, Madame has seen very, very much. Now Madame wants to be comfortable. Madame can't see your brother. Do you understand, Rokni? Madame can't see anymore."

She stretched out on the blanket, and as she was getting settled, she said, "If you want to stay, darling, it's up to you. You are dear, you are honored, this house is yours . . ."

She went to sleep. The basement grew quiet. A feeling of tiredness came over me, too. I stood up and prepared to go—not just to my own house, but to Ghaleh Bagh to see my Khan Papa Doctor. As I emerged from the apartment, it was getting light and the dawn was flowing down the empty streets—an outspread, soothing dawn, a dawn full of calm and dignity.

BOOK THREE

Solar Eclipse

1

My Uncle Aziz put the bedrolls on the roof of the Studebaker and tied them down with rope. When he saw me, he grumbled under his breath, "Well, so now we're going to Ghaleh Bagh. Does that set your mind at rest, Rokni?"

I couldn't concentrate, because I hadn't slept the night before. I rubbed my eyes and said, "I don't know."

"It's you who insisted; how come you've lost interest?"

My silence wasn't because I had nothing to say. He waited awhile. Then he shrugged and said, "Tell them to come. The car's ready."

I pushed back the curtain in front of the courtyard. My Bee Bee and Iran and Zahra Soltan were sitting beside the pool. I couldn't hear their voices from this distance. Their veils were whiter than the Arabian and white jasmine in the flower beds. The entire courtyard was swept and watered. The last of the sunlight anointed the tips of the branches and blazed in the windowpanes like the copper eyes of an idol. Gradually, with the approaching sunset, sheets of light rose to the sky from the invisible planes of the house.

It was exactly like the year when the sun became dark. My Khan Papa Doctor rubbed his hands together to clean off the smelting-furnace soot. Then he laid his geomancer's set and astrolabe on the ground next to the late Scholar of Gorgon's engineering machine. He said, "Now, you young people may laugh, but not all of the Scholar of Gorgon's work was crap. There was some truth to it. He could predict solar and lunar eclipses and rains and storms, and on a scientific basis, too. It was by this kind of scientific calculation that Xerxes was able to take so large an army to Greece. It was with similar calculations that Nader Shah set caldrons filled with fire on the humps of camels and sicced the frightened camels on the accursed Indian elephants."

He raised the tube of the engineering machine to the sky and put his left eye to the lens and continued. "If not for the British interference, the Scholar of Gorgon would have singlehandedly built an atom bomb before the Vosugh el Doleh's concessions. The British got wind of it and changed the machine's nuts and bolts. That's why now, even if you sent an elephant aloft, you couldn't find it in the sky with this machine."

When you looked up from the veranda you could see the sun. But the border of the disk was darkened like the crescent of a fingernail.

Standing at the edge of the pool, my Khan Brother Zia took off his outer clothes and assumed a diving posture. But he couldn't bring himself to dive. He shouted, "Should I dive, Rokni?"

I shouted back, "Dive, Brother!"

My Khan Papa Doctor grumbled behind the Scholar of Gorgon's machine. "Rokni, if you want to talk with this lunatic, this Agha Aziz II, go to the courtyard. Get away from here."

"Well, what's the matter? He's my brother."

"I wasn't forbidding you to talk with him. I just don't have the patience to listen. Last year he disbelieved everything and turned atheist and wanted to take a Polish wife. This year he's grown a beard and mustache. He's shaved his head clean and if you talk to him he answers you in Arabic. Oh, dear Father, I give up."

The solar eclipse was gradually becoming complete, corresponding to the Scholar of Gorgon's formula as my Khan Papa Doctor had calculated it. The sun's darkness gave an odd, other-

worldly mood to the atmosphere. It seemed the air was sprinkled
with soot. A deathlike pallor was cast across the surface of the
earth, and one by one the stars began to shine. My Khan Brother
Zia was visible in the distance. He shaded his eyes and looked at
the sky. I called, "Why is the sky changing like this?"

He called back, "The sun is entering the eclipse."

From the veranda, I jumped into the courtyard. I went over and
stood beside him and watched the sun. My Khan Brother Zia
said, "Didn't Khan Papa Doctor tell you not to look at the sun?
You'll go blind. You have to look through smoked glass so your
eyes won't get hurt."

"Why are you looking at the sun yourself without a smoked
glass?"

"You little donkey, I'm not looking at the sun. I'm looking at
the edges of the sky."

The washtub banging of the neighbors rose from here and
there. Veiled women came over the rooftop to watch the sky.
From the mosque at the head of the street, the call to prayers rang
out loudly. My Khan Brother Zia said, "Strange, how strange it
is. Look at the sky. How dark it's grown!"

"How long will it stay dark?"

He grinned and said, "You have to ask Khan Papa Doctor."

My Khan Papa Doctor's head came into view from behind the
Scholar of Gorgon's machine. He picked up his German binoculars and held them to his eyes, and he searched the sky for the
sun. By the time my Bee Bee and Zahra Soltan came to the veranda, he wore an exasperated expression. My Khan Brother Zia
nudged me and said, "In a moment, Khan Papa Doctor is going
to lose control. In a moment he's going to scream at your Bee
Bee."

But my Khan Papa Doctor disappeared behind his machine.
My Bee Bee circled her arm around a veranda column and, like a
boxwood branch, she arched and stared at the black sun. Behind
her was the silhouette of Iran, who sat cross-legged on the tele-
phone-room window seat and gazed at herself in the hand mirror
of Homayundokht, God forgive her soul. I said, "Look at her."

My Khan Brother Zia's mind was on the sun and he didn't
want to be bothered. He said irritably, "Look at who?"

"How prettily my sister studies herself in the hand mirror of the late Homayundokht!"

"She's playing. She isn't smart enough to study herself in a mirror. If she were, she'd take a little care of her appearance."

"I swear by your life, she's putting on makeup in front of the mirror."

Iran had opened a rouge box and was rubbing the cotton pad on her cheeks and enjoying her reflection. My Khan Brother Zia set his fists on his hips and looked at her. The sounds of people, of washtub banging and the call to prayers, rose in the street and on the rooftops. My Khan Brother Zia and I hunched our backs and ran bent over toward Iran. From close up, her face was odd. She had rubbed on spots of rouge like clots of blood. She looked like a circus clown who'd been beaten. You would shudder and laugh at the same time if you saw her. My Khan Brother Zia burst out laughing and said, "She wants to mimic. It's all playacting."

"Mimic what, Khan Brother?"

"Mimic our mother. When our mother passed away, Iran wasn't more than three and a half years old. But it had its effect on her. They say the mother's effect on her children starts from the earliest days of life. Except that it soon leaves their minds and they forget."

"Maybe Iran remembers. Maybe there are things left over in her mind. She imagines things we can't understand; maybe she sees things we don't see."

"Maybe. It's not so farfetched. I remember our late mother was standing on the rooftop. It seemed as though the street people were gathered outside the wall of our house. Our late mother removed her veil. I always ask why she didn't wait. Why did she remove her veil, especially in those days? It wasn't wise."

I was hoping he'd go on talking about Homayundokht, God forgive her soul, but he changed the subject. He said, "You should start saying your prayers, Rokni."

"Do you fast, too?"

"Yes."

We walked together to the other side of the courtyard. It hit me that he was right, I ought to start praying and fasting, and I ought to grow a beard and shave my head when I came of age. Even

better, I should wear a turban and a robe. Now the sky was really
dark. A crowd of people in black had lined up on the edge of the
rooftop like a row of burnt matchsticks, and they were watching
the stars. The circling flames and smoke of a bonfire leapt in the
sky behind the telephone wires. My Khan Brother Zia said,
"Rokni, do you hear that?"

"Hear what?"

"The shouting of the people in the street."

"Yes, I hear it, far away—far, far away."

"When you listen to a group, you don't appreciate that those
voices come one by one from people's throats."

"Yes, a group sounds just like a single roar."

Still sitting on the window seat, Iran moved the mirror up and
down in front of her face and put daubs of rouge on her ears. Next
to her, my Bee Bee and Zahra Soltan were entranced, motionless,
drowned in the sight of the sky. At the same time, the sun was
slowly emerging from the darkness. The chorus of the crowd was
fading and the line of people on the rooftop was breaking up. My
Khan Brother Zia shrugged and gave a beautiful smile that delighted my heart. My Khan Papa Doctor kicked the Scholar of
Gorgon's machine in a temper, and it fell heavily on its side into
the courtyard. Then he went to the library in disgust. My Khan
Brother Zia's eyes sparkled. He ran toward the pool and dove into
the water like a bullet.

The surface of the pool was calm now. They had changed the
water, and it was so clear that you could see the bottom. I yelled,
"Everybody here, the car's ready. Let's go."

My Bee Bee answered, "We're coming, Rokni. We're waiting
for Iran. Help to get her going."

I kissed Iran's face. I patted her hair. I said in her ear, "Are you
excited at seeing my Khan Papa Doctor?"

She didn't answer. I held her arm and she started limping along
on her bandaged foot. She was light as a paper boat that you blow
across the water.

Zahra Soltan teased my Uncle Aziz: "Agha Aziz, if you were to
make a thousand knives, not a one of them would have a handle."

My Uncle Aziz said, "All joking aside, Zahra Soltan, invest a hundred tumans and in six months it will triple."

"Agha Aziz, is this like the story of that stocking machine, when you said that in three months my fifty tumans would become two hundred?"

My Uncle Aziz tied the last knot in the rope. He wiped the sweat off his brow and said, "Is it my fault the customs agents confiscated my machine? Where can I find the money to wax their mustaches so they'll release it?"

"Agha Aziz, never mind the stocking machine, how about the chicken farm?"

My Uncle Aziz threw his hands up and didn't answer. The women climbed into the back seat of the car. I sat in front, next to Uncle Aziz.

When the car started moving, my Bee Bee settled back in her seat with a look of happiness that I hadn't seen on her recently. She recited the prayer, "Say That He Is Allah," and she blew it all around her for everyone's protection and ran her eyes over our faces with a thankful smile. Then she leaned forward and told my Uncle Aziz, "Agha Aziz, be careful."

"Sister, I told you not to take too long. Now it's already evening. If we fall into a valley it's your own fault, you know what I mean?"

"Don't say anything unlucky. If it's a man's fate to fall into a valley, it doesn't matter whether it's night or day. He'll find a valley and throw himself into it."

"Most accidents happen at night."

"Agha Aziz, man must trust in God. The servant of God is in God's protection."

Uncle Aziz started laughing and speeded up.

The closer we got to Fozieh Circle, the more crowded the streets grew. My Uncle Aziz stopped the car here and there to let horse carts, porters, and messenger boys pass in front of him. Beyond Jaleh Avenue, the crowd thinned. The hubbub was replaced by a bottomless vacuum of darkness, as though we'd fallen into a well. The women were soon asleep. My Uncle Aziz stared at the car's two columns of light that pushed back the darkness on the road. He asked quietly, "Rokni, is everyone asleep?"

"Yes."

"Put your hand in the glove compartment and take out that flask."

"Uncle Aziz, you're driving."

"Don't argue. The moon's coming up; it'll be wasted. We ought to enjoy ourselves."

I found the flask and gave it to him. He gulped from it and offered the flask to me. I took a swallow too. He said, "You say they're all asleep?"

"I guess. Do you want me to make sure?"

"No, no, let them sleep. Speak more softly."

"Uncle Aziz, why is it you don't come around anymore? You keep us at arm's length."

"I've gone in for passion plays."

"You wanted to start a business. How come you're back with passion plays?"

"You know me. I can't sit still. A man who's addicted to deserts and travel can't get used to city life."

"I guess you've used up Zahra Soltan's money."

"It's all gone. The stocking machine has its expenses."

His chuckle grew louder. He threw a glance behind him, checking to see if Zahra Soltan had heard what he said. Then he relaxed and smacked his lips, and his eyes flickered mischievously.

With no preparation, I attacked him. "You always cut a slice for yourself, Uncle Aziz. You even cut a slice from my Bee Bee."

"If a man can't cut a slice from his own sister, then from who else, dearest? In this family, everyone blames everything on me. When they want to put someone down, they call him Agha Aziz II. They say, 'He's become a knife wielder and a street Arab like Agha Aziz; he's turning out to be good for nothing.' What about you yourself, Rokni? What glory have you brought us that no one dares to say there are eyebrows over your eyes? Whatever you do, whatever stink you make, they say it's because of your intelligence and talent. Now, if I were to do the same thing, they would say it's because of donkey-headedness. They'd say, 'Agha Aziz is crazy, his mind is like a stone.' If you want to know the truth, let me tell you that your brother—I mean Agha Zia, you understand—"

"Yes."

"Agha Zia was like me. He was a real man, you know what I mean? They said something was wrong with his brain, his head was full of ambitious ideas. Then they destroyed him."

"Why do you bring him up out of the blue?"

He lowered his voice and said nostalgically, "He's been gone a long time, you know. It's not at all clear what they've done to him. In the days when we were young, the war was just ended and your brother and I found a job in the Russian circus. I looked after the tiger cage. Your Khan Brother Zia sold tickets."

He started laughing and continued: "In a month's time, they kicked us in the ass and threw us both out. We'd been going afternoons and sitting behind the Russians, watching them play chess. Our boss was a short, fat man they called Zhukovsky. There was always a stinking Russian cigarette in the corner of his mouth, and when he talked he would squeeze the pimples on the tip of his nose and pop them one by one. This one day, as soon as he caught up with us he jabbered something in Russian that we couldn't figure out. This little Armenian guy whose name was Jacob translated what Zhukovsky said. It seems that the comrade didn't need us any more and we had to get lost. Jacob used to do a lot of apple polishing for Zhukovsky. He was tall and thin like a thief's ladder. He had learned Russian and become a Tudeh Communist. He always wanted to sweeten up to the Russians and put a spoke in our wheels. One day, behind the Sangelaj slums in Khayam Street, we found that mother-fucking Jacob alone in front of the Etalaat Newspaper Building. I myself grabbed Jacob's hands from behind. Talk about Jacob: he was frightened. He thought we were about to send him to his prophet Jesus. He turned to us and said, 'What is this?' Your Khan Brother Zia gripped his throat and said, 'Why are you making trouble for us?' He socked Jacob in the ribs with his fist and said, 'Are you Iranian or not? Why do you betray us to the stupid Russians for nothing?' Jacob said, 'If I'm Iranian, then why do you punch me to make me talk? Why don't we discuss this together in a free and friendly fashion, so we can understand each other?' He was speaking bookishly, you see, like a member of the Tudeh Communist Party. Your Khan Brother told me to let go of Jacob so he could say what he wanted. Jacob put his hand out and asked your Khan Brother, 'Do you want to shake hands?' Your Khan Brother said, 'Up your ass.' Then they went and sat together in front of the Nezami Elementary School and talked. I don't know what Jacob told your brother, but it changed the kid completely. Somehow Jacob stole his dice and from then on your brother avoided me. I'm telling you, Rokni. They hugged each other and walked shoulder to shoulder in the direction of Firdosi Avenue. I said, 'All right, if that's the way the world is, then balls.' I got going and went to Melli Theater and saw the movie, *The Jungle Rooster.*"

"You could have followed them. Why didn't you?"

"How should I know? In Shah's Mosque I got hooked by Sayed Rajab's passion players. My voice was good. I was good-looking, too. Sayed Rajab said I could sing the young bridegroom, St. Ghasem."

From the back seat, my Bee Bee said, "Agha Aziz, a little lower. Iran's asleep."

"Sister, why are you awake?"

My Bee Bee answered him in her Kangavari accent, "I'll go to sleep, if your chattering allows it."

We stopped talking. In the deep of the night, the headlights opened the road and the moonlight spread everywhere. Below us passed the woods along the river and the darkness in the bottom of the valley. My Uncle Aziz's voice revived, but this time it was gentler and more cautious. "Yes, Rokni. If I could make a million tumans, there wouldn't be any more sadness and worry to put us at such a dead end. If luck allowed, if fate were with us. With a million tumans I'd buy a house in Shemiran, on the road to Darband, or in Golabdareh. With the rest of the money I'd live any way I liked. I'd invite the gang to lunch on Fridays and I'd spread a Sardar Azhdari table for them. In the old days they used to say a man's head is tied to his useless gut. If you don't look after your stomach, you'll meet your Creator. They'll put the lid on you and say the prayer for the dead. Your manner of dying, they say, depends on who you've descended from. Either you die of hunger

and poverty, or of the illnesses of the rich and upper crust, you
know what I mean?"

"What are these rich and upper-crust illnesses?"

"Heart attack, hemorrhoids, anal fistula, and gout. Then I say,
What do others have that I don't have? The same year they na-
tionalized petroleum—the year they kicked out the British, I
mean—I won a hundred thousand tumans in a card game. Your
Khan Brother was sitting beside me watching. He said in my ear,
'Don't let your father burn in hell, Agha Aziz. Stop the game.
You're going to lose, you know.' But do you believe a man's greed
has any limit? Just to prove your brother right, in forty-five minutes I lost the hundred thousand tumans to the last penny. That
was nothing. In addition, I borrowed fifteen thousand tumans
from your Bee Bee and added that to my losses and still came out
of the casino empty-handed. I wanted to kill myself. I found the
pearl-handled revolver of your Khan Papa Doctor and put it to
my temple to free myself. But your Khan Brother didn't let me.
He grabbed my wrist and said, 'Agha Aziz, stop it.' Instead, he
gave me his treasure map, so if I found the treasure we could split
it between us and get rich. Then, just my lousy luck, he started
chumming it up with Jacob. He got busy with Party activities and
forgot about me. I was left with that treasure map. No matter how
hard I looked for your brother, he didn't show his face. I heard he
wore Kermanshah slippers and carried an appointment book in
his shirt pocket. He sold the Party newspaper in front of the
university, he wrote slogans on the walls. I told myself, Finding
the treasure on my own is no fun. What did I want the treasure
for? You know what? The treasure map is a lie, too. Take it from
me, all of life is a lie and it's not worth a penny."

He drummed his fingers on the wheel. The moon was hidden
behind the car roof, but its light washed the windowpanes with
soapy water. A feeling of foreboding came over me. Some sort of
strangeness arose between me and my Uncle Aziz. All of a sudden
I wished that my Khan Brother Zia were sitting behind the wheel,
taking us for a ride to Tajrish Bridge to buy fresh walnuts and
roasted corn on the cob.

Uncle Aziz was really tipsy. He started singing under his
breath:

"Look at the separateness, that my love and I like
       two eyes
   Are neighbors to each other but haven't seen each
       other's houses."

As he quavered, he kept his eyes half shut and wore a lovesick
expression.

We had reached a point thirty kilometers from Ghaleh Bagh
and were circling the curve of Molah Felfeli Mountain. All at
once the air was saturated with the smell of water and greenery,
and our eyes caught the lights of Lamak flickering in the dark. As
we started downhill, the front of the car struck the embankment
and my Bee Bee jumped up and screamed, "Help, O Lord of the
Faithful!"

My Uncle Aziz opened the door in a daze, stepped out onto the
highway, and began to examine the car. Zahra Soltan stuck her
head through the window and said, "Finally, Agha Aziz has de-
livered his gift."

Then she softened her tone and asked me, "Dear, where are we?
Are we alive? Are we dead? Are we in this world? Are we in the
next?"

The shouts of my Uncle Aziz reached us from beneath the front
tires. "The fender's messed up, my car is demolished, and you
guys are leaning back in your seats gibing at me. I don't know
why I bother."

My Bee Bee rolled down her window and said, "Agha Aziz, did
you drink forbidden water again?"

My Uncle Aziz emerged from beneath the car and bent toward
my Bee Bee's window. As he spoke, his head wobbled like a loose
spring. "Sister, now you want to blame me for this? You're looking for an excuse? You want to hint that I'm not alert, that my
driving's no good?"

"Yes, Agha Aziz. I want to say just that."

My Uncle Aziz banged his fist on the car roof and said, "If
that's the way things are, then sit behind the wheel yourself and
drive."

He turned away in a huff and set off down the middle of the

road toward Lamak. I jumped out of the car and ran after him. I shouted, "Uncle Aziz, what's all this production for?"

He paused, but he didn't answer. I caught up with him and put my arm around his shoulders. Up close, he smelled of arrack and stubbed-out cigarette butts. He was breathing calmly and waiting for what I would say. I said, "What's this foolishness? In the middle of nowhere, with three women depending on you, you make such a production? Is this the way to do things?"

"Here are the car keys, they're yours. Please. Let it be you they depend on. At least, if the car falls into the valley, they won't yell at you."

"Uncle Aziz, I don't know how to drive. I can't tell a car from a horse cart. And you said yourself, this wreck of yours can't move at all. Even if I knew how, I couldn't drive it thirty kilometers to Ghaleh Bagh on this mixed-up, winding road."

"Me neither. I'm getting like an old car that burns too much oil myself, I swear by the saint Ali."

"What have we done, that you abandon us in the middle of nowhere with noplace to go?"

"To begin with, I don't know what's the use of my coming here with you. I don't have any business in Ghaleh Bagh. Ghaleh Bagh is fine for you who can stuff your mouths, but I have to look after my own life."

I couldn't see his eyes in the dark, but I could feel him glaring at me. I said, "I know, Uncle Aziz. But Ghaleh Bagh is of no use to *anyone.* We're all wasting our time."

He was taken aback. He looked intently into my eyes. He wagged his finger in my face and said, "Look, Rokni. I have the secret of the treasure map. I know how to go and find it. Don't tell anybody, understand? Rest assured. The key to the treasure map is in the hands of this Hadji."

"Really?"

"If I come to your front door next fall in a Mercedes Benz, what will you do? Will you dare to say Uncle Aziz's driving is no good? I swear by the Koran, as soon as I find the treasure I'll spend it nonstop. I won't be tight-assed. Whatever you want, you just tell me. Then see how I'll put the cash in the palm of your hand."

Then he said, a little more calmly, "Do you think I'll find the treasure?"

"How do I know, Uncle Aziz?"

"Pray that I find it. If I find it, your life will change. Your bread will be buttered."

We returned to the car. My Bee Bee asked anxiously, "How far is it to the teahouse at Lamak?"

Cross and sulky, my Uncle Aziz answered, "We'll be there in half an hour."

He reached through the window and began to guide the wheel. I pushed the car from the rear and we started down to Lamak. Iran was still asleep in the back seat, but my Bee Bee and Zahra Soltan followed the car on foot. When we arrived in front of the teahouse, we parked the car. My Uncle Aziz jacked it up and began to put the spare tire on.

The hours passed slowly, and I was gradually falling asleep on the bench in front of the teahouse. I didn't know anything about cars and I couldn't offer to help my Uncle Aziz. I sat alone and closed my eyes and dozed. When I woke up, the night had filled every space. My Uncle Aziz was still busy repairing the car. There was no trace of my Bee Bee and Zahra Soltan. A truck parked in front of the teahouse. When its flat front hood turned toward us, I glimpsed the driver's profile. He seemed to be bearded, and he had shaved his head completely in a way that recalled my Khan Brother Zia. Then I thought of the highway between Lar and Bushehr, and my eyes sank in darkness. I heard from afar the sleepy voice of Iran, talking to herself in another world. "Shambalee-doo, dolly, dolly, dolly . . ."

As I fell asleep again under the black dome of the sky, Capella grew distant from me like a dandelion.

2

It was an hour before noon when we arrived at the Ghaleh Bagh station. My Uncle Aziz nudged me and said, "You've slept long enough now. Wake up, we've got a thousand things to do. We have to unload the car and rent mules to take you to Takht Azhdar."

I went back to sleep. This time my Uncle Aziz shook me and shouted, "Good God! I want to see you get up! You have to go rent the mules."

He pulled me out of the car. He was so angry, it was impossible to argue with him. I descended the hill past the station and went to the river. The mules were scattered around Holy Jaafar Shrine in the middle of the cemetery. A peasant boy with a stick in his hand walked among them. When he saw me, he waved his stick in the air as if to ask why I'd trespassed on private property. I shouted, "This is a cemetery and I can come in!"

He called, "Boss, you're walking in our vegetable garden. We just planted it. It's going to be smashed under your feet."

I recognized what I'd done and stopped where I was. He knew why I was there. He took the mules' bridles and came toward me, clicking his tongue. I asked, "How much for five mules?"

"Fifty tumans, boss."

My Bee Bee poked her nose in and said, "Thirty-five tumans. Any time you see city people, you get greedy."

The peasant boy said, "Fifty tumans, no less."

My Bee Bee opened her purse and took out two twenty-tuman bills and said, "Forty tumans and the deal is closed. What greed!"

She threw the bills at the boy. The boy picked them up from the ground and said, "Dear lady, their straw and alfalfa alone cost more than forty tumans."

My Uncle Aziz untied the ropes, bitter as ever, and said, "Come on, hurry. I have to get back to Tehran, you know what I mean?"

My Bee Bee asked, "Why so soon, Agha? We'll wake you early tomorrow morning so you can reach Tehran on time. Spend the night, rest your feet."

"I'm used to being tired. Let the spoiled ones spend the night and rest; I don't want to."

My Bee Bee opened her purse again and took out two more twenty-tuman bills and put them in my Uncle Aziz's hand. Despite his disgust, my Uncle Aziz shoved the bills in his trousers pocket. He didn't glance at my Bee Bee, but she looked shocked by his childishness. She was about to start toward the teahouse when my Uncle Aziz screamed at her, "You think you've done me a favor with these few lousy pennies, Sister! You think you've broken the back of a monster. You try to buy me like a slave with this kind of generosity. But you don't read me right. You can't buy this Hadji, forget it."

The veins of his neck were thick with fury. He slammed the car doors shut, bang bang. He threw himself behind the wheel and started the engine. As soon as he put his foot on the gas, the car leapt forward. It circled the cemetery and disappeared in the dust of the road.

My Bee Bee seemed ashamed of my Uncle Aziz's behavior. She looked coldly at the dust that lingered behind his car. Farther away, the peasant boy had set Iran and Zahra Soltan on their mules and was tying our baggage on the back of another. The sleep had left my eyes. The fantasies that had pulled me to Ghaleh Bagh were emerging from the water like the awesome heads of submarine creatures. On the other side of the river, I could see a spindling, narrow road that stretched far among the trees to Takht Azhdar. It reminded me of my Khan Papa Doctor, and I conjured up the image of him walking around his herb garden with his hands clasped behind him. He inspects the herbs and gives orders for their care to Yadolah, the gardener, and his wife Mash Khadijeh. Then he walks toward his laboratory. The laboratory walls look dirty and splotched with repeated rains. The bindweed vines stick to its pillars like ticks and spread their branches everywhere. On the gray wooden shelves are jars of strange and rare herbs—poisonous herbs with mysterious effects whose names few people have heard. Anyone would hesitate to touch them. On the shelf below stand his specially ordered medicine jars—boric acid, cinnabar (which he calls red sulphur), and white and green and red tutty. Next to them are tin cans with Japanese labels, and cans of Indian mango, scorpion ointment, leech unguent. The smelting furnace is installed in the middle of the laboratory. Hanging from the ceiling is a circular rack holding prongs and pincers with carved wooden handles. These handles bear red marks that no one can understand. On a large table he has left open the twenty-pound dictionary, *The Deleted Beginning,* and Ptolemy's *Al-majist (Astronomy).*

In the laboratory's clutter, there is a kind of order that stimulates the viewer's curiosity and at the same time warns him to avoid direct questioning for fear of breaking the seal of a mystery and shattering the world to nothingness. But I said in my heart that I was ready for straight talk. I had to take the road to Takht Azhdar and get to my Khan Papa Doctor as soon as possible. When I looked at my Bee Bee, I saw she was aware of what was going on in my mind. She knew I couldn't rest. She stretched her long, slender fingers from her veil, and with a gesture she gave me permission to leave.

I took off. I walked the ups and downs of Takht Azhdar's narrow road and the alley behind the public bathhouse. When I arrived at the little bazaar of Ghaleh Bagh, the atmosphere grew shady and damp. The smell of raw fat and kebab and the cool fragrance of a summer resort floated in the air. Agha Kemal, the butcher, set his cleaver on the counter and welcomed me with an

open, unsure smile. I answered him with a wave and passed over
the river bridge. The closer I came to Takht Azhdar, the faster I
walked. Once again my heart was seething with worry. Every
stone, leaning wall, and crumbled building I saw, I told myself I
had seen before. Memories of past years of my life, and even of the
years before my life had begun, circled around my head like a
flock of restless, aimless birds. It seemed as though I had lived on
this land years before, or centuries before, with a different costume and a different occupation and a different name; as though
I'd walked step by step and shoulder to shoulder with the late
Sardar Azhdar. Above my head, the sky was turned over the
fields like a blue, uncracked enamel saucer; the sunlight pene-
trated every hidden spot.

I found myself in front of Takht Azhdar. I jumped over the
narrow stream and stood at the front door to knock, but I grew
cautious. I gently pressed the door till it opened just a crack.
Behind the door I saw the gravel road that stretched toward the
river. It wound around the gazebo and went forward to the edge
of the veranda. As I entered the orchard, I saw my Khan Papa
Doctor sitting cross-legged on a rug on the veranda. He didn't see
me, but when I approached he went through a sudden commotion
and pulled his Yazdi robe over his shoulders so he wouldn't catch
cold from the cool river breeze. He had put a pillow on his lap and
was watching the shimmering, crosshatched surface of the river
with a stricken expression. I walked past the plum and pear trees,
the marigolds and sunflowers. As I came close, he started to
move. He lowered his forehead slowly and rested it on the prayer
stone that he'd set on the pillow. Not only was I surprised to see
him praying, but I wondered why he was praying cross-legged.
Then I saw the wheelchair standing next to him. I thought to
myself, What if he's ill and crippled? Or maybe this was one of
those weird rituals he performed for growing his herbs. I tried not
to make any noise. I laced my fingers together, leaned my shoulder against one of the columns, and became absorbed in studying
him. A fluff of short, cottony beard, like a piece of white cloud,
circled his face. If you stretched out your hand to catch him, he
would pass through your fingers.

Almost by accident, his eyes fell on me. He wasn't surprised. It seemed he expected me. He blew his last Prayer of Praise around him and raised his beseeching hands a few times and then he said, "Rokni, if you can reach it, will you pour me a glass of tea."

I squatted in front of the samovar to pour the tea and asked, "What's this wheelchair for?"

His eyes were fixed again on the shimmering surface of the river. He answered me, "These good-for-nothing feet of mine don't have their old strength anymore. I can't stand on my feet. If there's a railing, a tree, something near me to lean against—well, I can do some shuffling around."

I put the glass of tea in front of him. He opened his mouth to speak but said nothing, and his mouth stayed waiting and half open. I asked, "What do you want?"

"Sugar lump. Sugar lumps, you know."

"The sugar jar's next to you."

"These crabbed hands of mine don't have their old strength anymore. They're no good even for washing your ass. Rokni, why is the weather so cold?"

"What do you mean, cold? It's so hot you can't stay in the sun."

"How would I know? It's old age, you see. Old age slows the circulation. Yadolah has gone to Kuhan Mountain to bring me back mountain mint and wild thyme. Percolated mountain mint is good for low blood pressure. It has a medicinal effect. You steep it like tea and drink it very hot to raise your blood pressure. And wild thyme is good for indigestion and laziness of the liver. It has another medicinal effect that I've discovered on my own, Rokni. If you raise wild thyme in a certain way it's good for the eyesight. You understand, we see the world in three dimensions, don't we? But wild thyme is good for the unconscious vision or, as the saying goes, for the fourth dimension."

His face looked thin and bony. He seemed transformed by a sudden, strong excitement. He had shed his skin and revealed his true self. I was sure that in such a mood he would talk—would say what he'd refused to say up till that time. Anxiety struck my heart, as if I'd come upon the scene of a crime. I was afraid to disturb the natural current with any movement. I had never before seen the sun shine so brightly, so clearly, and so cleanly in

Ghaleh Bagh. He lifted the teacup with difficulty and began to sip.
I said, "All this aside, how are you?"

He smiled and turned up a palm in resignation. "Oh, praise be
to Allah. How are you, Rokni?"

"Not bad. Things aren't going badly. The bad eggplant never
rots."

"Are you still busy acting and mask-making and singing?"

"What's wrong with that? It doesn't do any harm."

"That depends on how you look at it."

"What do you mean?"

"There's a famous saying that goes: you see the hair and we see
the curl of the hair. I'll tell you something, although I know for
certain you'll reject it. If you really want to see anything, you have
to close your eyes. Then the true nature of that thing will be
revealed to you. Look at those seven plane trees. Look at the
leaves. Look at this bright sunshine, and then close your eyes and
see what you see. Don't things like fish scales flicker in the dark of
your eyes? Then you understand that our nature, our basic passion, is not made up of those visible, momentary objects. As the
poet said, 'The flower lasts only five or six days. There is something else invisible that lasts forever.' "

I said, "You talk like Mirza Hassibi."

He laughed. But it was light, weak laughter. He said, "Where
have you seen Mirza Hassibi?"

"In his house."

"The same old house?"

"Yes."

"Why did you go there?"

"I was looking for my Khan Brother Zia."

"Allah be praised, you listened to what I said! I was afraid
you'd lose interest. I was afraid the Sardar Azhdaris would circle
around you and keep you from pursuing your business. You
know, they don't understand a thing. It makes no difference to
those mules that blood has been shed and the world has perished.
Well, obviously you haven't found your brother yet."

He put the tea glass on the brass tray. I said, "How do you
know I haven't?"

He shook his head and said, "It's obvious."

I bent over and said, with emphasis, "There's something you've kept secret from me. Why?"

He wrapped the Yazdi robe tighter around himself and said slowly, "In what grave is this Yadolah hiding? When will he be back? For the sake of his father's soul, he's only gone for mountain mint and wild thyme. He has some shopping to do, too."

"Why don't you answer my question? Khan Papa Doctor, for me you've always been the complete Heshmat Nezami. I always thought even Noah's flood wouldn't faze you. Now you act cautious with me. You don't say what you want to because you don't want to lose face. You're afraid I'll change my opinion of you. Do you know what Mirza Hassibi told me?"

When he spoke he didn't look at me. "You're getting upset over nothing. I've listened to Mirza Hassibi all my life. What he's told you is a dream and a fantasy, not real life."

"How do you know what he's told me?"

"Because I know him. I know how he's been waiting for this— to find a painter among the young Heshmat Nezamis and talk about the past. No doubt he's told you the story of the late Homayundokht, God forgive her soul. Hasn't he?"

"The story of Homayundokht?"

"Didn't he say that both he and she were studying with the Master Assar?"

"So that's what it is. Homayundokht, God forgive her soul, and Mirza Hassibi were the Master Assar's students. How far off base I was! What I don't understand is why Mirza Hassibi won't come to our house anymore."

"I don't know why. He was always hanging around. How attached he was to your brother! He always regretted that Zia had the character of a military man. He said Zia was unyielding, like all the Heshmat Nezamis."

His voice grew faint, and with an imploring, helpless look he said, "Rokni, I want to go to my room. It's chilly here. I'm afraid I might catch cold. Put me in this son-of-a-bitch wheelchair and take me to my room. Can you manage that much?"

I wanted to ignore him and ask one by one the questions that had come to my mind, but he did look tired and weak. I put my arms around his shoulders and under his knees, and I lifted him

from the floor like a molting sparrow. I set him in the wheelchair.
He said, "Mirza Hassibi shook his finger in my face and told me
Zia would make a good brigadier general. He was right. The officer's life was just the thing for Zia. I should have helped him
stay in the Army. I remember how his mother, the late Homayundokht, God forgive her soul, would sit on our five-doored room's
moonlit terrace and she'd put your brother in the sailor suit that
she herself had made to take him to the Master Assar and study
painting. Your brother wouldn't cooperate. He would fidget. But
as soon as I arrived and he saw me from a distance, he would
salute me like a soldier. He had such an attraction to the Army
that people were astounded. They'd ask constantly where this
little guy, half the size of a hand's breadth, had learned to ape
military men so well. He would salute you as though he'd practiced it for thirty years in the French military academy at St. Cyr.
I would stand at attention in front of him and click my boots and
return the salute. The late Homayundokht didn't appreciate this.
She would frown. She would take Zia's hand and lead him to the
telephone room. If it weren't for that God-forgive-her-soul, your
brother would have gone high places by now in His Great Majesty's Army staff. That God-forgive-her-soul spoiled your brother's
character. You can't expect any more than that from the Sardar
Azhdaris."

He grew silent and thoughtful. I pushed his wheelchair. From
outside rose the sounds of travelers and mules. My Khan Papa
Doctor raised his head and looked at me sideways. I said, "We all
came together."

He didn't say a word, but he continued to look at me with eyes
full of reproach and irritation. He motioned for me to take him to
his room immediately. Before we could reach his room, the door
to the orchard flew open and they all poured inside. The mules in
chains, with their riders and loads, came forward on the gravel
road and in the blink of an eye the yard was crowded. I turned the
wheelchair toward the door so my Khan Papa Doctor could see
the travelers. He smiled ironically and I started laughing. With
the tip of a finger he beckoned me closer. I bent over and he kissed
my cheek. His kiss was loose and limp and he smelled like the
basement of our house. I didn't know what he wanted to say or

why he'd kissed me. I asked, "How's your laboratory? Did you finally find your anticancer medicine?"

He raised his eyebrows clownishly. I said, "Isn't it important to you?"

"Of course. It's very important. But you have to be patient. There's plenty of time."

My Bee Bee and Iran came toward us. Iran staggered along in step with my Bee Bee, and her hands flew loosely and aimlessly in all directions. She looked like one of those dolls that people hang from their rear-view mirrors. My Bee Bee pulled her veil off her head. She narrowed her eyes and asked my Khan Papa Doctor, "How are you feeling, Doctor?"

"I'm tired. My hands and legs are weak."

"Who's cooking for you?"

"Mash Khadijeh, Yadolah's wife."

"Better to eat cement. I've tasted her food; she doesn't know how to cook. Would you like us to send someone to the little bazaar to buy you kebab?"

"I don't have the appetite. I want to take a nap. Maybe my appetite will be better when I wake up."

"We must make you some liver extract and pounded sparrow. You have to regain your strength. This is all because of anemia."

My Bee Bee pulled her veil back up. Whenever she was unhappy, she covered her face. My Khan Papa Doctor glanced at Iran. Iran's head was tilted on the stem of her neck and she was looking at the sky from the corner of her eye like a hunter aiming at a bird. I couldn't believe she was acting so indifferent, after we'd come all this way just for her to see my Khan Papa Doctor. My Khan Papa Doctor signaled me to take him to his room. I pushed the wheelchair forward.

His room was clean and cool. Its furniture smelled of perfumed soap and insecticide. The walls were newly whitewashed and the woodwork painted navy blue. His unmade bed was spread in the middle of the room. I lifted him from the wheelchair and carefully laid him on the bed. With a little moaning and groaning he settled himself, and very slowly he put his head on the pillow. He gestured for me to sit next to him. When I sat, he burst into that clownish laughter again. I said, "Why are you laughing?"

"Doesn't a man have the right to laugh with his own seed and flesh?"

"You're not the kind who does, usually."

"Rokni, I want to talk to you. Painting and singing won't make a man's living. You have to find a job that pays, so when you stick your hand in your pocket you'll find something besides your balls."

"What is it you're saying?"

"I want to get you a job in the Foreign Ministry. Maybe they'll send you overseas so you'll be out of this atmosphere."

"What can I accomplish in the Foreign Ministry? I don't have the head for that kind of thing."

"Do you think those in charge have the heads, either? What do they have that you don't have? If you want the truth, in the early years I thought you'd end up a leftist and a Tudeh Communist. What else could I expect, with all that playacting of yours? But you weren't even good for that. You don't even have the capability to be a revolutionary. Well, never mind. Working in the Foreign Ministry doesn't take a good head, or common sense, or know-how, or efficiency. I'll make a phone call. Maybe they can find you a place in the United Nations, so a piece of bread will come your way. Let the children of Cousin Abdolbaghi become Tudeh Communists, so if by any chance the government crumbles, and one day we wake up to revolutionary marches on Radio Tehran, we'll have someone to look after us."

I said, "My Khan Brother Zia is a revolutionary, and if the government changes he's not the type to be influenced by his blood ties."

He held up a hand and said, "Your Khan Brother Zia is no longer one of us. He doesn't have any connection with us. Now, don't give me a headache with your silly arguments. I'm tired. If you want to talk, come to the laboratory at seven o'clock tonight. We'll have our conversation there."

For a moment he paused, as if he didn't know what to say. Then he turned his back to me and pretended to go to sleep.

In the cool, insecticide-smelling atmosphere of the room, I heard only the buzz of a solitary fly trying to find a way outdoors. Behind the window, the cloudless square of the sky was a deep, deep blue.

3

A kerosene lantern was burning in the laboratory, which was as cluttered and as fascinating as ever. With his cane in his hand, wearing his blue striped shirt and suspendered trousers, my Khan Papa Doctor stood beside the sink. I said, "Hello."

He glared at me and said, "Hello, pain and illness. In what grave have you been until now?"

"I went to the seven plane trees to walk and think."

"Do you know what time it is? Seven forty-five. You've kept me waiting since seven and for what? If this were the Army, I'd give orders for your feet to be beaten."

I was about to explode when suddenly the cane fell from his hand. He put his palms on his abdomen and went to the sink and retched. I was worried. I ran toward him to help, but he waved, motioning for me to stay in my place and come no closer. He chose a sugar pouch from the shelf and took a pinch of an herb, something like dried mint, and poured it down his throat. He waited motionless a few moments for the herb to take effect. Gradually he seemed to feel better. He drew a deep breath. He picked up his cane from the floor and came toward me. Three paces away, he hooked his fingers to the edge of a counter and said, "Have you finally made a decision?"

"Decision about what?"

"About your future—a plan for a bit of bread and butter, enough so you can survive; a position in the Foreign Ministry."

"I haven't traveled sixty kilometers just to talk with you about a job."

"For what purpose did you come then, Rokni?"

"I don't know for what purpose."

"We haven't much time left, you mule. You want to spend your life aimlessly?"

I controlled myself in silence and only stared at him. In my Khan Papa Doctor's face, anger had been transformed into a kind of interrogation, a domineering force. His eyes were feverish, like two coals, above the cottony fuzz of his beard. He lowered his voice and said, "Are you still wrapped up in your masks and statues? Aren't you free yet of those half-baked fantasies?"

"You haven't seen my latest sculpture. If I had let you see it, you wouldn't be talking like this."

"Even if you were Michelangelo himself, I would say the same thing."

"You wouldn't. My statue bears a very close resemblance to you. If you saw it, you'd ask, 'What is this really all about? What is the meaning of these statues and masks?' "

"What questions! Crap!"

"You yourself, after a lifetime as a doctor and a soldier, don't you have your own half-baked fantasies that keep your heart happy in the middle of this lab, in a corner of Ghaleh Bagh?"

"Turds bigger than you are coming out of your mouth. What I do is a service to the country, you mule. You compare yourself with me?"

Once again his cane fell to the floor. He turned his back to me and suddenly raised both his shoulders. He went to the sink and retched into it. He became a little calmer. He took a new breath and retched again. Then he groped on the counter for the sugar pouch. It was out of his reach. I pushed the pouch toward him, trying not to let him see. My hand touched his. He turned and looked into my eyes. His face had grown white as chalk. The skin under his eyes had sunk and a thin string of blood flowed from the corner of his mouth down his white beard. I was looking at a weightless spirit, a ghost who was burning and melting away in the dark without a flame. I said, "You're really sick."

He shook his head emphatically and said, "It's obvious I'm sick. You're not blind."

"What's wrong with you, Khan Papa Doctor?"

"Call your Bee Bee to come here."

"What for?"

"Are you catechizing me? I said, call your Bee Bee to come here."

It was an order, but I didn't move an inch. He poured another handful of that special herb down his throat. Gradually he looked better and the blood returned to his cheeks and he breathed more easily. He continued talking. "After me, who will tend to our business? I've raised a flock of kids for myself, but in the middle of all this, there's only one person who listens to me. That's your Bee Bee. Thank God she was my lot in life. She was an angel of mercy who appeared in my life and answered our call. If not for her care and attendance, what would have happened to your sister after the incident of Homayundokht, God forgive her soul? What would have happened to your brother? Oh, dear Father, she sacrificed. She kept us together. Then those loose-assed Sardar Azhdaris say she's illiterate, backward, she doesn't wear fashionable clothes, and she won't set foot out of the house in jeans and with an uncovered head. I say let the washers of the dead take all fashionable, modern ladies. You ought to tie those women to the toilet brush and clean the toilet with them."

I said, "Khan Papa Doctor, what's wrong with you? Why won't you tell me?"

"You thought I'd live forever. In other words, you'd have me for the rest of your life so you could waste your time making masks and sculptures with no worries, so you could put on theatricals and entertain people. Now you'll have to open your eyes and look after yourself."

He'd been talking so fast that he ran out of breath. He sat down in the wheelchair and fell into thought. Then he lifted his head and said, "Everyone has a lot and destiny. These stupid struggles are useless. I was seven years old and I was going to Marvi Elementary School. A child thinks he can hoodwink his lot and destiny, that he can stick it to whatever comes his way. One day I got my sister Badi Zaman, the interpreter of the Koran, to do my homework for me. It was sisterly love. She cared for me and didn't want our mullah to hound me. But our mullah wasn't a donkey, he didn't eat hay and alfalfa. He could see the difference between my crab-and-frog handwriting and the neat, pretty handwriting of Badi Zaman. He took his stick from under his mattress and said, 'Mirza Sadegh, hold out your hand.' I said, 'What's my crime?' He said, 'Your crime is that you want to hoodwink your lot and destiny. This caning is so you won't forget. Every man is responsible for his own life and shouldn't dodge his responsibilities and cover up his shortcomings.' Now, Rokni, sixty-three years have passed since that caning. When I judge for myself, I can see that our mullah, God forgive his soul, was right. That old man wanted to teach me that, if it's our fate, we'll be successful in the end. Otherwise, our account is in the hands of the All-Merciful Accountant."

He was patting the bronze bust of Pasteur and he seemed absent-minded. I said, "What do you mean, lot and destiny?"

"It's very important. It has a scientific basis. Present-day people call it historical necessity, but the Scholar of Gorgon, God have mercy on him, used to say it's all the same thing: lot and destiny."

"Your mullah meant that a man is responsible for his own life. Whatever happens to him is because of what he's done."

He listened to me patiently. In his eyes was a sort of contemptuous compassion. He muttered, "You're too young. As the saying goes, your breath still smells of milk."

I pulled a stool closer and sat down and said, "What's wrong with you?"

He set a hand on his abdomen and turned his face away from me. "I'm dying."

"Of what?"

"Of cancer of the stomach. I know the symptoms. I don't need a doctor to give me the Tale of Forty Parrots."

"Why haven't you told anyone?"

He put a finger to his lips and whispered, "Ssh. There's no need to scream. I don't want anyone to know."

"Why not?"

"Because I don't want to lower myself in front of a herd of cows. People don't like a dying man. A dying man reminds them of their own coming deaths."

"Khan Papa Doctor, you look so different."

He nodded and went on. "One of the advantages of being a doctor is that, whenever you're tending a dying man, you say thanks in your heart that the man in the bed is the one who's puking his life out and not you, that he's the one singing his good-bye song and not you. But when the tailor himself falls into the pitcher, when they stretch out your own Excellency in the bed to die, then what? You look at the world from your bed and see that everybody's living a hodgepodge life. They're happy that their world has a tomorrow and a day after tomorrow. Those sons of bitches draw up plans for their tomorrow and their day after tomorrow: how they'll make an ass out of someone and ride him, how they'll cut off someone's ears and how they'll get somewhere. They don't care about a thing, but life in bed has no more tomorrow or day after tomorrow, Rokni-jun. Dying's not bad in itself, but life without tomorrow or day after tomorrow is hell."

"Khan Papa Doctor, you're not feeling well. You talk this way because of your illness. You have to see a doctor."

"So that's it? Now that I'm doing the talking, you say I'm talking nonsense? By the power of the Almighty, you young people have no more brain than a walnut. Go. Go and call your Bee Bee to come here."

I took advantage of the situation and left the lab. Talking to my Khan Papa Doctor had confused me.

It was getting dark. Sleepy birds whispered the arrival of evening with a sort of circular, metallic melody, like the sound of an old clock's gears. Ghaleh Bagh was sinking slowly into the moth-covered depths of the night. On the veranda, close to the kitchen, Mash Khadijeh had lit the clay oven to bake syrup-covered bread for us. Next to her, Zahra Soltan was sprinkling the balls of dough with flour and lining them up on the wooden tray. My Bee Bee held onto Iran's hand to keep her from falling into the oven, God forbid. Both of them were bending to look inside. Now and then flames leapt out the door and red reflections jittered on the faces of Mash Khadijeh, Iran, and my Bee Bee. Behind them, Zahra Soltan with much care and finesse pressed the wooden mold into the balls of dough, imprinting them with flowers and bushes. I called, "Bee Bee, Bee Bee!"

She turned and searched for me in the darkness. She said, "What is it, Rokni?"

"My Khan Papa Doctor needs you. He wants to talk with you."

"Tell him I'm coming."

Reluctantly, I went back to the lab. I was split by feelings of anger and regret, but finally I made my decision. I wouldn't give up until he answered my questions. Never mind the stomach cancer, or the anemia, or his premonitions of death.

Quick and shrewd, he asked, "Where's your Bee Bee?"

"She's coming."

I sat on a stool. He looked at me inquiringly. With the tip of his tongue, he wet his parched, cracked lips. He asked cautiously, under his breath, "Did you find any trace of your brother at all?"

"I went to Farzaneh, but he didn't help."

"That pimp didn't help? That lackey of Police Commissioner Mokhtari?"

"No. There was nothing he could do."

"Shit on his father's grave. Let him refuse to help. I know what it is that's burning his ass. We Heshmat Nezamis are not the ball-massaging types and we don't pay anyone hush money. Mokhtari wanted to make me the special prison doctor so whenever they decided to do a man in I could finish him off with an injection of air just like the physician Ahmadi. But I didn't go along with it. I said, 'Commissioner, I have sworn I'll do no harm.' That's why Sohrab Farzaneh is angry."

"This Army that you've spent a lifetime of drudgery on, what has it done for you?"

"I didn't have any expectations. What I did in the Army was only for my country, not for this man or that man."

"Was the Hoseinabad incident for the country, then?"

His gaze grew soft and velvety. He smiled philosophically and said, "No doubt Mirza Hassibi has given you some song and dance and filled your ears with Sardar Azhdari gibberish. No, Rokni-jun, nobody exiled the Master Assar to Hoseinabad. He went to Hoseinabad of his own free will. We didn't have any quarrel with the Master Assar. We only wanted to put down the disturbance that Mirza Kazem Feshangchi's followers had created. You understand? I myself went with two orderlies to see the Master Assar. He was in fine condition and feeling well, happy and fat, the blood was running in his cheeks. I greeted him and said I had orders to arrest Mirza Kazem Feshangchi and his followers."

This is how I imagined the scene he spread before me. The Master Assar stepped out of the orchard and came to the field. He walked by himself along the edge of the field. Mirza Hassibi and Homayundokht, God forgive her soul, walked behind him. Mirza Hassibi wore the fortuneteller's costume and from far away he had the jerky, trembling movements of a cartoon figure. Homayundokht, God forgive her soul, had folded her veil and she carried it under her arm like a bathhouse bundle. In her white lace dress that reached her ankles, she took slow and stretchy steps, as though she were in a dream. Then the Master Assar set up his face-making equipment in the corner of the field and sat on a stool that he'd placed in front of his easel. He crossed his legs and fanned himself with a straw fan. Mirza Hassibi approached him and said, "Master, please forgive it."

"Forgive what?"

"Forgive their insolence in trespassing on your property without permission. These people don't understand. They're on orders. What they do isn't intentional."

The Master Assar said, "The forgiveness of God's servant lies with God. Agha, I have given up my rights; God may also give up His rights. If possible, I ask only this: that there be no bloodshed. Blood wants blood. Blood will become a trap and demand more sacrifices, generation after generation."

Now Homayundokht, God forgive her soul, had put on her veil. At the edge of the field, next to the walnut tree, she searched for a shady place to sit. My Khan Papa Doctor stepped forward and tucked his baton under his arm. He stood at ease and watched the Cossacks get into position. The merciless midsummer sun toasted the field. My Khan Papa Doctor said, "Mirza, you're a respected man; what's this costume you're wearing?"

"Major Sadegh Khan, only once in a lifetime does such an opportunity arise, that a man can sit in front of the Master and enjoy his presence."

"Haven't I told you not to bring Homayundokht here, especially unveiled?"

Before Mirza could answer, Homayundokht said, "Mirza Sadegh Khan, you married a wife and not a slave. Besides, you don't know what you're doing here. This will brand your forehead till the end of time, and you'll pay for it."

My Khan Papa Doctor always belittled Mirza Hassibi in front of everyone. He used to say that Mirza was raised in the Chaleh Maydon section of the city, and whatever he saw struck him as big and unbelievable. Sarcastically, he would tell him that Mirza had not seen the museums of Berlin, Paris, and Florence. In Mirza's eyes, anyone who picked up a paintbrush and copied a few bits of scenery was a second Rembrandt. My Khan Papa Doctor said, "Mirza, if you like this kind of thing, why don't you take a trip to Paris? In Paris, if you hit any dog on the head a hundred painters will fall off, big and little, and the Master Assar wouldn't be able to keep up with the dust of a one of them."

Mirza said, "Mirza Sadegh Khan, you see everything with superficial eyes. You judge everything by its appearance. If it's my lot, I'll go to Paris. Maybe I'll go to Paris next year. But not for the reasons you say."

My Khan Papa Doctor always taunted him and said Mirza was stupid. Mirza only knew how to drink vodka and watch Homayundokht, God forgive her soul, up on the rooftop. Homayundokht was strutting on the rooftop in her blue décolleté dress, and with natural pomp she was puffing on the pipe her Dear Daddy had brought her from Petersburg. Mirza Hassibi burst out singing:

> "I have a bath pouch, pumice stone, and white
>   powder from Tabriz.
> I have a pouch full of beautiful combs.

Dear lady, buy them cheap,
Buy them at Tehran's prices."

Homayundokht, God forgive her soul, answered:

"A person whose heart is full of the blood of
    suffering and sadness,
What need does she have for powder and soap?
My lot in life is sadness and pain,
My face has turned dark and yellow."

Mirza Hassibi answered:

"Dear lady, if you don't want soap,
And you don't want a bath pouch, pumice stone,
    or white powder from Tabriz,
Give me a penny, I'll do book divining for
    you
And uncover your enemies.
I do book divining.
I'll reawaken, once again,
Your sleeping fortune."

Then the peasants appeared among the trees at the edge of the
pasture. They swarmed like a bunch of leeches. Mirza Feshangchi
rode a horse and he snapped his whip in circles in the air. As soon
as my Khan Papa Doctor saw him, he raised his hand and gave
the order to shoot. The Cossacks fired. A bullet hit the Master
Assar's eye. All of a sudden the blood started bubbling like a
boiling spring in the middle of his left eye. Homayundokht, God
forgive her soul, ran around the Master Assar and screamed like a
crazy woman. The Master Assar stayed calm. He pulled a handkerchief from his paintbox, put it over his eye, and walked toward
the orchard. Homayundokht, God forgive her soul, ran after him
with a thousand wails and screams. But Mirza Hassibi sat in the
corner of the field in his fortunetelling costume, and with fixed
and deadened eyes he watched my Khan Papa Doctor. Apparently my Khan Papa Doctor wanted to say something, but he held
himself back. For the first time in his life, he avoided talking to
Mirza Hassibi, and it seemed he dreaded even looking at him.

The following morning, the Cossacks were cleaning the field and the Army photographer was taking pictures when the Master Assar reappeared. Tall as the standard in a funeral procession, wearing a Nozari robe and dark glasses, he came forward over the large stones in the riverbed.

Once again, Mirza Hassibi started up with his stupidity. He called my Khan Papa Doctor to come close and watch him posing as a fortuneteller. My Khan Papa Doctor asked irritably, "What is this business? Have you lost your mind, Mirza?"

Mirza Hassibi answered, "Watch, Major Sadegh Khan. That's what they gave you eyes for: watching."

"What do you want me to watch?"

"Master Assar, in the field. He's in the field."

"Yes, he's in the field and he's busy painting. Where did you want him to be?"

Mirza glanced at the field and said, "You see, Major Sadegh Khan, the Master is standing in the middle of the field."

"Well, so he's standing there, so what? He's not a bogeyman, to come and eat you."

"Major Sadegh Khan, you Heshmat Nezamis take everything lightly. One of the Master Assar's eyes has been blinded. Do you see those dark glasses? He wears them so no one can see the wound."

"My dear Agha, the Master is fine. Come see for yourself. He's brought his equipment into the field and now he's painting the field with his good eye."

"Major Sadegh Khan, doesn't it matter to you? Is everything you do in life just a military mission? Are you satisfied now that you've completed your mission and done your country a service?"

My Khan Papa Doctor grew furious as he listened to Mirza. The Master Assar was still standing in front of his easel. When he sensed that my Khan Papa Doctor and Mirza Hassibi were approaching, he adjusted his glasses, as though to make sure that his eyes were covered and protected. Then he turned his head and from behind the dark glasses he gave my Khan Papa Doctor a look that my Khan Papa Doctor never forgot.

"Rokni, he looked at me with such conceit, as though he'd

fallen from heaven's asshole, with such pride that he'd become a peacock of the highest rank."

The Master Assar asked, "Have you carried out your mission?"

My Khan Papa Doctor didn't answer. He only looked at Homayundokht, God forgive her soul, who was crouching in her veil in front of the Master Assar and gazing at the sky with purple, opaque eyes. Now Mirza Hassibi had spread his fortunetelling kerchief on the grass next to Homayundokht, God forgive her soul, and he was waiting, awestruck, for directions from the Master Assar. The Master Assar said gently, "Very well, Agha. This kind of incident doesn't require questions and answers. Whatever happens is the will of God, and God is compassionate; He will forgive."

My Khan Papa Doctor's reminiscence was interrupted just then by my Bee Bee, who entered the lab in confusion and said, "Doctor, don't tire yourself over nothing. You're pale and out of breath. Tell the rest of the story tomorrow."

My Khan Papa Doctor circled the tip of his tongue over his dry lips. With difficulty he said, "If there *is* any tomorrow."

My Bee Bee said, "What did you want me for?"

"I don't remember, Miss Asiah."

She asked me, "What did your Khan Papa Doctor want me for?"

"I don't know."

My Khan Papa Doctor said, "Miss Asiah, I wanted you to be with me. Sometimes a man feels horrified at being alone. I wanted you to talk to me so I could hear your voice."

My Bee Bee motioned for me to push my Khan Papa Doctor's wheelchair back to the main house.

Outside it had grown completely dark. The stars had appeared in the sky, and behind us the murmur of the river was combing Ghaleh Bagh's blackness. As we approached the house, I whispered to my Khan Papa Doctor, "You have to see a doctor."

He turned and looked me up and down with an expression of disappointment.

I asked, "Are you sleepy?"

He snapped, "No, Rokni."

"Where do you want us to spread the tablecloth for your supper?"

"I don't want supper. I don't have an appetite."

"What do you want to do, then?"

"I want to sit on the edge of the veranda and watch the river."

My Bee Bee heard our conversation and jumped in. "Why do you act this way, Doctor? We've cooked you a nice soft rice and chicken dish."

My Khan Papa Doctor seemed really tired. He didn't have the strength to talk. He gestured for us not to bother him. Then Yadolah and I brought the wheelchair up the stairs and placed it on the veranda. On my own, I pushed him around the veranda until we arrived on the river side. Suddenly a cool breeze hit our faces and my Khan Papa Doctor revived at the feel of it. He pointed to a spot between two columns and said, "Stop right here. Let's enjoy the view awhile."

I stopped the wheelchair at that spot. I tried to leave him alone. I leaned against a column behind him with my arms folded across my chest, and I grew absorbed in watching Ghaleh Bagh's evening. The disk of the moon was visible over the shoulder of the Mountain of Mountains, and the moonlight had turned the hills and humps to velvet. My Khan Papa Doctor sighed. He put his hands on the crook of his cane and rested his chin on his hands and sank into thought. Yadolah, carrying the drinking tray in one hand and a kerosene lantern in the other, came forward from the dark of the orchard. He put the drinking tray on the veranda and disappeared without a sound. My Khan Papa Doctor pointed with his cane for me to pour him a drink. I did so and handed him a glass. He emptied it down his throat. Once again he rested his chin on the crook of the cane and fixed his penetrating gaze on the Mountain of Mountains. The kerosene lamps of the country houses burned among the crowded trees like glowworms. He murmured a verse from *Rumi:*

"I said we had found that which is not findable.
He said, I long for that which is still not findable."

I whistled an accompaniment. He turned toward me. He grinned and said, "Rokni, are you still here?"

"Yes, I'm here."

"Well, now you understand all I was telling you?"

"I'm thinking about it."

He laughed. "Do you have any wits to think with? Take it from me, your head's hollow, it's empty."

Instead of answering, I began whistling again. My Khan Papa Doctor interrupted me and said, "Oh, warbling nightingale, the urge to sing has hit you again. You've turned completely and solidly into a Sardar Azhdari, you know."

"At least Sardar Azhdaris have feelings and compassion, at least they don't have blood on their hands."

"No doubt you learned this shit from Mirza Hassibi. He always used to say that in time he would hook some rootless yes-man of a Heshmat Nezami and stuff him full of nonsense."

"What nonsense?"

"The long tales about Homayundokht, God forgive her soul, that he himself made up. He used to sit in a corner of the Sufis' monastery and imagine that whatever came to his good-for-nothing mind was true. These bums are good only for fortunetelling, poetry, and astrology. They should be lined up in front of Bagh Shah's Wall and executed with a machine gun. You don't know how I begged Homayundokht, God forgive her soul, to listen just once to logic. But where were her ears? She constantly screamed at me, and, because of Mirza Hassibi's evil suggestions, she claimed that I'd killed people and blinded the only painter in the country, and a handful of other rot. All the Sardar Azhdaris are cut from the same bolt of cloth. All of them are wishy-washy, loose-assed, and crazy."

He motioned for me to leave him alone. I shoved my hands in my pockets, rose up on tiptoe, and resumed whistling. He lifted his cane in his wobbly, weak hand and hit it against the veranda railing with a strength I hadn't expected. He screamed, "Are you going to get lost, puppy dog?"

My Bee Bee heard his voice and ran onto the veranda, calling, "Doctor, what's the matter?"

He was so tired he couldn't answer. His head was bowed over his chest and he was breathing very slowly. I dug my hands in my pockets and went toward my Bee Bee, whistling. She stood in the middle of the veranda like a shadow, looking at me anxiously. Behind her, the silhouettes of Mash Khadijeh, Iran, and Zahra Soltan were visible at the flaming red mouth of the oven. As I came close to my Bee Bee, she gripped my arm and asked, "What's going on? Rokni-jun, your Khan Papa Doctor isn't feeling well."

"He's dying. Do you know he has cancer of the stomach?"

"Yes, I know. It's not news, Rokni."

"Well, I just found out. My Khan Papa Doctor has a special fear of cancer."

"Heshmat Nezamis have always had a special fear of cancer."

I saw that she was right. The Heshmat Nezamis were always afraid of things that possessed them without an open battle.

BOOK FOUR

꘍꘍꘍꘍꘍꘍꘍꘍꘍꘍꘍꘍꘍꘍

The Prayer of Light

1

I came down the rooftop stairs and put on my clothes outside the kitchen. I didn't have any appetite for breakfast. I wanted to go skinny-dipping in the river, but this early in the morning the water would be cold, so I changed my mind. I looked across the orchard. It was silent, but a kind of disorder was visible everywhere. A few suitcases, traveling bags, and other odds and ends were piled by the gravel road in front of the veranda steps. In the middle of the veranda, I saw our big brass tray with the unwashed dishes and leftovers from last night scattered across it. My Bee Bee had tightened her veil around her face like a scarf and was whispering to Yadolah in front of the door to my Khan Papa Doctor's room. In her movements and her manner of speaking, there was something that worried me. I stepped forward and asked quietly, "Bee Bee, what's the matter?"

She turned. Her eyes were hollow from a sleepless night. She put her finger to her lips and said, "Ssh."

"Has my Khan Papa Doctor taken a turn for the worse?"

She shook her head. She started walking in silence and descended the steps, indicating that we should go to the orchard and find a private place to talk.

When we arrived at the gazebo, she gathered the hem of her veil under her knees and squatted by the spring. I sat down in front of her. I pointed to the pile of luggage by the road and asked, "Who do those belong to?"

"Last night some guests arrived. It's nothing important."

Still I felt anxious, and I asked, "Where's my Khan Papa Doctor?"

"In his room. They've sent him a doctor, Dr. Amir Sina, a special Army doctor."

"Are you hiding something from me?"

She shifted her body. With her fingertips, she made parallel, wavy lines on the surface of the stream. I insisted: "Has something happened?"

She pushed her veil back from her face and said, "Rokni, you're not a child anymore. You've guessed for yourself that your Khan Papa Doctor's condition isn't good."

I said, "He's gone. Isn't he?"

Again she shook her head. She squeezed the corners of her lips between her thumb and index finger. She said, "He couldn't sleep well last night. He struggled all night. Constantly he turned from one side to the other. Then he fixed his eyes on the ceiling and wouldn't answer anybody. Just the spoonful of soft rice and chicken that we put in his mouth, he threw up. He seemed confused. He kept calling your brother's name and moaning, 'Where's Zia, when is he supposed to come?' After that Dr. Amir Sina and Mirza Hassibi and Masoud arrived, in the middle of the night. As soon as your Khan Papa Doctor saw your Khan Brother Zia wasn't among them, he buttoned his lips and didn't say a word to any of them. Maybe that was because of his confusion; maybe he didn't recognize them."

"Why didn't you wake me?"

"Wake you for what? Nothing was going on."

"Maybe he would have talked to me. Maybe he wanted to talk to his own son."

"No, Rokni. Dr. Amir Sina examined him and said the cancer has spread to his brain. If it weren't for Dr. Amir Sina's shots, he might already be gone."

I stood up and walked toward his room. My Bee Bee called, "Rokni, come back."

"I want to see him."

"You'll see him. There's no need to hurry. Come here. We haven't finished our talk. I want to tell you something."

I turned back. My Bee Bee motioned for me to sit by the spring. I sat and asked, "What did you want to say?"

She lowered her eyes and arranged herself. It was as though she were shy and couldn't bring herself to speak openly. She murmured, "Well, you know his condition isn't good. You shouldn't argue with him. He doesn't have the strength for these struggles. You're a young man and you have a future. You're our hope. But your Khan Papa Doctor has lived his life, he's eaten the dust of the desert and labored all his life. It's over for him now, there's not much time left, and he doesn't have the strength to argue with you."

"What arguing?"

"Well, like last night."

"Bee Bee, someone has to look after me, too. I have to go on my own and ask this and that so I can figure out how he's lived his life, what's the meaning of it. I have to find out somehow where my Khan Brother Zia is. Is he in prison? Are they torturing him in prison? Whatever happens in our house, there's not a word from anyone. Everyone's deaf and dumb."

My Bee Bee lowered her eyes again and said nothing. She took hold of the stem of a tobacco flower and plucked it. I said, "Why don't you speak?"

"What shall I say?"

"That's exactly what I mean. In this house, all tongues are paralyzed. Whoever gets involved with my Khan Papa Doctor, his tongue is paralyzed—from Homayundokht, God forgive her soul, to Khan Brother Zia, to you."

The tobacco flower fell from her fingers into the spring, and the current took it away. A few paces downstream, the flower turned around and disappeared inside the water pipe from the well. Then my Bee Bee said, "Rokni, haven't you complained enough?"

I shrugged my shoulders. I was still angry. We stood and the two of us started up the gravel road. My Bee Bee went to see what was going on in the kitchen and I climbed the front steps. I saw Masoud standing in front of my Khan Papa Doctor's room, squeezing a piece of wax in his fist to strengthen his grip. He wore jeans and an open-collared silk shirt. A chain with a gold prayer medallion, "Those Who Cheat," shone on the hair of his chest. As soon as he caught sight of me, his mouth drooped and he put on a tragic expression. I didn't pay him any heed.

I opened the bedroom door and entered. My Khan Papa Doctor was stretched on the bed in the middle of the room with a pale and washed-out face. He seemed likely to drop his chin at any moment and roll back his eyes to the ceiling; but, as soon as I closed the door, he noticed me. He raised his head from the pillow with an effort and pulled the edge of the checkered blanket over his chest, as if I were a stranger he had to welcome with gestures of courtesy. After that, for no apparent reason, he turned his face from me. He looked out the window. A blue square of sky was visible beyond the frame, and shadow birds, bored and lazy, were circling and bothering no one. I imagined that they had been circling like this outside his window from the beginning of creation, and, as long as the world existed, that circling would continue.

The smell of iodine sterilized the atmosphere. Dr. Amir Sina was squatting at my Khan Papa Doctor's feet. He poured a little alcohol into a big basin and lit it with a match. He picked up surgical tongs and gripped the edge of the basin and twirled the basin like a millstone. The soundless blue flame coated the inner surface of the basin and sterilized it. Dr. Amir Sina got up and offered a perfunctory greeting. "O Allah. How are you?"

"I'm fine. How are you, sir?"

"Busy, you know."

The bulge of his abdomen didn't reduce his height; it only made movement difficult for him. That was why he put down the basin. He took off his coat and hung it on a hanger. He rolled up his sleeves. He firmed the hazelnut-sized knot of his tie and squatted once again, and with more commanding and confident movements swirled the basin with his surgical tongs. I asked, "What are you doing?"

He chewed the tip of his toothbrush mustache and said, "Noth-

ing can stay in his stomach any more. Food has to reach him by
way of an I.V. At every mealtime he needs a liter of glucose
serum—"

My Khan Papa Doctor raised his weak voice. "Give this pimp a
slap on the neck and throw him out of here."

He lifted his hand and pointed to Dr. Amir Sina, but his face
was still set toward the window and he was watching the shadow
birds. Dr. Amir Sina stopped swirling the basin and looked at him
with tired, surprised eyes. Then he shrugged, as though to say my
Khan Papa Doctor was talking nonsense. My Khan Papa Doctor's voice rose again. "I told you. Kick this good-for-nothing out
of here. I don't have any need of doctors or medicine."

He stopped talking. Dr. Amir Sina pulled down the corners of
his mouth and continued swirling the flame in the basin. Then the
door opened and Mirza Hassibi came in. It was obvious he had
smoked his opium. He wiped his lips with the palm of his hand.
He wore a clean black suit that apparently didn't belong to him.
The sleeves and the trousers were too short. His tie was a flaming
red and its stripes contrasted oddly with the worn-out, second-
hand look of the suit. When he entered the room he didn't glance
at anyone. He bent over my Khan Papa Doctor and said, "Greetings to you, Mirza Sadegh Khan. How are you feeling?"

My Khan Papa Doctor seemed to have lost consciousness. The
curdled whites of his eyes were fixed on the ceiling. Mirza cleared
his throat and continued talking. "Mirza Sadegh Khan, we have
to get ready to go to Tehran."

Then he looked at me like a man whose heart was empty of
compassion. He put his hand in his jacket pocket and took out a
silver cigarette case. As he tamped a cigarette on the case, he
continue looking at me. He asked, "Are you ready to go?"

I said, "Go where?"

He lit his cigarette and exhaled the smoke. He said, "There's no
point staying in Ghaleh Bagh."

Dr. Amir Sina said, "In ten minutes his I.V. will be finished.
Then we can leave."

My Khan Papa Doctor came to and moaned, "Mirza, I don't
want to go. I want to stay here."

Mirza Hassibi pushed out his lower lip and shook his head. Dr.

Amir Sina filled his syringe with the serum he had poured into the basin. He pulled back a corner of the blanket. He lifted the loose skin of my Khan Papa Doctor's thigh like a crumpled bath rag and stuck the needle under it. My Khan Papa Doctor took on a look of pain and protest, but not a sound came out of his mouth. He only remained motionless for a few moments, waiting for relief. Bit by bit the serum accumulated under his skin, creating an oblong prominence. He groaned, "It's burning. It's burning badly. When are you going to stop all these cuckold doings and let me die in peace?"

Mirza took a puff from his cigarette and said, "Mirza Sadegh Khan, the famous Sufi sage Hajviri said that God's servant will choose the will of the righteous over his own will."

My Khan Papa Doctor said, "Fuck Hajviri. Mirza, your beard has grown white and reached your navel, and still you have a head full of stupid ideas."

Mirza Hassibi listened to him carefully, like a doctor with a stethoscope on his patient's chest. Dr. Amir Sina threw the empty syringe into the basin. He rolled down his shirtsleeves and fastened his gold cufflinks. He made the hazelnut knot of his tie even firmer and stood up. It was clear that everything was finished and we were ready to go. Mirza Hassibi stubbed out his cigarette in the ashtray. He rubbed his hands together and looked around as though he'd lost something. But my Khan Papa Doctor lay spread on the bed and seemed in no hurry to leave. His bitter, sickly gaze passed over the faces of the others and fell on me. He gestured for me to come forward. Slowly, I went and sat next to him. He was unconscious again. His eyes were open, his mouth was half open, and he was snoring. The room was silent as Mirza Hassibi helped Dr. Amir Sina put his instruments in his leather bag. They did everything cautiously, with dainty, fastidious movements, like ballerinas dancing without music. My Khan Papa Doctor put his hand on mine, and without preparation he started speaking. "Rokni."

I said, "Yes."

He closed his eyes and asked, "Did you see the sun coming up in the east?"

"Go on talking. I'm listening."

"Do you hear a voice from far, far off? Do you hear them leading a bride to her bridegroom—I mean from far, far off?"

"Go on, Khan Papa Doctor."

"Today, in the early dawn, I saw the sun. What a glare, it nearly blinded my eyes. When a person looks at the sun, he has to keep a smoked glass over his eyes; otherwise he'll go blind."

He sank into a coma again. I said nothing. Now Mirza Hassibi had lifted one end of a steamer trunk, and with Dr. Amir Sina's help he was carrying it out of the room. My Khan Papa Doctor resumed speaking. "Greetings to you, Agha Ass Dass Dolah. Say that I'll be in his presence day after tomorrow. . . . I'm waiting for the son of the house, Agha Ziadeen. . . . Rokni, where is Zia? When will Zia come? I have to talk to him."

His eyes were open and he was looking at me. I squeezed his hand and said, "He'll come, Khan Papa Doctor. I promise he'll come."

He was relieved, and he closed his eyes again. But he continued to talk as before. "His Majesty made utterance: 'Heshmat Nezam, do you still think the spirit of the Regent Abbas Mirza has entered your body?' Heshmat Nezam submitted, 'Yes, Your Majesty.' His Majesty made utterance, 'Why, among all the rednecks sponging on our court, has the late Regent chosen your body for a dwelling place? How do you account for that?' Heshmat Nezam submitted, 'Because we are created this way.' Then His Majesty turned his blessed face to the late Sardar Azhdar and made utterance: 'Why is your brother, Heshmat Nezam, so stubborn? He doesn't know his manners. Was he raised in a barn? The Hamedani Sadats say one must learn kindness and compassion from Agha Sardar Azhdar. Look at the circles around his slanted eyes. Look at the arch of his uneven, braidlike eyebrows. That's the face of a dervish or a hobo, with its modesty and humility. It's not the face of the highest Army authority.'"

Mirza bent over and cupped a hand to his ear, as if listening to a weak and distant sound. Dr. Amir Sina approached and said in a low voice, "Mirza, we have to get going."

Mirza said, "Wait a minute, Doctor. Let me see what Mirza Sadegh Khan wants to say."

Then my Khan Papa Doctor continued his monologue. "Rokni,

how dark the sky has grown! It's not a good omen. In the street there's fire and smoke. Have you called the Fire Department? We have to make a phone call and tell the Fire Department. Otherwise, there'll be blood and killing. . . . I've done what I could. I told her, 'Lady, I'll be your servant, your attendant.' The people in the street gathered in front of the bakery and watched Homayundokht, God forgive her soul, on the rooftop. They didn't so much as chirp. Then, imagining that the quarrel was over, they scattered and left. But the caretaker of the mosque screamed and pointed to Homayundokht, God forgive her soul. . . . That God-forgiven, that knuckleheaded woman had poured a tin of kerosene over her head and lit it. The neighbors thought it was another display of her Sardar Azhdari playacting. They said it was witchcraft and she'd created a hollow around herself. But that God-forgiven woman was standing in the midst of the fire and wouldn't move from her place. The flames were licking all around her body. That God-forgiven woman was enchanted. Someone had cast a spell on her. The neighbors couldn't believe it. They thought they were looking at an icon, not at that God-forgiven woman. Then she fell on the rooftop like a sack of rice and the neighbors screamed. You understand?"

Now his eyes were open and the last of his life force was concentrated in them. He was giving me a straight, focused look. He tightened his fingers on my arm and said angrily, "You understand? We were disgraced."

His nails scratched my arm and hurt me. I tried not to let out a sound. In the corner of the room, Mirza Hassibi stood behind my Khan Papa Doctor and wiped an invisible dust from the windowpane with his palm. He was reflective. I didn't know if it were my Khan Papa Doctor he was thinking about or Homayundokht, God forgive her soul. My Khan Papa Doctor kept on clutching my arm and staring into my eyes as though I owed him something. I couldn't wait any longer. I released my arm from his grip and stood up. He shouted, "Why aren't we moving? What are we waiting for? Where is this good-for-nothing Mirza Hassibi?"

He had regained his strength and was speaking with authority. I opened the door and left the room. Colonel Bayat and his orderlies were bringing the stretcher up the gravel road toward the veranda. On the veranda, Masoud leaned against the wall, facing the sunshine. He had his legs crossed like a pair of scissors and he was waiting for something. As soon as he saw me, he said, "Rokni, what have you done now?"

I said, "Nothing."

I left in a hurry and went toward the river. He followed. I turned and said, "Masoud, let's go south."

"Rokni, what is this game you're playing? Didn't we decide that first we'd look after your Khan Papa Doctor?"

"We'll get in a car and go south. We'll go to Bushehr and stand on the beach and watch the ships anchoring. We'll watch the sea gulls in the sky and we'll listen to them calling. We'll go after them among the reeds and the waters of the white marshes along the bay, and the farther we go the farther away the gulls will get and the weaker their voices."

My face had grown wet and my arm was burning from my Khan Papa Doctor's scratches. Masoud sat down on the ground. He said, "I don't have time to travel south. Find yourself another traveling companion. They've given orders to free your Khan Brother Zia. As soon as we get to Tehran, we have to go to Mr. Farzaneh and claim your Khan Brother Zia."

"How come Farzaneh changed his mind?"

"Because of your Khan Papa Doctor. Because the Army owes a lot to your Khan Papa Doctor."

"I don't believe you. I know how the Army rewards people's services."

Masoud frowned and said, "I don't feel like arguing with you. We have to get going to Tehran and receive your Khan Brother."

Mirza Hassibi spoke up behind us. "What are you going to do about face making?"

I turned around. I asked, "What do you mean?"

"Don't you think you could still do your face making while you're working in the Foreign Ministry?"

"I'm not going to the Foreign Ministry."

In a hushed, stern voice, he said, "Please put your stubbornness aside. You have to get out of here. This place is no longer your place."

Dr. Amir Sina opened the door of my Khan Papa Doctor's

room. My Bee Bee, Yadolah, and Mash Khadijeh came to the center of the orchard, and their shadows clung to the ground like a paste. Then the orderlies brought my Khan Papa Doctor's stretcher from his room. Mirza Hassibi was whispering in my ear, "It's to your advantage to get out of this environment. A man can do face making anywhere in the world. He doesn't need any special place. All a face maker needs is a pair of hidden, seeing eyes. If you have the eyes for it, you don't need anything more. The late Master Assar himself said, 'Mirza, suppose they shot and blinded both my eyes. Very well. Let them do it. But they don't know what I see with, how I see and what I see.' You understand what I'm talking about? Nobody can blind your hidden eye. The hidden eye belongs to no one. It's impossible to own it like a worldly good. It's impossible to register it under somebody's name in the Registry of Documents, or to bequeath it to someone. The hidden eye is free. What the hidden eye sees is not color; it's pattern and composition. It's connection and disconnection; it's mood and change of mood."

The orderlies were taking the stretcher out through the orchard. My Bee Bee, Iran, and Zahra Soltan followed, and with their exit a frightened silence stilled the atmosphere. Mirza shaded his eyes and peered at the sky. Then he bent his head and, walking with his cane, he went down the gravel road toward the orchard door. I paused for a moment. It occurred to me that my Khan Papa Doctor had left his laboratory behind him. I felt the mark of his fingernails on my arm.

2

Walking behind the stretcher, we passed through the alleys of Ghaleh Bagh. We passed over the bridge and arrived at the little bazaar. My Khan Papa Doctor's struggle with cancer had increased his air of contempt and pride. With every shake of the stretcher, a knot was tied in one corner of his mouth, giving him the stubborn expression of someone who had tasted something bitter. Mirza Hassibi and Dr. Amir Sina, their heads bowed, took slow and measured paces. My Bee Bee and Zahra Soltan walked on either side of Iran's mule, watching so she wouldn't fall, God forbid. Iran had a hopeful smile on her lips. Her thin, knobby fingers searched for each other over her head as though counting the days of the week.

Masoud was walking in step with me. The way he smoked his cigarette struck me as inappropriate. It was repulsive to me. It made me angry. He was puffing with the haste and nervousness of a civil servant, as though he were waiting outside a government office till he could go in and fling his exaggerated, ministerial signature on the bottom of official documents. His expression of readiness, instead of giving him authority, made him look false—a no-account, one-dimensional man. The old rage clutched my throat. He noticed and watched me from the corner of his eye, trying to figure me out. He threw down his cigarette butt and rubbed it with the tip of his shoe.

"You're always thinking of yourself," he said. "You think you're the only one who's breathing, and others don't have the right. They have to stand with their arms folded on their chests like slaves, waiting for Your Excellency's orders."

"If you want to get to Tehran without a fistfight, you'd better start talking like a human being."

I imagined how Masoud would look in his sixties—an overripe fruit, fat and juicy, puffy and fermented. The swelling of decay would have softened the sharpness in the lines of his face. I seized his sleeve and pulled him behind the public bath furnace. A feverish steam came from the bathhouse dressing room, turning the alley heavy and cloudy. The heat made Masoud look as if his face had been slapped. He pushed back his hair from his forehead. He looked right and left and lowered his voice. "Rokni, what's wrong with you? Why are you doing this?"

I held his shoulders and shook him. "Never again put me on."

"What do you mean, put you on? Who am I doing all this for? It's for your own Khan Brother. Otherwise, why would I be knocking on everyone's door and begging this man and that for your Khan Brother's freedom?"

I couldn't answer. Somehow, he had stumped me. When he saw I'd stopped talking, he said, "Look, Rokni, it's because we're relatives that I don't want to embarrass you. Have you ever just once come and said, 'Masoud, I hope you're not tired from all you've done for me'?"

"Relative, my foot. You knew my Khan Brother Zia was in prison. Why did you hide it from me? Why did you send me to Farzaneh?"

"After all I've done, you're still not satisfied? Now I have to give you money too, so you'll forgive me?"

He took my arm to lead me down the alley behind the bathhouse. I resisted and didn't move. He tilted his head and looked at me inquiringly. I felt his face was moving in front of me; like shadows at sunset, it was growing darker and more opaque. I reached out and grabbed his collar and brought him close. With the eyes of a slaughtered lamb, he looked at me. I let him go. I took a step back to see what he'd do. He searched around himself, confused and dense. He found a slab of stone and sat on it. He adjusted the creases at the knees of his ironed jeans. Then he held his head between his palms and grew motionless. Gradually he felt better. With his fingertips, he removed a piece of tobacco from his lips. My rage had faded. Masoud asked, "What did you do that for? Is it because of your Khan Papa Doctor's illness? Maybe you're having a breakdown."

"I warned you not to argue with me. Don't forget that."

I sat on another slab of stone. He pointed and said, "It's dusty, Rokni. Blow off the dust. Your pants will get dirty."

"Don't you want to give up this Sardar Azhdari caretaking?"

"Sardar Azhdari, Heshmat Nezami, it doesn't matter. We shouldn't fight over trifles. We're relatives. We have to protect and look after each other. If one falls, the other has to pick him up and dress his wounds. If you have something bothering you and you want to pour out your anger, this is my head, please come and hit me. What are you waiting for?"

He had stumped me once again. I didn't know what to do. He put his palms together and said, "Sincerely. If I hurt your feelings, it wasn't out of meanness. As soon as we arrive in Tehran, I'll collect your Khan Brother Zia myself and bring him to your house safe and sound, so at least your Khan Papa Doctor can see him at the end. Now, get up and let's go. We've fallen behind."

We started down the alley. We passed under the shade of the apple and plum trees and turned into a narrower alley and came out in Ghaleh Bagh station. The air was filled with the smell of manure and crushed grass. The orderlies had set my Khan Papa Doctor's stretcher down and they were waiting for us. Yadolah was putting the mules' loads on top of the ambulance. A wind blew toward the cemetery and the river, fluttering the women's veils like flags. When Mirza saw us, he waved his cane and shouted, "It's getting late. Where have you been?"

We quickened our pace and went toward Masoud's car, which was parked near the teahouse across from the station. Again Mirza Hassibi waved his cane in the air, this time a little more loosely and less enthusiastically, as though he'd given up expecting us to answer him. Then the orderlies opened the back door of the ambulance and lifted my Khan Papa Doctor's stretcher and put him inside. We were closer now and we could see his glaring, determined eyes. The orderlies asked him something that he left unanswered, and he kept looking at us as if warning us not to forget some request of his. Masoud said, "You ride with your Khan Papa Doctor in the ambulance. When we get to Tehran, we'll go after your Khan Brother Zia together."

But my arm still smarted from my Khan Papa Doctor's fingernails. I said, "I'm not riding with him. I want to go to Tehran by myself."

He shrugged and opened his car door for me. From my place in the car, I saw Mirza Hassibi pivoting his hands on his wrists as if asking a question. I gestured for them to go ahead and not to wait for me; I wasn't riding in the ambulance. Mirza Hassibi twisted his hands again: why? Before I could answer, the wind puffed the women's veils, blocking my view. Then the women got in Dr. Amir Sina's Mercedes. Masoud started the car, stepped on the gas, and we left.

To our right, Ghaleh Bagh's river crept gently on its gravel path in the bottom of the valley and, like a silver wire, it slit the valley under the needling of the sunlight. I was looking through the rear window at the Army ambulance and Dr. Amir Sina's Mercedes, both of which were gradually falling behind and disappearing in the winding of the road and the dust of the horizon. Masoud looked serious, refusing to talk. Whenever we passed over a pothole, the "Those Who Cheat" holy medal swung around his neck. I thought the pieces of his face were put together according to careful calculation. With every blink, the lines around his eyes disappeared. I said, "Do you have a Winston?"

He put his hand in his shirt pocket and took out a pack of Winstons and gave it to me. I wasn't a smoker, and I don't know why I took the pack from him. I gave it back. He said, "Azra's right. You're like one of her balloon men. Your head isn't connected to anything, nor are your feet. You're forever dangling."

I was looking at his "Those Who Cheat" holy medal, and in my mind the words of the prayer revolved: "Those who cheat commit blasphemy, those who cheat commit blasphemy. . . ."

I expected Masoud to repeat the same words, imitating me— like the Masoud of olden days who used to echo whatever I said. Without a question, without a doubt, without any struggle, the Masoud of olden days believed what I told him.

"Well, what else did she say?" he used to ask when I told of seeing the spirit of Homayundokht, God forgive her soul, on the roof.

"Who do you mean, Masoud?"

"Homayundokht, God forgive her soul. God bless her, what else did she say?"

"What else did you want her to say? Nothing."

"Was that all?"

"Yes, that was all."

He was silent for a while, thinking. Then he rubbed his hands together and said, "Oh, my soul. Tell me, did she let you touch her?"

"No. Can you touch a spirit? A spirit is as cold as cold wind. If you touch it your finger is frozen. You suddenly grow cold. Your hair stands up on your skin like pins."

Then he swore that he too had seen Homayundokht, God forgive her soul, in the hall of their house. That is, she had brought her painting equipment so she could paint the pine tree and the awnings of the rooms at the end of the courtyard. He didn't dare tell anyone. Homayundokht, God forgive her soul, had told him something he was afraid to reveal. Even with me, he spoke in generalities. He wouldn't give the details. At first, I didn't believe him. I thought he was making things up. Later on he began to talk about my Khan Brother Zia as if he had some message for him from Homayundokht, God forgive her soul. I said, "What kind of message? Cough up. Out with it."

He grew absent-minded and dreamy. He said, "Homayundokht, God forgive her soul, says being a soldier is not a useful occupation for your Khan Brother Zia. She says he'll become an artist. He'll learn painting and get himself free of all the Heshmat Nezamis and Sardar Azhdaris."

I said, "You're lying. You're making things up."

Next day in school he claimed he had once again seen Homa-yundokht, God forgive her soul. She had appeared near the spigots deep down in our quarter's water house. She had said, "Masoud Sardar Azhdari, you are about to leave this trivial and impermanent world. Soon they will look you up and send you away."

Masoud had said, begging and beseeching, "Why, lady? What have I done? I'm not involved in art. I had to repeat my language and composition courses."

Homayundokht, God forgive her soul, answered, "Don't you want to be free? Don't you like freedom? I know people who burned themselves up for freedom."

Masoud answered, "Dear lady, I don't want to go. I'm only a puny kid. I haven't tasted life yet. Life in the other world is no fun."

He kissed my face and tears filled his eyes and he said, "Rokni-jun, whatever good or bad you've seen of me you have to forgive. 'If we were unkind, we are gone anyway. If we were a heavy load, we are gone anyway.' "

I said, "All right," and burst out laughing. Masoud didn't get the joke, and with the same orphaned face he said, "See you on Resurrection Day."

Two days after that he changed his story. He ran toward me on the playing field, happy and excited. When he reached me he beamed and said cockily, "Homayundokht, God forgive her soul, says it's too early yet for me to go to the next world. I'm still a kid and too stupid to understand these things. Instead she bought me a lottery ticket and said to keep it carefully because it's a winner."

He reached into his pocket and took out the lottery ticket. He flattened the crumpled ticket. He showed it to me and said, "This number's a winner."

I said, "If you win, what will you do with the money?"

"I'll find a good painter to paint an excellent tableau of Homa-yundokht, God forgive her soul. I'll put the tableau over her grave."

"They won't allow it. It's forbidden. It's not possible to hang the unveiled face of a woman in the cemetery."

"No, they let you. Conditions have changed and it's not that difficult."

In the car now, the grown-up Masoud said, "Rokni, do you remember?"

"Remember what?"

"Remember when Homayundokht, God forgive her soul, sent a message for us not to pass by the Bastion? If we passed it, we'd go blind?"

"Yes."

"All that was a lie. I made it up to see if you were a fool or not."

"All right, a bouquet of flowers for you."

"Rokni, are you still cross? If you could, you'd really let me have it, isn't that so?"

He wiped the sweat off his forehead and continued: "You know it's impossible to say everything. As soon as you start to speak they won't give you a chance to explain. Right away they condemn you. You understand?"

"What are you talking about?"

"Son of a bitch, how hot it is! Have you ever asked yourself why, wherever you've gone, I've followed you? Have you ever asked yourself what's bugging this Masoud, that he measures the streets behind you for no reason?"

"Why do you, Masoud?"

"I'll tell you. But it's hot and I'm getting exasperated."

He slowed the car and turned down a narrow path. We passed beneath crowded branches. Then a wheatfield appeared in front of us. Clattering and jolting, the car traveled through the field to the riverbank. I asked, "Masoud, what are you doing?"

"I want to take a dip. Son of a bitch, how hot it is. I'm dying for a dip."

"I have to get to Tehran."

"You have to get to Tehran for what? Are they flying elephants in Tehran?"

"We need to go after my Khan Brother Zia. Time is passing. My Khan Papa Doctor's condition isn't good at all. I don't know how long he can last."

"You worry over nothing. A swim won't take long. The ambulance is about six kilometers behind us. Till it catches up, we have plenty of time."

He pulled the emergency brake and jumped out. He hurried toward the river. Then he kicked off his shoes. He took off his outer clothes and threw them on the grass. Bewildered, I climbed from the car. The sun beat directly on my head and I was dripping with sweat. I removed my vest and tossed it on the car hood. From a distance I watched Masoud, who by now was creating a whirlpool in the middle of the river. After that, he swam underwater and his body was marble white and wavy, like a peeled willow trunk, creeping on the green and steel-colored stones of the riverbed. I had no desire for a dip. I was in a hurry to get back to Tehran. But I did take off my boots and my socks. I wriggled my toes till the tiredness left me. Then I went to the riverbank. Two hoopoes leapt into the sky from the trees on the other side. They circled over the wheatfield. They rose and disappeared again among the trees. There wasn't a trace of a human being around us. The width of the field and the chirping of the crickets created a kind of nostalgia, like an echo in the mountains.

Watching that wheatfield alone was strange. Like most of the Heshmat Nezamis, I wasn't used to being away from my family. As Agha Ass Dass Dolah used to say, we didn't belong to any place or any person except our own relatives. Wherever we went, whatever we touched, we behaved as if we had no connection with anyone. Even in the court of the Martyred Shah where everyone else was scared silly, the late Heshmat Nezam could not control his tongue. If it hadn't been for the late Sardar Azhdar, the Mecca of the Universe would have finished off the late Heshmat Nezam in the wink of an eye and, in Agha Ass Dass Dolah's words, his name would have been erased from the page of life forever. But the late Sardar Azhdar was valued and respected in the presence of the Mecca of the Universe. They called him a paragon of good manners. How civil—a poet and a scholar. When he opened his mouth, everyone fell silent and listened. He donated all his possessions to the Humanity Association. Money didn't stay with him. Hamedani Sadat said the melancholia must have hit him in the head, otherwise he never would have thrown himself on the blessed likeness of His Majesty with a sugar hammer.

Masoud called, "Rokni, come on in. The water's perfect."

In the middle of the river he stopped splashing, expectant. I paid no attention. I was figuring out how to pick up my unfinished sculpture from the Art School and take it to my Khan Papa Doctor. I turned over on the grass. The wheat stood around me in a circle. Big maroon ants were running after food in every direction. I caught sight of a handgun that had emerged a few inches from its leather holster. I pulled out the gun. It was cold and heavy. The steel barrel smelled of gunpowder, as though it had recently been fired. I touched the handle with the tip of my tongue. It was acrid, like a flashlight battery. I rose and went to the riverbank. Masoud saw me and stopped swimming. Again he smiled and gestured for me to dive into the water. I waved the gun in the air. I called, "Masoud, look what I've got."

He wiped his face and said, "Where'd you find it?"

"Over on the grass."

In a more serious tone, he said, "It belongs to me, Rokni. Be careful. Don't fiddle with it. It'll go off and destroy you."

"You know me, Masoud. If I find something, I won't let it go until I know it inside out."

He pulled himself from the water in a hurry. He hitched up his underpants and lunged for the gun. Maybe he was afraid I'd been seized by an evil thought. I lifted the gun beyond his reach. As he charged toward me, I dodged. He fell on the grass, but he didn't give up. He rose and said, "Hand it over, Rokni. That gun belongs to me. I wanted to show it to you myself. I brought you here to show you a lot of things. Stop acting so spoiled and silly."

His eyebrows slanted above the arches of his eyes. The water had washed his hair over his forehead like a paintbrush, giving him a stupid expression. He took advantage of my being momentarily off guard and grabbed my wrist and tried to squeeze the gun from my fist. With all his practice squeezing wax, he should have been able to crush my bones. But I resisted, and the more I resisted, the more his begging expression changed to one of stubbornness and rage. He drew back his lips and showed me his clenched teeth. He couldn't get the gun from my hand. He threw me backward with a punch. After that, he hit me in the side. My eyes darkened and I saw red. With the butt of the gun, I hit him on the head so hard that it sounded like a crock of yogurt. It didn't matter to me; if his skull had cracked, I wouldn't have minded. On the contrary, I would have been all the angrier. I fell on him and I hit to kill. He might have been a piece of raw meat that I wanted to tear apart.

Suddenly, the light seemed to fade and darkness fell everywhere. The continuous, eternal stillness of the wheatfield was transformed into a hushed murmur. Far away on the horizon I saw Homayundokht, God forgive her soul. In the midst of the dusty yellow light she had opened her green umbrella above her head. She was walking parallel to the horizon, and the long tail of her silk dress trailed over the wheat. She had wrapped a blue ribbon around her straw hat and its tongues were fluttering from the bow in back. There was a smile on her lips that was calming and soothing. There was a sweet smell in the air. The earth started to breathe again, and in the depths of the sky's hollow, way high up, shadow birds were circling each other like a flock of dreamy butterflies. On the horizon Homayundokht, God forgive her soul, strutted away as before. When she reached the end of the field she turned and threw a glance at me over the curve of her shoulder. A satisfied expression appeared in her eyes, as if she wanted to say, "Didn't I tell you?"

I got up. I was still dizzy. My eyes were glued to the edge of the field and the empty place left by Homayundokht, God forgive her soul. I threw the gun on the grass and started walking toward the car. I saw Masoud, bloody and battered, moving on the ground. My joints grew inexplicably weak. My knees touched the ground and impulsively I muttered, "Oh, Merciful of Mercifuls."

The trunks of broken trees came into view, scattered here and there over the field. At this distance they resembled burnt bodies, charred and clutching. Behind them, the wheat stalks had put their heads together in the wind and were stirring restlessly.

I felt Masoud's hand on my shoulder. Before I could look at his face, he set a white card on my palm. He shrugged and went away. I was still giddy and couldn't read the writing on the card. I could see Masoud in the distance, wandering and tired, hunting his clothes in the grass. He found them one by one and put them on with a look of dejection. I brought the card closer and saw these words:

Masoud Sardar Azhdari
Number 379
National Organization of Information and Security
SAVAK

The features of Homayundokht, God forgive her soul, appeared again on the edge of the horizon. She wore a frown and was questioning me with her eyes.

3

We had reached Baharestan Circle. The air smelled of gunpowder
and tear gas. It wasn't clear what was going on. People walked the
sidewalks with a peculiar pull, and there was a hint of haste and
worry in their movements as though they were skirting some danger. In the distance was the tap-tap of a solitary machine gun, like
the roasting of a handful of cantaloupe seeds. Masoud drew his
eyebrows down and said nothing. If these had been the old days,
no doubt he would have tilted his head and lightly slapped his
own face and said, "By the soul of Masoud, let this body die!"

But now he remained silent. Nor did I lift my gaze from his
purple, puffy face. When he saw this, he turned away and said,
"We have to go to a hospital first so I can get fixed up. These
damned swollen eyelids don't let me see to drive."

I said, "Stop. I want to get out."

"We have to claim your Khan Brother Zia. We don't have
much time."

"I told you to stop. I want to get out in front of Safi ali Shah."

"If you won't go to a hospital, at least let's find a drugstore and
buy a bandage or something for these wounds. It won't take
long."

As the car circled Baharestan, I reached for the handle and opened the door with a jerk. Two small cars and an orange taxi honked behind us. Masoud grew worried and shouted, "What are you doing? You'll be run over!"

"If you don't stop I'll throw myself into the street."

"All right. Wait till I change lanes."

He slowed down next to the sidewalk and slammed his foot hard on the brake. The car hadn't completely stopped when I landed with a jolt on the sidewalk. I paid no attention to traffic. I ran toward the kebab shop from the center of the circle. Masoud put his head out of the car and called, "I know you very well, Rokni! Do you want to say something? Let your soul come out! Say what you want! There's no need for all this, there's no need for these dramatics. Don't get the wrong idea. If I'd wanted to, I could have settled your account right there on the riverbank, so you'd know you had peed on hard ground. I go along with you because you're my relative, because we've been good friends, because we've eaten bread and salt at one table."

When I reached the other side of the circle, a peddler was standing in front of his pastry tray, holding a mosquito-net pole in his hand. Pinned to the top of the pole was a copy of a painting of a woman from the Ahmad Shah period. Her golden hair, all curly and finger-waved, descended from the top of her head to the white of her neck. She pursed her mouth flirtatiously, like a blossom, as though she had swooned in the midst of making a kissing sound. As I came close to the peddler, he brought the pole forward and said, "Boss, do you want some pastry? If you don't have the money, it's dog food; for you it's free."

I drew back. The man slapped his charcoal-blackened hand on his hip and burst into laughter. I ignored him. I unbuttoned my shirt and sat down on the curb. Then a vanguard of Army trucks appeared from the direction of Shahabad. They came screeching around the circle and went off toward Sarcheshmeh like a train of prehistoric turtles. A helicopter was descending over Baharestan's statue. I caught sight of Azra Hamedani, who had appeared somehow from the west side of the circle. She carried two canvases under her arm. She looked around her cautiously, and when the road was clear she started running. I shouted, "Azra!"

She glanced in my direction, but she didn't see me. She took a jump, rose in the air like a straw, and landed on the sidewalk. Then she kept running. The rapid shadows of her legs scissored the edge of the sidewalk. The peddler pointed to the sky and grinned. After that, his face disappeared in the dust. Again the tap-tap of the machine gun reached my ears. I dashed into the street and began running toward the Art School.

When I entered the school garden, I saw a group of outsiders gathered around the pool—people in a variety of outfits, some in jeans and open-collared silk shirts, some in suits and ties with briefcases, some in suits without ties and with unshaven faces. Among them was an assortment of children. They were moving in wide paths and without any order. As I came close, they parted and made way for me. The garden was more like a loan office or a passport bureau. I circled the steps and walked along the corridor. From the back windows, the drawing hall appeared cluttered. No one was in it. I passed the audiovisual section. I saw Azra Hamedani, who was hanging her paintings on the wet and mildewed wall of the balcony. Balloon men, big and little, in motionless silence, continued their eternal descent on the brick wall. Azra ran this way and that, worried and in haste, adjusting the paintings. I said, "Azra."

She paused for a moment and looked down at me. She waited to see what I would say. I said, "Want to go to Lazarian for a beer?"

She pounded a hammer on the nail that she held to the wall and said, "Rokni, don't you see what's going on in the streets? Don't you see there is chaos everywhere and the killing is beginning?"

"If that's so, why are you here yourself?"

"For my exhibition that's scheduled to open next week. It's not for the fun of it."

"In this mess, who has time to come to an exhibition?"

"For some, it's important. Even if it rains bombs, they get themselves to an exhibition."

I fell silent and she continued to hang the painting. She spoke again. "Rokni, I hear they're going to release your Khan Brother Zia. Is that true?"

"That's what they say. Masoud says they'll free him in a few days. But no one can trust what Masoud says."

"No doubt you're happy. Isn't that right?"

"If you want the truth, I don't know."

She stopped working. She squatted on the edge of the balcony and said irritably, "I know what you're talking about. If I were in your situation, I would have given up all this crap and gone on with my own business. When Jahangir says we should go here and there, I pull down the venetian blinds and keep working in my darkroom. Working in my darkroom takes courage because you might hit on a new idea. When Jahangir says it's not prudent to come to the Art School, I say I don't mind the danger, you've got to have courage."

She got up angrily and turned back to her paintings. I said, "The problem is that my father's dying. I can't tell a dying man I'm going on with my own business."

She flung up her hands and said, "Oh, Rokni. Stop acting so childish. If you don't take your work seriously, one day you'll wake up and see you're not connected to anything around you and you don't know where you're going."

She went back to hanging her paintings. I opened the door and entered the drawing hall. The interlaced, borderless shadows of the crowd swirled behind the front windows. Children pressed against the panes with flattened faces, peering inside. I saw my unfinished sculpture still standing on its pedestal, rebellious as ever. The cloth I had wrapped around it had dried out in the heat and it looked starched. It molded the hollows and prominences of the statue. I lifted the statue from the pedestal. It was light. It rolled in my arms like lath wood.

Bit by bit, people were joining the crowd behind the window. They pressed against the panes and watched the drawing hall. It wasn't clear to me why they were watching. I put the statue on my shoulder and left the hall. No one was in the corridor. In the garden, the sunlight was slanted. The smoke of the tires they had set afire was twisting in the air and here and there it spotted the sky. Several children, ten or twelve years old, walked behind me. Wherever I went, they followed me politely and in silence. I stood on the curb of Safi ali Shah and turned to see what they wanted. They stopped twenty paces away from me, and under the harsh sun they looked at me with crumpled, India-ink eyes. I reached in my pocket and pulled out a handful of coins and poured them on the sidewalk. The children started collecting them as I began walking again toward our house.

I was feeling dizzy and walking was hard for me. At a distance, the children still followed me from shadow to shadow. There seemed to be a purpose in their movements. They were after something, but I didn't know what. I stood on the curb near the bus stop. Of course it was ridiculous to ride a bus with that statue. Then a cherry-colored car appeared. Masoud had put a big white bandage over his left eye and sunglasses over that. When he reached the bus stop, he braked and gestured for me to get in. I didn't. It was obvious he was exasperated with me. He turned down an alley and went as far as the arches at the entrance of the bazaar. He parked in front of the mirrored water shrine. As he got out of the car, he was forced to lean back against the tiles of the water shrine and rise up on tiptoe to make way for a procession of religious mourners beating their breasts. The torrent of the crowd flowed toward Shahabad with standards and banners. A young man with a shaven head, wearing a black shirt, stood on the counter at the bakery. He reached inside a pouch and brought forth handfuls of straw to sprinkle on the mourners and on their henna-colored horse.

> For the dry throat of St. Ali Asghar,
> For the cut hand of the Moon of Bani Hashem,
> For the loneliness of the Lord of Martyred Saints.

Upraised hands bearing chains came down on the bloody, blackened backs. The dust beneath the dome of the bazaar clouded the hanging columns of sunshine. I pushed toward Masoud. He was pressing his hands behind him on the water-shrine tiles and looking nervously at the crowd. Although I was close to him and he could see the statue on my shoulder, he didn't open the car door for me. I opened it myself and rolled down the window. I rested the foot of the statue on the seat and closed the door in such a way that the head of the statue stuck out the window. Meanwhile, Masoud was tracing the grouting of the tiles. I said, "Is my Khan Papa Doctor dead?"

He didn't answer. He didn't look away from the tiles, either.

Behind him, the icon of the Moon of Bani Hashem leaned in the
niche of the water shrine on a clean doily. Written on the doily
was, "Help Abalfazl al Abbas." Next to the kerosene lamp and
electric candles, a horse without a rider and without eyes, like a
chalk statue, smelled the brown land of Karbala. A bouquet of
roses wrapped in plastic had been placed in front of the wooden
bridal chamber of the young martyred saint, Ghasem. The water
shrine had a sort of newly built feeling and a brightness that
seemed unsuitable. It was like a peasant house whose clay walls
had been whitewashed and sprayed with DDT.

Masoud started down the alley and I followed. Pigeons were
circling above Mirza Hassibi's rooftop like a handful of papers
torn to pieces. I said, "My Khan Papa Doctor's dead, isn't he?"

Masoud averted his eyes from me. I said, "Why don't you say
something?"

He put his hand on the doorknob and knocked. He said, "Well,
no doubt you expected it."

"Expected what?"

"You weren't so blind you couldn't see. You could see that only
Dr. Amir Sina's shots were keeping him going."

"He's dead, then. Isn't he?"

"When I called, Mirza Hassibi gave me the news. He said your
Khan Papa Doctor was finished along the way, before they
reached Tehran."

I felt I was about to throw up. I hadn't expected to hear that
news. I felt double-crossed and angry. I asked Masoud, "Did
Mirza Hassibi say how my Khan Papa Doctor died?"

"What do you mean? How does anyone die?"

"For example, was his mind alert till the last moment? Could
he recognize people around him? Could he talk?"

"I don't know anything about that. We didn't have much time
and I couldn't ask about these little things. Mirza only told us to
think about the shroud and burial."

"You call them little things?"

I wanted to raise my fists and knock them both against
Masoud's head. Any time I saw his pitiable face and bent neck, I
grew furious. I wanted to scream and burst out crying at the same

time. I said, "You see to the shroud and the burial. Go ahead and eat whatever shit you want."

"Look, Rokni. In these circumstances, I don't have any wish to argue with you. We have your Khan Brother Zia's release order. They'll set him free tomorrow so he can take part in the funeral. Now if you don't want to believe it, who cares?"

"Are you putting on this pathetic farce again?"

"Whatever I do is for the sake of your Khan Papa Doctor's soul. He was the only one of his kind among our relatives. You understand? If he had wanted, he could have been minister of war. But he didn't, because he didn't care to give anyone a piggyback ride. You understand? I do these things for him, not for you."

"Don't bring my Khan Papa Doctor's name up for nothing. You are a spy, you are a mercenary of the Security Organization and you should be put against the wall and shot by the firing squad."

Masoud turned his back toward me and knocked on the door of Mirza Hassibi's house. I grew worried. I dreaded seeing Mirza Hassibi. I was afraid he would say something, he would show me something that frightened me.

A servant opened the door for us and we entered. From beneath the vaults of the hall we saw Mirza Hassibi in an undershirt and pajama pants. He had an aluminum bowl full of millet under his arm, and he was scattering it to the birds from the side of the pool. The flock of scissortail pigeons around him gave him the look of someone standing in a cotton field. They were fluttering and cooing and snatching the grain from each other.

Evidently Mirza Hassibi was expecting us. As we came close, he started speaking. "So nice you came. It's growing late now. I have to get ready to travel. But you're in my thoughts. You have other business to see to, you have to think of the shrouding and burial."

I made my way among the pigeons. I stood beside the pool and said, "You were with him till the last?"

"Yes, till the last moment."

"Did he tell you something? Give you a message? A testament?"

"No, as we arrived at the Lamak's teahouse, he asked us to take him to the teahouse and leave him alone with your Bee Bee. We took them to a clean room and left them alone. You have to ask your Bee Bee what message or testament he gave. I myself stood outside reciting for him the Prayer of Light from St. Fatima, greetings of Allah be upon her. It works miracles for cutting fever. 'In the name of Allah the Light, in the name of Allah the Light over Light, in the name of Him Who writes the affairs, in the name of Allah Who created light from light . . .' "

"Does reciting the Prayer of Light take a long time?"

"It wasn't only that I was reciting the Prayer of Light. I was in a trance of discovery. I mean a vision had been caused to appear to me. God forgive her soul, it was the late Homayundokht."

He put down the bowl of millet. He focused his feverish eyes on me and said, "Tonight at seven-thirty the Mashad bus will depart from Kothari Garage. If I delay, I'll be left behind. There's no allowance for delays any more."

"Don't you want to attend my Khan Papa Doctor's funeral?"

He rubbed his hands with regret and looked at me helplessly. He ducked his head and said, "Agha Rokni, I beg your forgiveness. Are you listening to me? Are you paying attention to your big cousin?"

"Of course I am listening to you. But how soon you want to forget my Khan Papa Doctor!"

"Why can't you understand? Ghazali was delivering a lecture when someone brought news of the death of his son, the apple of his eye. He turned to the students and said that, in religious tradition, it's a virtue to attend the procession for the dead. Those who wished to follow could go. Then he looked at his book and continued his lecture: 'In the name of the Compassionate, the Merciful.' "

I said, "I don't want to follow the dead either."

Surprised, he asked, "What do you want, then? Tell me what you want from me."

"I want your vision. I want you to describe your vision to me."

He mumbled. He looked around for something and scratched his head. Masoud had picked up the bowl now and was scattering more millet for the pigeons. His movements were automatic. His face was thoughtful and his forehead was lined as though he were alone, as though he'd gone from us and was flying in a distant sky. Mirza Hassibi said, "Masoud, would you let me take your cousin to a private place and explain something to him?"

Masoud only nodded. Mirza immediately led me to his brazier room. The room was completely empty. In one corner a cloth bag leaned against the wall, tied at the top with grocery twine. I said, "You really want to go. No doubt it's because of your vision. Isn't it?"

He folded his hands and tipped his head and started talking like a prayer reciter in a shrine. "The late Homayundokht, God forgive her soul, who appeared to me in the vision, was very happy, just like in the days when we were going to Nishapur. Her face was radiant with light. Not a line in her expression spoke of sadness or bewilderment. She was standing in the middle of the cloister and there were others present as well, people with turbans and robes all sitting around cross-legged, not talking. The late Homayundokht, God forgive her soul, with her own special daintiness and dignity pulled back the lace hem of her sheer dress and showed me her small white feet. Then I sensed that something had changed in the structure of that cloister. The change appeared to me strange and impossible. It occurred to me that it could only happen in a different world beyond this external, perishable one. I understood that the pattern on the soft white foot of Homayundokht, God forgive her soul, was nothing but the seal of the Prophet himself. Then I prostrated myself and kissed the pattern of the seal. The deceased woman addressed me with the thin, echoing voice of a crowd of young boys and said, 'Mirza, from the day of my last journey, not a bite of food or a drop of water has passed my lips. The tree full of fruit is only a morsel for the hungry birds of the desert, so they can sit on its branches and consume it piece by piece with their crooked, hungry beaks.' "

As I listened, I could see in my mind Homayundokht, God forgive her soul, in the spring of the year, when people were on their way to the pastures and fields. The Heshmat Nezami ladies were throwing parties and gathering around each other and expressing concern about the mood and general condition of Homayundokht, God forgive her soul. They were saying that she was upset and frequently conversed with the fetus in her belly, that she was making predictions about the future and the calamities at the end of time. Every day, with the excuse that the Master Assar was busy painting a new portrait of her, she wore odd new clothes and talked constantly about the Master's paintings—the painting of Hafez's beloved in his youth, the painting of the Baghdad gypsy, the painting of Mary in blue satin. Major Sadegh Khan was generally absent. He was frequently busy in Bagh Shah with bicycle-riding contests and airplane-flying contests and he was almost indifferent to Homayundokht, God forgive her soul, when she sang for the festivals of the saints' births and martyrdoms. He took lightly everything she did. They said that a person born in Petersburg was distant from the world of saints and passion plays; no matter how you figured it, it didn't fit. There must be more to it than met the eye. She ought to see a doctor. Aunt Badi Zaman, the interpreter of the Koran, answered that to understand the moods of Homayundokht, God forgive her soul, required knowledge and research. The late Homayundokht should not be compared with ordinary singers at the saints' birthday festivals. Ordinary singers gathered people at private parties and public assemblies merely to open a business for themselves.

From the courtyard, the ladies called, "Miss Homayundokht, we implore by the five saints under the Prophet's robe, implore by the tears of the Prophet's daughter, innocent Fatima, implore by the ill body of St. Zaynol Abedin, by the martyrdom of the disciples and the fourteen innocents: sing for us the passion of the Lord of the Faithful talking to the skull, the miracle of the blind girl seeing the rumbling wild camels in the night, the elegy of our Master the Lord of the Faithful as he shared his secrets with the well and the well grew bloody, the elegy of the red-faced man from Damascus and Jafer Temple, the elegy of Lady Narjess and the King of Rome . . ."

Homayundokht, God forgive her soul, didn't answer. The ladies were about to repeat their requests when my Khan Papa Doctor arrived in his military uniform. There was dust on his Pahlavi hat and his boots. His face looked hot. He was walking toward the tent as though someone had informed him of something. In front of the tent, he put his hand on the hilt of his sword and spoke mildly. "Lady, what do you want from me? You have disgraced me, what more do you want?"

The voice of Homayundokht, God forgive her soul, came from inside the tent. "What disgrace, Mirza Sadegh Khan? The disgrace of the spit they've spat on your epaulets for blinding the Master Assar and killing a handful of hapless peasants? What disgrace?"

My Khan Papa Doctor snatched off his hat in a rage and slammed it hard on a chair. Then, indifferent to the lip-biting of Aunt Badi Zaman, the interpreter of the Koran, he went to his library and pulled down the shades. Still Homayundokht, God forgive her soul, shouted from inside the tent as before: "Mirza Sadegh Khan, remember why it was that you brought a fourteen-year-old girl from Petersburg to Tehran. Remember that, as my late Dear Daddy and the rest of the Sardar Azhdaris promised, I kept my word. In sickness and in health, I poured on the table whatever was in my bag, just for you, the top flower in the Heshmat Nezamis' basket. But you didn't appreciate it, you belittled me. Now you put me down on account of the children. You say they're better off raised by a mere servant, Zahra Soltan, instead of on their own mother's knees. Let me tell you something. We Sardar Azhdaris are different from the others. Even if you kill me, even if you tear my flesh piece by piece and throw it to the birds of the sky, I won't become like the others."

The people, young and old, big and small, scattered and kept as great a distance as possible. Any time Homayundokht, God forgive her soul, invited them and wanted to spread a royal table for them, they excused themselves and said they had a headache, their problems wouldn't allow it, walking wasn't good for their hearts, their livers, or their stomachs; and no one came except Aunt Badi Zaman, the interpreter of the Koran, who until the very end followed Homayundokht wherever she went. No matter how much Homayundokht, God forgive her soul, displayed excessive behavior and lack of care, Aunt Badi Zaman didn't cut her ties. She stuck with her, and she backed her up in front of relatives and strangers.

Now Mirza Hassibi was beckoning me into the storeroom. He wasn't paying much attention to me. Thinking about Homayundokht, God forgive her soul, had excited him. That indefinable excitement was rubbing on his nerves, making a hump on his back and pushing his neck down into his chest. He walked bent and, like someone afflicted with palsy, he counted imaginary coins with orderly, repetitious movements of his fingers. He walked as though propelled from behind. When he reached the safe box he turned and said, "All this belongs to you. It's yours. For us old folks, it's over now and we don't need anything. But you should think of assuming ownership and taking possession of the family inheritance. The family inheritance belongs to no one but you. It doesn't belong to the Heshmat Nezamis, it doesn't belong to the Sardar Azhdaris. It belongs to someone who can give it up and let it go at a moment's notice. You understand what I'm saying?"

I looked carefully at Mirza's face. In his excitement, he seemed suspended between earth and sky, suspended without movement, like a doll hanging by a thread. I said, "These things won't help me. You have to talk to me more clearly. You have to say something, show me something."

"What do you want me to show you?"

"I don't know, I don't know, Mirza."

I rested my head on the wall and grew tearful. Mirza Hassibi didn't say a thing. It seemed he understood everything and was of two minds about what to say.

He took a big iron key, like an old stable key, from the top shelf and put it on my palm. Then he bent his head and said, "Keep this. Be careful not to lose it."

I asked, "What is it for?"

"It's the key to this house. I want to leave my house to you during my absence. I'd be grateful if you'd look after it now and then. Any time you get bored walking the streets, any time you get tired of struggling with the people of today, come to this house for a while. It's not bad. The courtyard's pleasant and the house has character. You can search every part of it you wish and examine all its nooks and crannies."

He raised his head high. He gave a wavering smile. He cleared his throat and pointed to the opposite wall and said, "There are motifs in every corner of this house to remind you of yourself. The late Master Assar always used to say that life is face making. He used to say that face making is not just drawing faces; face making has to have a motif, too, to give it life, and to keep it alive. You have to find these motifs in out-of-the-way places without names and addresses, like this tiny house, or the water shrine in the little bazaar."

I said, "Don't go. Stay right here. If you let me, I'll come too and live with you."

Searching for an answer, he looked at the door and the walls. He said, "More important than anything else, you must find a position in the Foreign Ministry. You have to think of your late Khan Papa Doctor's shrouding and burial as well. When you're free of those worldly chores, come to this house for a while. I've left something in the storeroom for you to see and take a motif from."

I said, "You know very well I'm not the type to work in the Foreign Ministry, or to go to memorials and processions for the dead."

He smiled and gestured for us to return to the courtyard. I said, "What are you smiling about?"

He walked ahead of me and said, "All of you are stiff-necked. There's nothing that can be done about it, either. Maybe what I've left here for you will make some impression. Maybe someday you'll step inside the storeroom and look at the Master Assar's painting of the naked Homayundokht, God forgive her soul, and that will change your mind."

I didn't know how to answer him. After a short pause, he said, "But now we have to get going."

When we emerged from the brazier room, it was darker. Masoud was leaning against the wall in front of the courtyard door. He was twirling his key chain around his finger and whistling the Mahoor scale. I glanced at Mirza Hassibi one more time. He waved both hands as though shooing a flock of hens. I said, "Working in the Foreign Ministry? Funeral processions, mourning ceremonies? It makes you sick."

"Agha Rokni, all these are life's motifs, the same motifs the late Master Assar used to talk about."

He locked the door behind us. The clicking of the latch made me feel empty and cold. I thought, Closed doors, like blind eyes, are without light. The nausea still wouldn't let me go. At the head of the alley, children were gathered around Masoud's cherry-colored car, and they had broken my statue to pieces with their bats.

BOOK FIVE

⚜⚜⚜⚜⚜⚜⚜⚜⚜⚜⚜⚜⚜⚜⚜⚜⚜

The Absence

I took the fairy lamp from the hall and started walking toward the courtyard. My Bee Bee called out tearfully, "What do you want to do, Rokni?"

"I want to open the doors of Homayundokht's room."

"Rokni-jun, I beg of you, hold back and wait so we can think this through and learn what sort of dust we have to pour on our own heads. The sealed door is not so easy to open."

"I'll show you how easy it is." But when I examined the lock, I saw that to undo it was the work of an elephant. I couldn't kick it open either. I searched for an ax or a hatchet, but I couldn't find any. I was losing my mind, pacing from one room to another, and cursing for nothing. Wherever I went, my Bee Bee came sobbing behind me. Her crying was getting on my nerves and I was growing angry.

Finally, when even the late Sardar Azhdar's sugar hammer couldn't break the latch, I gave up. I knew then that it is not easy to open sealed doors in our family.

Why the mood came over me I don't exactly understand. I know this much: that a strange strength was generated in me and I felt unafraid. I couldn't understand what my Bee Bee and Zahra Soltan were saying. As soon as I felt a little calmer I told my Bee Bee, "Now I want to go to the library and be alone."

"Dear, do you want to harm yourself?"

"No. I don't have any such plan. I just want to be alone with Khan Papa Doctor for a little while."

I went to the library. On the floor in front of the dais my Khan Papa Doctor lay stretched beneath the late Heshmat Nezam's cashmere shawl with his feet toward Mecca. I picked up a chair from the corner of the library, set it at the head of the body, and sat. I couldn't understand anything of what I was doing. My brain was not working right, and the inside of my head was hollow. The library ceiling seemed very high. Undefined, wandering lights swarmed in the honeycomb of hollows and knobs inside the arches.

My Uncle Aziz opened the library door without a sound. He stuck in his head and looked around cautiously. Then he tiptoed to the center of the room. He bent over the candle burning in its tulip-shaped glass above my Khan Papa Doctor's head, and he blew at it. The flame fluttered and died. It wasn't good luck to extinguish the candle of the dead before the first night in the grave. I said, "Why did you blow out the tulip lamp?"

"We have to get ready to go."

"It's supposed to burn till the first night in the grave."

"I know more about these things than you do. It's I who's the passion player, not you."

He started to laugh, but he swallowed it. The usual humble, wasted expression returned to his face. He stepped out of the library and took his shoes off and came back in. The black suit he wore made him look strange and artificial, his black tie and socks weren't becoming to him, and he walked as if mindful of his old backache. How aged and haggard he looked, too! He had combed back his white hair on both sides so that his face looked longer, especially with that stretched and bladelike nose. He seemed stricken by a vague illness, not truly sick and yet not healthy. He straightened the old photos on the wall. He couldn't decide what else to do. He came back to my Khan Papa Doctor's body and smoothed the late Heshmat Nezam's cashmere shawl. He picked up the Koran holder from the foot of the body and placed it at the head. He bent to take two corners of the Kashan rug in his fists and move the body a little more toward Mecca. He poured rose water onto his palm from the rose-water jar and rubbed it on his head and face. He sauntered over to the fireplace and grew busy studying a photo of my Khan Papa Doctor as a youth. In this photo my Khan Papa Doctor has his woolen Cossack hat, shaved face, and waxed mustache. A triumphant smile tugs at the corners of his lips. Unconsciously, he has brought his hand through the slit of his cloak and laid it gently on the hilt of his sword. My Uncle Aziz said, "How chic your Khan Papa Doctor was in his youth! Alas, no one recognized his worth."

My mind was on the funeral escorts who were gathering in the courtyard and muttering respectful greetings, asking one another how they felt. Hadj Ali was leading the black-garbed ladies toward the orangery. The men were grouped in front of the sealed room of Homayundokht, God forgive her soul. They were whispering and looking around as though they wanted to keep an eye on things. My Uncle Aziz said, "Rokni, how crowded the courtyard's grown! Everyone who's anyone has come."

"Not a one of them could free my Khan Brother Zia."

"Have a little patience. Masoud's gone to receive him and bring him to the mausoleum for the burial."

"All that's a lie."

"All right, so it's a lie. What's important now is, do you know in whose trust your Khan Papa Doctor left his money? You have to think of these things. Now's the time you must look after your father's household."

Again the voices of the funeral escorts rose from the courtyard. The men in front of the sealed room of Homayundokht, God forgive her soul, collected to one side and fixed their gazes on the courtyard door. They stopped whispering. Aunt Badi Zaman, the interpreter of the Koran, entered with the help of two young men who were holding her arms. When she reached the courtyard, she raised her head and walked with slow and measured steps. The edge of her black voile veil covered half her face. As she passed the line of closer relatives, the men bowed and murmured greetings. When she reached Hadj Ali, she lifted the edge of the veil from her face and glared at him. Hadj Ali tucked one hand in his armpit and with the other he hit his forehead; his shoulders trembled with silent weeping. Aunt Badi Zaman started walking again. A few steps farther on, she reached Cousin Agha Abdol Mehdi. He bent and kissed her hand. My aunt went ahead, and the crowd of funeral escorts followed her.

My Uncle Aziz said in a mournful voice, "Of course, she's the older sister. She has the right. Of all the children of Heshmat Nezam, only she is left. The rest are gone. You were born so late, you didn't see any of them. You didn't see Uncle Agha Abdol Majid. He was epileptic. He had a seizure in the pool at Ghaleh Bagh and choked to death. Aunt Lady Najafi died the year you were born. I mean she died of grief over her crazy husband, Sayed Kazem, the owner of *The Book of Divine Graces.* Now no one's left. How fickle this world is!"

Aunt Badi Zaman and the two young men supporting her appeared on the veranda. Her head shook with palsy, and for a few moments she didn't move. My Uncle Aziz was urging me with exaggerated gestures to prepare myself for a confrontation with her. They opened the library door and she came in. My Uncle Aziz immediately raised his voice in wailing and lamentations. "O Agha Doctor, rise up. O head of the Heshmat Nezamis, rise up, your dear sister has come to visit you. Agha-jun, rise up and say, 'How are you?' Why don't you speak, Agha-jun? Why aren't you saying sweet things to your honorable sister?"

The wailing of the ladies came from the orangery. Aunt Badi Zaman, indifferent to all sounds, approached the body of my Khan Papa Doctor. Again my Uncle Aziz began reciting lamentations. "The head of our family, our leader, has departed this transient world."

He pulled up the leather chair for Aunt Badi Zaman. She didn't sit on it. With the two young men still holding her arms, she paused beside the body. Now I could see her watery eyes behind her veil. She was looking at the body with an old person's astonishment and hunger. One of the young men shouted into her ear, "Where do you want to sit?"

She listened and then asked, "Where is Mirza Sadegh?"

The second youth pointed to the body. My aunt raised her trembling eyebrows and asked in surprise, "This is Mirza Sadegh?"

"Yes, ma'am. This is he."

"No, Mirza Sadegh is not under this shawl."

"If you wish, we'll pull the shawl back so you can see for yourself."

"I mean that you, you children of time, can see only the superficial face and not the internal one. 'And we indeed created man; and we know what his soul whispers within him, and we are nearer to him than the jugular vein.' As the poet says, 'The one whose heart is animated by love will never die. Our immortality is imprinted upon the scroll of the universe.' "

Addressing the funeral escorts, she swept the library with her hand. Then she folded like an accordion and sat down on the floor next to the body. She placed an index finger on the body and spoke slowly. "Mirza Sadegh, in these few years of my absence I haven't forgotten you. Give my greetings to our honorable brothers and sisters, especially our sister Lady Najafi, and our late

mother and our late father, all the prisoners of the dust; and tell
them the journey of life is short. I will be in their presence soon."

She glanced up at my Uncle Aziz and said, "Uncle, do you
have a handkerchief?"

My Uncle Aziz searched his pockets nervously and took out a
handkerchief and offered it to her. Aunt Badi Zaman waved it
away and said, "I didn't want it for myself, Agha. I wanted you to
blow your nose. Your sniffing is giving me a headache."

My Uncle Aziz looked defensively at the funeral escorts. He
searched for a witness to back him up. He raised his shoulders
and said, "Is my nose running? Has anyone else heard me sniffing?"

The funeral escorts only stared at him. He backed away and left
the library. Aunt Badi Zaman focused on the body again and
continued her conversation. "Brother, why have you allowed
these ruffians in your house? These people weren't brought up to
understand decency and politeness."

She motioned for the young men to take hold of her arms and
lift her from the floor. Once she was on her feet, she pursed her
lips and said, "How this library has changed! Brother Mirza
Sadegh used to change anything that came his way. He wasn't
satisfied till he'd fiddled with it."

Her eyes skimmed the faces of the men surrounding her. When
she came to me, she said, "Why have you come here in this outfit?"

I folded my arms across my chest and didn't say anything. The
funeral escorts whispered among themselves. Aunt Badi Zaman
exploded: "What sort of getup is this? A shirt with no tie? Loose
pants? Barefoot? Don't you have a decent suit, like respectable
people?"

I said, "I'm not the type to wear a suit and tie."

She sized me up and said, "Are you one of Mirza Sadegh's
sons?"

Hadj Ali said, "Agha Rokni, the younger son of Mirza
Sadegh."

She passed a palm as rough as fish scales over my face. She
asked softly, "How old are you?"

I didn't answer, but Hadj Ali said, "He's twenty-three, praise be to Allah."

She asked, "Are you in the Army?"

I said, "No."

"Then they must have found you a job in the Foreign Ministry, wheeling and dealing. Isn't that right?"

I said, "I'm unemployed at present."

"If you were a Sardar Azhdari, you'd say that unemployment is employment in itself."

She smiled faintly and went over to the funeral dishes that sat above my Khan Papa Doctor's head. She stroked a bowl and said, "These belong to a pious foundation and they're forbidden possessions. Dustali Khan Sardar Azhdari stole them from the pantry of Sepah Salar Mosque. He used to say he'd only borrowed them, but he didn't return them during his lifetime."

She chuckled with a brittle sound like a sheet of gold leaf crumpling. Uncle Abdolbaghi and the first-rank cousins entered the library. Uncle Abdolbaghi was searching for something in his vest pocket, and his asymmetrical eyes wearily surveyed the funeral escorts on both sides. Aunt Badi Zaman coughed and said, "Agha Abdolbaghi, greetings to you. How are you?"

Uncle Abdolbaghi took his fingers from his vest pocket and absent-mindedly looked around for her. "Greetings to you, Cousin Badi Zaman, interpreter of the Koran. Where have you been, Cousin? Do we have to be stricken with grief before we can see you?"

Aunt Badi Zaman pointed to the funeral dishes and said, "These are forbidden possessions, Cousin. Why have you put them at my brother's head? It's a scandal."

"What are you talking about, Cousin?"

"I'm talking about these funeral dishes that Dustali Khan stole from Sepah Salar Mosque. Have you forgotten about it?"

"What sort of slander is this, Cousin? They're all borrowed goods."

"Anyhow, Cousin, where are you planning to plant Mirza Sadegh?"

"In our own mausoleum, of course. I've ordered a grave dug in the left cloister."

"Isn't the late Homayundokht, God forgive her soul, buried in the night porch, next to her father, Mirza Yousef?"

"Yes, as I remember, that's right."

"We have to plant Mirza Sadegh in the night porch next to the late Homayundokht, God forgive her soul."

"Mirza Sadegh is a Heshmat Nezami and has to be buried in the left cloister."

"Abdolbaghi, listen carefully to what I say. If you don't want to share the dead man's load of sins, you have to do his will. He wished to be buried between the late Homayundokht and her father."

Uncle Abdolbaghi smiled and said, "You're still thinking of him, after all."

"Thinking of whom?"

"Thinking of the late Mirza Yousef. Look at me, I thought after fifty years he'd have left your mind."

"Abdolbaghi, eighty and some years old and you still talk nonsense. Your back's grown a hump and your beard has reached your navel, but still your eyes and ears are closed. As the noble Koran would put it, 'They are deaf, dumb, and blind, and do not change their ways.' "

Uncle Abdolbaghi wore a grin that gave his uneven face a light, childish look.

Then the shopowners entered the courtyard with the casket, reciting, "There is no God but Allah." They lined up behind the library door. Aunt Badi Zaman glanced at them and said, as if to herself, "They've come to carry Mirza Sadegh away. We have to get going."

She motioned for the young men to take her arms and help her. Then she passed slowly before the funeral escorts. When she reached the library door, she turned her head and called to me, "Roknideen, if you don't want to go to the funeral on foot like everyone else, you can be my companion."

I knew instantly that was what I would do. I got up and went toward her. The embarrassed, worried whispers of the Heshmat Nezamis and the Sardar Azhdaris floated beneath the library ceiling.

When I reached Aunt Badi Zaman, she offered her arm. In an

encouraging tone she said, "Roknideen, now you have to be the cane of my old age. When a person gets to be my age, she cannot tackle anything and her thoughts are always on the cane and the life buoy for the journey to the other world until, by the grace of the Holy Ghost, the sunlight on life's roof darts safely out of this house of horrors and dangers."

In the courtyard, a crowd was rippling. The neighbors had grown on the rooftops like crabgrass and they watched the courtyard. My aunt rested her hand on my shoulder. We came down the stairs slowly and cautiously. She muttered to me, "Look at how foolish they are, see how they've fastened the wind to a spool and tied knots in the water. But, Roknideen, you keep busy with the work of your heart. Nowadays, in this crazy bazaar, no one hears the voice of the voiceless. People are swarming together like ants and grasshoppers. Alas, these are terrible, voiceless times. Let no one be their prisoner. 'That Egypt of happiness that you have seen has become a ruin, that Nile of abundance that you have heard has become a mirage. Our days have lost substance and our fate has grown harsh. Our dreams are dragging and Providence is hastening toward the end. Expect no water from the well of wealth. Those buckets are broken and those ropes are severed.' "

We left the courtyard. It was somewhere around noon. From the end of the alley, behind the broken shadows of the walls, the call to prayers could be heard.

2

Aunt Badi Zaman got into the back of her Cadillac and pushed her voile veil off her face. She had drawn two jagged indigo lines in place of her eyebrows, and they gave her a dissatisfied, surprised expression. She called to the young man who was driving, "Mehdi Khan, take us to the mausoleum."

Mehdi Khan said, "Don't you want to go first to the bathhouse of the dead?"

"Let the washer of the dead go to the bathhouse of the dead. The bathhouse of the dead belongs to the dead. Our business is with the living. Isn't that so, Roknideen?"

As the car lurched forward, she frowned. She held her pompous Heshmat Nezami head high and she looked down her nose at the street. I wondered why it was that, after so many years of keeping her distance, she'd shown herself now among the relatives. I grew more aggressive and asked, "Do you remember my Khan Brother Zia?"

"Khan Brother who?"

"Zia, Ziadeen."

"You mean Homayundokht's son?"

"Yes, the son of the late Homayundokht, God forgive her soul."

"Where is he now? I didn't see him today. Is he alive? What does he do for a living?"

"They plan to release him from prison today so he can come to the mausoleum."

"Why's he in prison? Was it Article G, cheating the government?"

I lowered my voice and said, "Aunt Badi Zaman, interpreter of the Koran, don't you know? Don't you know he's a political prisoner?"

"Political or not, it makes no difference. Every prisoner's a political prisoner."

"That's not so. You don't know that my Khan Brother Zia was politically active in the Army, in secret. He also did away with a few Security agents. It was a serious business. They say he played a lot of pranks to make the Security agents suspect each other and he had them at each other's throats."

My aunt said irritably, "Roknideen, you're giving me a headache with this talk. In my lifetime, I've heard many such stories. Your Khan Brother Zia's no different from the others."

I said, "I think about him constantly. I tell myself that if his late mother, Homayundokht, God forgive her soul, were still alive maybe the page would have turned and his fate would have changed, he'd have become like all the other Heshmat Nezamis."

Aunt Badi Zaman said, "As long as Homayundokht, God forgive her soul, was alive, Ziadeen was comfortable. He was easygoing, and what came out of his mouth made sense. But after the hand of the God-forgiven lost touch with this world, your brother fell under the care of Miss Asiah, who was brought for your father from behind Kangavar's mountains. By the power of the Almighty, she couldn't tell up from down. If you sang her a popular song, she thought the Antichrist had risen. Now, forget she's your mother. Maybe what I'm saying offends you, but the fact of the matter is that Homayundokht was something else. Once in a century you find someone like her. Not everyone can be Homayundokht, God forgive her soul."

With her glittering eyes, Aunt Badi Zaman might have been a

lunatic. I said, "They say you conveyed my Khan Papa Doctor's marriage proposal to the family of Homayundokht, God forgive her soul."

"Roknideen, the things I do in this life don't have any bearing on my personal and heartfelt beliefs. I'm only a go-between. Your Khan Papa Doctor wasn't the type to let anyone interfere in his business. He had seen her and chosen her. He threw me in the middle to satisfy tradition."

I said, "I want to ask you something. I know there was something about Homayundokht, God forgive her soul, that made her different from the others. But I don't know why she set herself afire on the rooftop. What was her problem? Why, after thirty-odd years, won't she leave us alone?"

With her rough, cardboard fingers, Aunt Badi Zaman began to scratch a loose piece of skin that hung like chitterlings below her chin. The mingled sounds of the street slid downhill behind the car windows. A crystal silence fell, and the air grew as clear as a mountain stream. Aunt Badi Zaman was going to make me see.

It was as if I'd stepped into a scene from years ago. Homayundokht, God forgive her soul, clutched the hem of her silk dress and ran barefoot across the grass with a wild, childlike joy. She snatched her matronly kerchief from her head and, as she approached the orchard pool, she hastily, impatiently tore off everything she had on and flung it in the middle of the flower bed. She screamed and threw herself in the pool. Aunt Badi Zaman jumped back and said, "Homayundokht, for heaven's sake, you've got me wet. There's a limit to these excesses. That's enough now. If your Dear Daddy arrives and catches sight of you, you'll be sorry. Your Dear Daddy has forbidden skinny-dipping to keep you from the eyes of strangers."

Homayundokht, God forgive her soul, giggled and answered, "Don't worry, Badi Zaman. My Dear Daddy's asleep in the stable next to Hazel, the horse. You know how soundly he sleeps. He won't wake up."

"He will, Homayundokht. I swear to God, he'll wake up and it'll be a scandal."

"Badi Zaman, what have you brought for Hazel today? Chickpeas and raisins? Almond candy? Butter mints?"

"By the dust on my grave, Homayundokht, don't scream like that. The neighbors will hear and come running."

"There aren't any neighbors around here, Badi Zaman. There's only one orchard, and behind that a field and a pasture. It's God's refuge, ha-ha. . . ."

"May God set fire to your soul, Homayundokht, we've disgraced ourselves."

"No, no, Badi Zaman, why should He set fire to my soul? Rest assured, we won't be disgraced. A person who doesn't care can't be disgraced. Forgive me for saying it, but it's other people who should be disgraced for gossiping behind our backs and finding fault. From oldest times it's been said that people get what they deserve."

She came out of the pool as naked as the day she was born. She picked up her towel from the stone edge of the pool. She wrapped it around her carved marble thighs and knotted it at one hip. She set a foot on the stone bench, tilted her head, and took hold of her pitch-black hair and wrung it out. She tried to tease Aunt Badi Zaman with a slanted, hinting smile. But Aunt Badi Zaman was still worried and restless. Homayundokht, God forgive her soul, came forward and laid a palm on Aunt Badi Zaman's cheek. A little more seriously, she said, "Badi Zaman, listen. You and I don't have to stand on ceremony. After all, I know why you come to visit us so much."

Aunt Badi Zaman drew back so she wouldn't get wet. She opened her mouth to protest. But Homayundokht, God forgive her soul, with the same coquettish smile set her wet hand on Aunt Badi Zaman's mouth and said, "Ah-ah, Badi Zaman. First you listen to me a minute."

Aunt Badi Zaman couldn't stand it anymore. She pushed aside the hand of Homayundokht, God forgive her soul, and said, "I come here to learn Russian, to look at your Dear Daddy's photos of Baku and Petersburg. You know that, Homayundokht, if no one else does. As God is my witness, life in our house is hell for me. I'm not created for life in that cancerous Tehran. I understand poetry and literature. I've memorized the whole of St. Ali's *This Highest Eloquence.* My soul belongs somewhere else. My heart flutters for another sky. When I come here, my heart opens up. I tell myself, 'Oh, God, is it possible that one day I, too, will go to Petersburg? Is it possible that one day I, too, will hold jewel-studded binoculars to my eyes and watch an opera, or sit on a sailboat and go sightseeing on the Neva?' Dear Homayundokht, when I close my eyes, you don't know what things I see. You wouldn't believe it."

"Oh, Badi Zaman, you're wasting your life in the wind. Petersburg doesn't exist any more. Nobody sits in a sailboat to go sightseeing on the Neva any more. These are all fantasies."

Aunt Badi Zaman closed her eyes with a dreamy expression. She nodded regretfully as she listened. "You're right, Homayundokht. You've seen more of this world than I have. In your short life, you have much more experience than I do. But I can't control myself. When I close my eyes, Petersburg appears in front of me. I see your Dear Daddy and your Mamushka, we're all going together to Pavlovski for sightseeing, we're going to chic and first-rate restaurants. Your Dear Daddy says to your Mamushka, 'Olga, Olga, my heart pines for you. Olga, those Russian eyes of yours are killing me.' Your Mamushka fans herself with her mother-of-pearl fan out of embarrassment."

"Badi Zaman, none of this is true. You don't know what a torture life is for my Dear Daddy. It's because of life's torture he's addicted to spirits."

"You're right. You're telling the truth. But your Dear Daddy's behavior comes from courage and daring. Now, if a drop of vodka goes down his throat the world won't end. Suppose that, once in a blue moon, he gets a little hotheaded and pulls out a broadsword in the cabaret in the face of Russian officers to defend his national honor, what's wrong with that? Is that going to cause a famine? He's a Sardar Azhdari and he has to dive in headlong every once in a while. It's better than the Heshmat Nezami way of doing things. It's better than the lives of Lady Najafi and Mirza Abdol Majid. In fact, none of the descendants of my father, Heshmat Nezam, turned out well except for my brother, Mirza Sadegh."

"I know, Badi Zaman. But swear by your honorable brother, Mirza Sadegh, aren't you in love with my Dear Daddy?"

"Oh, may the dust of the universe be on my head, what is this nonsense? It will disgrace us."

"Why, Badi Zaman? What's wrong with it? Being in love isn't a blasphemy."

"Well, thank you very much. What being in love? For heaven's sake, two dry words come out of my mouth to tell my heartache. I never dreamed you would blare it all over the neighborhood."

"Badi Zaman, sometimes the person herself doesn't know she's in love. You talk like someone in love."

Aunt Badi Zaman was reduced to silence. She raised her arms at her sides like those fastidious people who don't want to get dirty touching anything. She wiped her face on her shoulder and turned toward the pool. Homayundokht, God forgive her soul, didn't press further. She got up and went behind the paisley curtain that hung from a branch of the weeping willow tree. She put on her clothes, and her talking machine started working again. Out of the blue, she said, "Badi Zaman."

"Hmm?"

"May my Dear Daddy become the target of the Invisible World's arrows if you refuse this request I have of you. After my Mamushka passed away, my Dear Daddy had no head and no mind. Drinking spirits is destroying his life. He needs a caring person like you to be around him and pull him together."

Homayundokht, God forgive her soul, stuck her head out from behind the paisley curtain and waited for Aunt Badi Zaman's answer. Instead of speaking, Aunt Badi Zaman rested her chin in her fist and seemed struck dumb. When Homayundokht saw this, she emerged from the paisley curtain. She put her hand gently under Aunt Badi Zaman's arm and helped her get up and go into the orchard for a stroll. They passed beneath the shade of the willow and mulberry trees and reached the late Mirza Yousef's stable. They stepped on the crooked, lowered branch of the almond tree and climbed up the trunk. When they reached the stable roof, they put their eyes to the vent holes and peered inside. As their eyes adjusted to the darkness, Hazel, the horse, became visible. A column of light fell from the small window in the wall to the tip of the late Mirza Yousef's boots. The late Mirza Yousef was spread on a mound of straw next to Hazel, drunk and crazy. In his twill jodhpurs and black boots, he resembled an abandoned marionette. His white silk shirt had wide, puffy sleeves, like a

Russian Cossack's. Wrapped around his waist was a red satin cummerbund. He was slugging vodka from a Ghamsar rose-water flask, and in a nasal voice he sang to himself, "Tonight she is beside me, that essence of preciousness . . ."

Homayundokht, God forgive her soul, threw her arms around Aunt Badi Zaman's neck and said, "I beg you, be my Dear Daddy's wife."

Aunt Badi Zaman examined her doubtfully. Homayundokht, God forgive her soul, continued speaking. "Promise me you will."

Aunt Badi Zaman chewed a corner of her lower lip and said, "I don't want to promise, Homayundokht."

"Why, Badi Zaman? Why?"

"I said no, that's all."

Homayundokht, God forgive her soul, lost heart. She tossed the strands of her wet hair over her shoulder and said no more. Aunt Badi Zaman fiddled with the hem of her skirt and said in a cautious tone, "To tell the truth, I've come here on other business."

Homayundokht, God forgive her soul, was absent-minded. She asked indifferently, "What business?"

"I've come on behalf of my brother, Mirza Sadegh. He himself has seen you and chosen you. Before opening a discussion with your Dear Daddy, he wants to hear your opinion."

Homayundokht, God forgive her soul, suddenly emerged from her dejected mood. She straightened and with a mischievous, expectant look said, "Of course I'll be his wife. Why shouldn't I? But on one condition."

"What's that?"

"That he ask acceptance from me and not from my Dear Daddy."

Aunt Badi Zaman joyfully embraced Homayundokht, God forgive her soul. "Oh, Homayundokht, you're no taller than half a man's palm and still such a devil. No doubt you've learned these notions in Petersburg, I mean in the theaters of Petersburg. Isn't that so?"

"Badi Zaman, from ancient times they've said, 'Don't look at the size of the pepper, break it and taste the sharpness.' "

"What a devil you are. A little girl like you, knowing all this sleight of hand! God be praised, a person marvels."

Now the sickening smell of the tannery entered the Cadillac. Aunt Badi Zaman rolled up the window with her shaking hand. Clay huts and brickmaking kilns passed like a strip of ribbon. On both sides of the road, ruined patches of earth full of potholes stretched under the hot sun like dried potato peels. The landscape of the Shah Abdol Azim shrine—mud houses, abandoned domes, and minarets—took on color, and their details grew visible on the dusty breadth of the horizon. Aunt Badi Zaman said, "That God-forgiven one was no ordinary woman. When she was thirteen years old, she could spin a hundred men around her little finger; it was as if she'd gone to Europe for a diploma in handling men. Her presence had a pull. When your eyes fell on her, you were lost. From that very first encounter with Mirza Sadegh, she behaved the way you read about in stories."

"I know."

"You think you know, Roknideen. You imagine you know, but you're mistaken."

Her braided white hair swung between her shoulder blades like a silk rope. Her fingertips passed over the mud houses, and she wore the expression of someone who had summoned a spirit.

Maybe she was imagining Homayundokht, God forgive her soul, sitting on a rattan chair on the landing, her elbow resting on the wooden railing. Under her elbow, the balusters trailed down to the entrance hall. She held a bouquet of pink roses and she sniffed it daintily. In the entrance hall below, behind a folding screen for propriety's sake, my Khan Papa Doctor sat on a leather chair in a serge riding coat and black broadcloth fez, one leg crossed over the other, and listened carefully to Homayundokht, God forgive her soul, who must have been no older than fourteen. From his humorous expression, it was obvious he had made his choice and was assured of possessing Homayundokht, God forgive her soul. I said to myself, How he's assumed control!

The Cadillac traveled around Shah Abdol Azim Circle and entered the yard of the mausoleum. Suddenly the mausoleum's walls, upper chambers, and cloisters appeared before us in the midst of their two-hundred-year-old cobwebs. The yard was swept and a few geese and ducks loitered around its mossy pool. Sayed

Jaafar, the custodian, and his wife Omlayla stood at the right, in front of the Sardar Azhdari cloister, both folding their arms across their chests and waiting for the mourners' arrival.

Aunt Badi Zaman had trouble walking on the uneven bricks and flattened old tombstones. Nonetheless, she pushed toward the cloisters with her ancestral single-mindedness. As she drew close to Sayed Jaafar and Omlayla, Sayed Jaafar bowed and said, "Madam, may your head be healthy. Let the dust of Mirza Sadegh be added to your life span. Please come into the tearoom so you can rest a bit."

Aunt Badi Zaman said, "Sayed Jaafar, are the cloisters open?"

"Of course, madam. All three are open. May I tell Omlayla to bring you tea?"

Aunt Badi Zaman motioned to the two young men to take her arms and help her upstairs. She no longer paid me any heed. Willy-nilly, I followed her till we reached the top of the stairs.

Only the late Sardar Azhdar's cloister was carpeted. Although the french windows were open to the yard, it was too dark inside to see the photos of those who had passed away or to read the black writing on the marble plinth. In the center of the cloister the late Sardar Azhdar's tombstone rose about one meter from the floor, like a steamer trunk. A piece of green cloth covered it, and on the cloth another tulip lamp was burning. Aunt Badi Zaman stood beside the tombstone. She closed her eyes and set a finger on it and hastily recited the prayer for the dead. Then she asked Sayed Jaafar, "The grave of Cousin Agha Jalal must be in that corner, isn't it?"

"No, madam. That's the grave of the unfulfilled Nasrin."

"You're right. I'd forgotten we planted the unfulfilled Nasrin beside the late Sardar Azhdar."

"It was the order of your honorable late mother. She swore that if we buried the unfulfilled Nasrin in the Heshmat Nezam cloister she would level the mausoleum as flat as the palm of her hand."

A smile appeared on Aunt Badi Zaman's face. She nodded and told me, "My late mother was like that. When she rejected the unfulfilled Nasrin, she never again spoke a word to her till the last breath left her body. If she wanted to tell her something, she would set me in the middle to speak for her. She'd say, 'Badi Zaman, *you* talk to her. You're our go-between, you talk to her.' "

She went to the northern wall of the cloister and squatted on the floor beside it. The tombstone of her honorable sister, Miss Najafi, and her faded photo were limed to the wall. In this photo, Miss Najafi's head was covered with a white, gauzelike kerchief. She had her hands laced together in her lap and her pious smile reminded one of Ayatollah Kashani. Her late mother, the Lady of Ladies, had repeatedly suggested to Miss Najafi that, instead of the family mausoleum, she should go to Najaf and find herself a burial place in the yard of the saint's shrine. "Miss Najafi, why don't you go to that good-for-nothing husband of yours? Go to the owner of *The Book of Divine Graces.* You want to stay here for what? Suppose they buried you in the cloister of the late Sardar Azhdar; in the Desert of Resurrection no one knows the late Sardar Azhdar and he can't put in a good word for you. Get up and go to the owner of *The Book of Divine Graces.* Maybe he can intercede for you with his ancestor the Prophet."

Miss Najafi, silent and resigned, looked at her mother. But her mouth was sealed by the same pious smile. The Lady of Ladies was infuriated. She screamed, "Miss Najafi, why are you looking like that? Haven't you ever been a human being? Cough up! Say something, you're suffocating me."

Still Miss Najafi didn't speak. The late Lady of Ladies turned to Aunt Badi Zaman and said, "Badi Zaman, you've read the Koran and you understand its interpretation. Say something to this sick-in-the-head sister of yours. I can't tolerate her stare any longer. She makes you lose your mind with that stare. From childhood, she was this stubborn. She drove her wet nurse crazy and sent her to the nuthouse with that very same stare. Oh, dear God, I'm becoming delirious."

Aunt Badi Zaman answered, "Dear Mother, intolerance is a blasphemy and a sin."

"For ten years I listened to her weakling husband, the owner of *The Book of Divine Graces.* It's enough. He talked so much of his asceticism and his miracles, we were fed up. He whined so much about his suffering and his mortification that now we're sick of all the oppressed and victimized. Do you remember how he used to hoodwink his followers? He would throw his carnelian ring into the pool and order fish to bring it up from the bottom. Why do Heshmat Nezamis always have to marry a descendant of the Prophet in rags, so that he may intercede for them in the Desert of Resurrection? Is the Desert of Resurrection like the Ministry of Justice, that you have to have an attorney?"

Aunt Badi Zaman put her arms around Miss Najafi and embraced her and comforted her. Miss Najafi blinked like a chalk doll, swallowed, and remained motionless. Aunt Badi Zaman took a deep breath and said, "God is merciful. He Himself will forgive."

Miss Najafi pulled away from Aunt Badi Zaman's embrace. Exactly like the photo above her grave, she sat with dignity and calm on a chair opposite the late Lady of Ladies, laced her hands in her lap, and again smiled her pious smile.

Aunt Badi Zaman turned her eyes away from Miss Najafi's photo and said, "God have mercy on all that have passed away."

She got up and went to the middle cloister, the one belonging to the Hamedani Sadats and to relatives by marriage.

The middle cloister's walls were freshly whitewashed. Our footsteps echoed as we walked on its uncarpeted floor. Behind the french windows, the mud wall of the mausoleum garden leaned to the south. The wooden door was scarlet. Its glossy paint distinguished the doorframe from the worn-out, dusty wall.

Aunt Badi Zaman looked tired and beaten. She pointed to the night porch in front of the cloister and said, "Sayed Jaafar, let's see if you can help me. I want to go to the night porch."

She moved toward the french window. Sayed Jaafar looked worried and said, "Why do you want to use the french window? Let me take you there the right way."

"Sayed Jaafar, you're giving me a headache with your nagging. Hold my arm."

She stepped out onto the night porch with Sayed Jaafar's help. When she reached the tombstone of Homayundokht, God forgive her soul, she pulled her voile veil down to the tip of her nose. She pointed to a spot on the ground and said, "Sayed Jaafar, you must plant Mirza Sadegh right here, according to his will."

Sayed Jaafar shook his upraised palms in her face and said,

"Madam, is this reasonable? If I bury Mirza Sadegh here, where can I bury Miss Asiah, where can I bury Miss Motlagh? The night porch belongs to the Sardar Azhdaris, not the Heshmat Nezamis."

Aunt Badi Zaman was upset. Her face trembled and tears welled in her eyes, but she held back. I said, "To the dead it makes no difference where they're buried, the left cloister or the night porch."

Aunt Badi Zaman crumpled the corners of her mouth and said, "Whatever you asked I answered, Roknideen. Still you pretend to be ignorant. 'He whose heart comes alive with love will never die.' "

"All right. 'He whose heart comes alive with love will never die.' "

"May you never leave this world tongue-tied. Say it again."

We said it together: " 'He whose heart comes alive with love will never die.' "

Sayed Jaafar shrugged and said, "Whatever. We've dug Mirza Sadegh's grave in the Heshmat Nezami cloister, by order of Agha Abdolbaghi. There's no point arguing. It stays that way."

Aunt Badi Zaman sat next to the grave of Homayundokht, God forgive her soul. She brought her veil over her face and down to the level of her shiny black shoes. She covered herself completely and withdrew into privacy. From a distance, she looked like a crow on snowy ground. Her fingers emerged from her veil like two cautious spiders and groped for something on the tombstone. She asked, in a croaking, sniffling voice, "Sayed Jaafar, where is the statue of Compassion that Mirza Sadegh imported from Petersburg?"

Sayed Jaafar answered, "I don't know, madam."

"Mirza Sadegh told us to put that statue on the grave of Homayundokht, God forgive her soul."

"Agha Ass Dass Dolah didn't agree. He said those things were forbidden by Islam."

"Agha Ass Dass Dolah wasn't literate enough to read a two-word letter. He would say things out of fanaticism that could make you grow horns."

Aunt Badi Zaman got up and went to the garden. The walnut

and almond and plum trees stretched their arms in every direction and protected the dusty, ancient mausoleum like a big umbrella. Aunt Badi Zaman stood between the graves of the two sisters, Superior Venus and Great Pride, like a go-between, like someone who wanted to bring about understanding without participating in it—a role she'd played all her life, and in which she had all her life been defeated.

From the day the two sisters built the partition down the middle of their ancestral home and severed their ties from each other, Aunt Badi Zaman became the mediator. She insisted they put a door in the partition so that once a year, at least, they could visit each other on the night of the Ninth of the First Rabbee, the night of the killing of Omar, the enemy of the Shi'ites, and celebrate together, invite the relatives, sit around, speak sweet words and hear sweet words. The two sisters promised they would. All that year, they lived separately on either side of the partition in their twin, symmetrical rooms. Their sole communication was the clutter of sounds from their toilets or their bedrooms—the sounds of their nightly insomnia and their solitary pacing before the dawn prayers, the sounds of their morning incantations, full of obsession and doubt. Then the festival of the Ninth of the First Rabbee arrived. They invited the Sardar Azhdaris and the Heshmat Nezamis to an evening party. Early in the morning they went to the bathhouse together, and with henna they drew flowers and leaves on their foreheads and the backs of their hands. Early in the evening they dressed in their flashy red dresses. They sat in front of a mirror and, old as they were, they applied their makeup with seven brushes. As the guests arrived, the sisters poured pumpkin seeds and cantaloupe seeds into a pan and insisted that everyone put on a toothy grin so the seeds would burst open and smile like Damghan pistachios. Two hours into the evening, they set fire to the effigy of Omar, made of tissue paper and wearing a red costume, and they cried together with joy. They started the fireworks—paper rockets and mortar shells exploding in the air, making millions of red, yellow, and lavender stars and decorating the sky with amazing patterns.

Then Mirza Hassibi arrived unexpectedly with the Master Assar's painting of Homayundokht, God forgive her soul. He insisted he must hide the painting somewhere so it wouldn't fall into the hands of Mirza Sadegh Khan, and then he told everyone the news about Homayundokht. First, the guests were stunned. They didn't know what to say. All together they burst into wails. An hour later, when their wailing was finished, they started fighting over the burial of Homayundokht, God forgive her soul. Superior Venus, bareheaded and barefooted, went to the middle of the courtyard. She held up her hands and told her heartaches to her late grandfather, Agha Sardar Azhdar: "Agha, I swear by whomever you worship, wherever you are, and whomever you're with, lend me your ears. From the time you laid your precious head on the ground, life has become a hell for your children. For us no water is left, and no honor. Our days have grown dark and our nights sleepless. My sister, Great Pride, has allied herself with the Heshmat Nezamis and given her consent for Homayundokht, God forgive her soul, to be buried in the Sardar Azhdari cloister. No matter how I swear that my father, Agha Ass Dass Dolah, has your promise that *he* will be buried there, no one believes me. They say that Agha Ass Dass Dolah is a relative by marriage, he's a stranger and he should be buried in the mausoleum yard. But now they want to bury Homayundokht, God forgive her soul, in your own cloister—Homayundokht, who laid down her head in a world of disgrace. A Moslem shouldn't gossip about the dead but, Agha, I implore by my ancestor the Prophet, please somehow get it through to the Heshmat Nezamis that they shouldn't do this. Otherwise tomorrow on Judgment Day, in the Desert of Resurrection, I will grasp the robe of my ancestor and ask for vengeance."

Now Aunt Badi Zaman, with the help of the two young men, approached the Cadillac. I called, "Aunt Badi Zaman, where are you going? The body hasn't arrived."

She didn't answer. Sayed Jaafar rubbed his hands together and blocked her path. "Madam, if I have offended you, please forgive me. I've saved you a very good spot in the left cloister. Please don't forget your servant in your prayers."

Aunt Badi Zaman held her head high and said, "Sayed Jaafar, I have written my will. No one has a right to plant me in this mausoleum."

"Then where do you want us to bury you?"

"I've left instructions to be cremated."

Aunt Badi Zaman threw herself in the back seat. As the Cadillac traveled along the right side of Shah Abdol Azim Circle, the funeral escorts and the casket they bore approached from the left. The mausoleum yard looked silent and forgotten, and it gave no hint of anything unusual. Then the crowd of funeral escorts flowed in like the tongue of a flood, and they covered every inch of the ground.

3

The Heshmat Nezamis and Sardar Azhdaris played with ease the roles assigned to them. They needed no teachers or rehearsals. As Agha Ass Dass Dolah would have said, knowledge of family tradition is not like learning calculus in school; it comes to human beings from the moment of conception. Of course, this made life very simple for the Heshmat Nezamis and Sardar Azhdaris. But in some respects it created problems for them. They often asked themselves, what if they'd been caught in a trap, what if the braid of their destiny had fallen from their hands and, no matter how hard they struggled, how loudly they screamed, how high or low they jumped, escape from the family's spell was no longer possible?

For instance, in his youth the late Mirza Yousef, the Dear Daddy of Homayundokht, God forgive her soul, sold all his worldly possessions with his heart's blood and moved heaven and earth to get to Petersburg. When he arrived, he put on a Russian Cossack officer's uniform and spread the rumor that, underneath, he was a Heshmat Nezami and, in the war with the Russians, his great-great-grandfather was a riding companion of the late regent,

Abbas Mirza, and had singlehandedly sent two hundred rough and red-neck Russians to the depths of hell. Then he developed an obsession and without obtaining permission or consulting the Koran he went ahead and married a Caucasian woman. Every month he sent several photos of himself and his bride, Olga, to Superior Venus and Great Pride. Initially the two sisters, scandalized by the photos of a man and woman together, hid them under the mattress and didn't show them to anyone. After gaining confidence, they put the photos in gilt frames and hung them on the wall in the gatehouse as a lesson to relatives and strangers. Fridays, after lunch, they read aloud to the Sardar Azhdari ladies the late Mirza Yousef's ten-page letters about how Mirza Yousef, excuse their saying so, went to the opera with such-and-such cancerous count or poisoned himself with veal steak and lamb shashlik at such-and-such ownerless restaurant. The Sardar Azhdari ladies said, For heaven's sake, he married a Caucasian woman for what? What did Iranian women lack in comparison to Caucasian women? If it was the Caucasian woman's cooking, any little Sardar Azhdari girl could cook such excellent and out-of-this-world Tabrizi meatballs that a Caucasian woman would be flabbergasted. The unfulfilled Nasrin, in her very last year, cooked a Tabrizi meatball the size of a bath bundle. When they sliced the meatball in half, a canary flew out of it and sat on the morning glory trellis and twittered for the guests. No doubt there was something wrong with the late Mirza Yousef that he couldn't find an Iranian wife. But every night the young Sardar Azhdari ladies could not sleep for thinking about Petersburg and the late Mirza Yousef. From the start of the night till the end they tossed from side to side thinking about the drugged eyes of the late Mirza Yousef, about his silky mustache, his velvety lashes that looked as though they'd been darkened with some sort of natural collyrium powder.

Agha Ass Dass Dolah listened attentively to the two sisters' conversations and said nothing. He only bowed his head and sighed. Superior Venus asked with the utmost respect, "Dear Father, why do you sigh?"

Agha Ass Dass Dolah put on a philosophical and world-weary expression and answered, "I always sigh for those who go to war against their lot and destiny. My sigh, in fact, is a plea for forgiveness. I am mediating for him with my magnanimous ancestor, the Prophet."

Eventually, bits and pieces of news reached Tehran via the Iranian Consulate: how the Caucasian Olga had eloped to Italy with a Russian officer. Everybody worried about the condition of the late Mirza Yousef and his fourteen-year-old daughter, Homayundokht, God forgive her soul. They feared the late Mirza Yousef would go crazy and put an end to such torture and misery with his Russian revolver. But some of the eligible young ladies and some of the old, pickled spinsters were happy, and a grain of hope sprouted in their hearts. They reflected that no one had received a guarantee of his fate and no one could figure out the mysteries of Providence. When you throw an apple in the air, it will turn a thousand times before it lands. As the old people used to say, this wheel-of-fortune world has a lot of funny games up its sleeve. Maybe it so happened that that Caucasian slut Olga fell from Mirza Yousef's grace. Maybe Mirza Yousef desired to marry a lady from among his relatives. How long could he continue drinking medicine-water and fighting with the short sword? Especially they worried about that precious daughter of his, every joint of whose fingers dripped with a thousand talents. If you offered her rose water she would give you a rose-water flask in return. She spoke French and Russian like a nightingale. She answered gentlemen with such elegance and charm that the gentlemen grew nervous and forgot to speak. They burst out coughing, they took handkerchiefs from their pockets and dusted off their shoes because of the intensity of their admiration.

Agha Ass Dass Dolah didn't want to say, "I told you so." He only gave a meaningful smile, and with artificial shyness drew lines with the tip of his cane on the ground in the courtyard. Of course he was very glad, and inwardly he danced with glee. All his predictions, one after the other, were coming true. And the late Mirza Yousef, after all, despite his stubbornness and his camellike coyness, returned to the bosom of his family. The things that Agha Ass Dass Dolah knew about the Heshmat Nezamis and Sardar Azhdaris, not even they themselves knew.

The men, obeying ancestral tradition, poured into the left cloister. They wiped their faces and necks with their handkerchiefs. They gave way so the pallbearers could lay the body on the ground beside the empty grave with the proper respect. Then they squatted around the body, hit their foreheads with the palms of their hands, and burst into sobs. Only Mirza Kamal, the lecherous, atheist son of Rafi Khan Sardar Azhdari, withdrew to a corner of the cloister and without any shame or consideration began puffing on a cigarette. In the mausoleum yard Sayed Jaafar, forced into a straddling walk because of his old backache and his other chronic affliction, led the black-garbed ladies toward the garden. But the ladies couldn't be hurried. My Bee Bee was too exhausted and hysterical to walk on her own. One of her hands was in Nosrat Aghdas's, and Miss Motlagh was pulling at the other. My Bee Bee's mind wasn't on Iran, either. She had left Iran entirely to Zahra Soltan, to follow like a shadow wherever she went and not bother her and avoid arguing with her. Zahra Soltan had only to see that Iran acted rational and normal.

They hadn't yet passed the cloisters when suddenly Iran started running. Zahra Soltan could not recall being so frightened since the day the late Homayundokht, God forgive her soul, refused the ladies' requests to sing the elegy of St. Fatima the Pure's conversation with her unborn baby and instead took off her muslin jumper and showed everyone her sheer Parisian underwear and said the Master Assar was going to paint her last portrait in this same Parisian underwear.

In front of the stunned eyes of relatives and strangers, Iran grabbed her black dress and began to unbutton it down the front. The ladies screamed and gathered to circle her lest the eyes of a stranger fall upon her. But back in the days when Homayundokht, God forgive her soul, showed her Parisian underwear to these same ladies, they froze and their tongues were paralyzed as if they'd been cast under a spell. That distant, glassy expression of Homayundokht's astounded the ladies. She always flowed like mercury and she behaved with such sinuous smoothness that they were pulled to her. In contrast, Iran's behavior had a kind of trapped force, a sort of locked energy that made them anxious. They were afraid she might suddenly snap and go to pieces. The day my Khan Brother Zia brought her the fresh walnuts, Iran came out of the kitchen in just such an agitated state. She nervously set a foot on the stone edge of the pool and raised her fist like that icon of the saint holding the Mohammedan scrolls.

Perhaps now, too, she felt the presence of my Khan Brother Zia. Maybe that was why she looked so tense. Perhaps this time that unprincipled Masoud, that SAVAK Masoud, had actually kept his promise and brought my Khan Brother Zia to my Khan Papa Doctor's funeral. I jumped up from my seat and shouted, "Ladies, please go back. I can calm my sister."

They took two or three steps backward in surprise. I could tell from their wide eyes that they hadn't expected me to charge in and give orders like that. I told myself that no doubt my Khan Brother Zia was somewhere around, loitering alone behind the row of boxwoods. If I didn't look for him, he wouldn't think of stepping forward. The ladies began to chatter and rushed to circle Iran again. I pushed them away and said, "Please go back, go to the garden. I will talk to Iran and quiet her."

I motioned for Nosrat Aghdas and Miss Motlagh to take my Bee Bee's hands and lead her away. The ladies silently did as I said. As she left, my Bee Bee turned her face to me and said, "Dear, you must take care of your sister. Don't think of me. Go, dear, you don't owe me a thing."

When they had gone, Iran raised her eyebrows and thinned her lids like Homayundokht, God forgive her soul. But that haughty, self-congratulatory expression looked ridiculous when combined with her shaggy appearance. I said, "Iran-jun."

It was clear she heard me. She sat on the stone bench very naturally. If a stranger had seen her in that position he wouldn't have known her from an ordinary person. A calmness had come over her and her movements were executed with patience and serenity, as if she were a passenger seated in a bus. I sat next to her and pretended that my mind was elsewhere, and I searched for my Khan Brother Zia in the crowd. A group of late arrivals passed us hurriedly and went straight to the left cloister. My Khan Brother Zia wasn't among them. They were walking as though they had a sealed message to deliver. I thought, what if something bad had happened? What if we'd done something wrong again and broken a law and the Security agents suddenly poured into the mausoleum and searched everyone? But Masoud always said that if Security agents wanted to arrest anybody they didn't need to make a carnival of it. Secretly, they would block his way with a car in a narrow, empty alley and throw him in a dungeon without a sound. After that the only way you'd see him was with the eyes in the back of your head.

I told Iran, "It looks as if they might have brought my Khan Brother Zia."

She gave a little shake, as if to ask what this nonsense was.

In the cloister there were so many people that if you dropped a pin it wouldn't have reached the ground. The crowd moved with a strange excitement, like a stirred pot of soup. Some men were going from the cloisters to the garden, muttering a message into the ladies' ears and then hastily returning to the cloisters. One by one, the ladies rose, pulled up their veils, and rushed to the french windows. When nobody stopped them, they tried to enter the cloisters by way of the night porch. Sayed Jaafar and a few of the younger Heshmat Nezamis rushed toward them and blocked their way. Sayed Jaafar shouted, "Ladies, it's shameful! There's a men's section and there's a women's section."

Nosrat Aghdas wailed, "Sayed Jaafar, please let us see him."

I told Iran, "We have to get up and find out what's happened."

We were about to rise when Hadj Ali came forward and told me, "Agha, everything's finished and now we must cover the grave. Everybody's waiting for you."

I said, "What do you need me for? If you want to cover the grave, go ahead and cover it."

"Agha-jun, it's not good to cover the grave in front of strangers without you. They'll make up stories behind our backs and ask why his son wasn't at the burial."

"In that case, we should wait till my Khan Brother Zia comes too."

"He's just arrived and given his permission."

I said, "Hadj Ali, are you telling the truth?"

"I swear on your father's grave it's the truth. Agha Zia is waiting for you in the cloister. Don't you see how the ladies are pushing to catch a glimpse of him?"

I threw my arms around Iran and kissed her cheek. I said, "Iran-jun, get up, let's go, Khan Brother Zia is back."

Sayed Jaafar said, "Where are you taking her? The cloisters are only for men."

He took Iran's hand from me and led her to Zahra Soltan, who was standing by the pool. Zahra Soltan dragged Iran toward the orchard. Iran leaned back limply like a Raggedy Ann. She raised her free hand and moved her fanned-out fingers as though weaving a complex pattern in the air.

I opened a way through the crowd and went to my Khan Papa Doctor's gravesite. The shrouded body lay on the brick floor in the cloister. On the edge of the grave, a turbaned mullah was jabbering a prayer in Arabic. The gravediggers stood waiting to receive the body. Masoud, with his bandaged head, made shooing motions in front of the french windows, forbidding the women to rush toward the funeral escorts.

My Khan Brother Zia stood alone at the foot of the grave. I recognized him at first glance. In those eleven years his face hadn't changed by so much as a hair. Only his temples were a little grayed. He wore a black shirt and pants, and he looked more like a breast-beater from Chaleh Maydon than a political prisoner. It was obvious from his frowning, serious expression that he was a committed man who insisted on understanding the meaning of everything. He was listening to the Prayer of Suggestions with strange attention and soundlessly repeating it word for word, as if he were sitting on a prayer rug lost in meditation.

With a gesture, Masoud asked what I was waiting for. Why didn't I step forward to say hello to my Khan Brother Zia? The answer was obvious. I didn't have the guts. From behind his dark glasses, my Khan Brother Zia looked at me in such a way that I was glued to my place. Maybe he wanted to discourage me from making too much fuss and interrupting the ceremony. The funeral escorts circled us, expecting some event. Talking was inappropriate under those conditions. With so many people around, how could I approach and ask my Khan Brother Zia: "How are you? In these eleven years, what has happened to you? Why didn't you let anyone hear from you?"

The Sardar Azhdaris murmured: Suppose they have made

Agha Zia a wanderer in the desert, suppose they have thrown him
in prison and put him under the pressing machine. Well, at least
he could set the minds of his relatives at ease with a two-word
letter. Eleven years without any news is no joke. In these days a
stone can't rest on a stone. In the clear light of day, in the middle
of the street, people disappear, they fly to nowhere, they go where
the Arab throws his reed. For Agha Zia to keep all the secrets to
himself, for him to keep his distance from everyone, is utterly
absurd. Look how he holds his chin, standing at the foot of his
father's grave, fixing his eyes on the cloister's tiled floor. Acting as
if he's the only one here. What do you call such behavior? the
Sardar Azhdaris continued to murmur. Now, if they'd given him
a bad time in prison, tortured him, paralyzed his limbs or made
him a cripple, all right. We could feel sorry and we'd be consider-
ate. But, God willing and a thousand God-willings, he hasn't suffered any harm in these eleven years and he hasn't lost even one
hair. He seems stronger and healthier than anybody else. It seems
he's grown younger each year. Then his brother, poor Agha
Rokni, goes to him to say welcome, shows a little human kindness
and pays his respects. In return, Agha Zia draws back, making
the excuse that now is not the time to express emotions and act
like a lower-class woman. Without any rhyme or reason, he dis-
graces his poor brother in front of relatives and strangers. One
would like to ask him: "Agha, have you brought some novelty for
us that you think people owe you something?"

The Heshmat Nezamis discreetly made it known that my Khan
Brother Zia's cold behavior was due to the great trauma he'd
suffered as a result of my late Khan Papa Doctor's death. Of
course, it was clear that from then on his heart would no longer be
attached to this unworthy and temporary world. A man who lives
eleven years in prison will forget how to live among his relatives.
He will always want to go back to his cage and crouch in one of
its corners and moan of his helplessness, of being a stranger in the
world.

But I knew that my Khan Brother Zia was not a willow that
trembles in such winds. He wasn't a man who would allow his
eyebrows to be bent simply because of my Khan Papa Doctor's
death. Perhaps secretly he was even happy, and told himself, Well,

balls, if he's dead, he's dead. What is it to me? I have to look after my own life.

If you observed him closely you would understand that, beneath the well-arranged but indifferent appearance, something had changed. His face didn't have that old expression of cunning and there was no trace of that famous embarrassed, anxious smile. He seemed gloomy and wooden. His movements were performed with effort and not with joy or excitement.

It seemed just yesterday that he entered the house with those old, split-seamed suitcases. I couldn't figure out why he wasn't wearing his officer's uniform—the one he'd struggled over with my Khan Papa Doctor. Instead, he had on a civilian outfit, with a striped, open-collared shirt, worn black trousers, and a touring cap. As he walked, his shoes squeaked, as though he'd just bought them from the Shoemakers' Bazaar. What a beard he'd grown for himself! You wondered for what purpose he had put on that St. Abbas face. It was six months since he'd returned for the holidays, and he was a stranger. He circled the pool. He passed by the flower beds and he bent in front of the sealed room of Homayundokht, God forgive her soul. He peered through the windowpanes. Perhaps he wanted to break the seals, enter, and take possession of the furniture for his wedding. But he only tilted his touring cap in the windowpane. I felt shy about greeting him. I couldn't bring myself to go say hello. Instead, shadow to shadow I followed him. We hadn't gone far when he heard my footsteps. He turned and looked at me from behind his dark glasses. I said, "Hello, Khan Brother Zia."

He said, "Hello to you. Why didn't you speak up?"

"I didn't want to disturb you. Shall I call Iran? She's gone to the kitchen to get some sweet soup from Zahra Soltan."

"No, it's not necessary. I gave her some fresh walnuts just a minute ago. Your sister likes walnuts very much."

"My sister likes whatever you bring her."

"No. She likes bread and feta cheese and walnuts. If you want to make her happy, give her bread and feta cheese and walnuts."

He started laughing. But then he collected himself and said,

"Pick up this suitcase and let's go to the basement. Don't let anyone know I'm here, especially Khan Papa Doctor."

I picked up the suitcase and said, "My Khan Papa Doctor's asleep in the pool house. He asked that nobody wake him. If his nap is interrupted, he'll be cross, he'll get a headache and scream at all of us."

He raised his eyebrows and began to walk. I followed him, panting, down the basement stairs. In front of the door to the basement he took the suitcase from me. It was heavy and lumpy. I thought he had put dumbbells or scale weights in it. I said, "How heavy it is! Are you keeping your treasures in it? What happened to your treasure map, Khan Brother Zia?"

He didn't answer. He entered the basement and locked me out. I felt awkward. I stood behind the door, embarrassed. I thought maybe after a few minutes he would open the door again and ask me to come in and watch him cleaning his Bruno rifle. He would teach me how to aim and how to set the stock against my shoulder so it wouldn't kick and break my collarbone.

His voice came from behind the basement door: "Rokni."

"Yes."

"If anyone asks for me, say I'm not home. Don't forget. Say, 'Agha Zia's gone and we haven't heard from him at all.' "

"All right, Khan Brother Zia. I won't say a thing. May Allah turn my lips to stone."

"God bless you. Now go back to your business."

I climbed the steps and went to the courtyard. I had figured out for myself that my Khan Brother Zia's return with all those suitcases wasn't just a vacation. Surely, in half an hour one of those annual arguments would start up between my Khan Papa Doctor and my Khan Brother Zia. My Khan Brother Zia would become enraged and, like that time in the typhus year, he would break a drinking glass on Hadj Ali's head, throw the lunch tray into the pool, and kick my Khan Papa Doctor's rose-and-bird china service to pieces.

In the courtyard, Iran was standing in front of the kitchen with her fresh walnuts and she was staring at the outer door. The outer door was locked, as usual. The curtain was tied to one side. In the entrance hall it was dark and cool and damp, like the water house.

The courtyard awaited the day's events with a natural silence and calmness. Under the fig tree, Zahra Soltan and my Bee Bee were peacefully washing the laundry and talking. I went to the balcony, and I was watching the courtyard from behind the railing when all of a sudden the agents burst in. They didn't knock or ask permission from anyone. They kicked open the door and ran to the center of the courtyard. When they reached the sealed room of Homayundokht, God forgive her soul, they stopped and with rapid, jerky movements examined their surroundings. They examined them as if they knew every inch of that house like the palms of their hands. My Bee Bee took notice and immediately she pulled her veil over her head. She tiptoed to the end of the courtyard, where she hid herself under the awning of the five-doored room. One of the agents saw Zahra Soltan. He came close and said, "Old biddy, we don't bother women. Where are your men?"

The hapless Zahra Soltan lost her composure and started stammering. She ran toward the pool house with her uncovered head and bare feet. Then the fear got to me, too. If I stayed on the balcony, the agents would see me and come after me. I backed into the cloakroom and stood at attention behind the curtain. But it was useless. No one could fool the agents. As soon as you say F., they know you mean Farahzad. Before you have a chance to see your own cards, they know your hand. It wasn't a minute before they opened the door and without any search came straight to the cloakroom. The first agent gave a humorless smile, and in an oily voice he said, "Well, well, how strange. We were looking for you in the sky and caught you right here. Well, you ass, you big fat bear, why are you hiding behind the curtain?"

He raised his hand to slap me in the face. But the second agent, who had a naked gun in his hand, stopped him and said, "Let him go, Hormoz. He's only a boy."

The first agent lowered his hand and said, "What's your name?"

I said, "Rokni."

"What is your relation to Zia Heshmat Nezami?"

"None."

He boxed my ear, bang. He said, "What are you here for, then?
Are they giving out free halvah?"

"I'm a guest. I'm here for a party."

The second agent nudged me in the side with the tip of his gun
and said, "Cough up. Tell the truth. You think we're suckers?"

I said, "All right, I'll tell you anything you want."

"Well, sonny boy, isn't Zia Heshmat Nezami your brother?"

"He's my half brother."

He replaced his gun in its holster. He ran his thumbs around
the edge of his belt and started advising me. "Agha-jun, when a
question is asked of you, tell the truth. Haven't they told you a
man must be truthful?"

The first agent said, "If you lie, I'll cut off your ear with a
knife."

He raised his hand to slap me again. The second agent told him,
"He's just a boy. Let him go."

But the first agent still hadn't cleared his account with me. He
continued, "Come on, boy, where's your brother hidden himself?
If you don't tell me, I swear by St. Abbas, I'll put your head on
the edge of the balcony and cut off your ears with a knife."

I burst out crying. The first agent became more irritated. He
boxed my ear again and said, "Son of a bitch, you've started
playacting. This time, you can't get out of it."

He reached into his trousers pocket and took out a switchblade
and snapped it open. No matter how I tried to avert my face, he
didn't let me. He took my chin and turned my face to him so I
could see the switchblade. I grew confused. They knew every
place in our house. They surely knew where my Khan Brother Zia
had hidden himself. Why did they need to interrogate me? What
was the use of putting the screws on a twelve-year-old boy?

Because of my sobs, I couldn't finish the last sentence. I didn't
have the strength for any more. They left me alone then. The first
agent said, "Until we've gone, you don't have permission to step
out of this room."

He showed me the switchblade as a warning. After that they
both ran down the stairs to the basement.

Stunned, I stood in the cloakroom. I didn't know what to do. I
saw them bring my Khan Brother Zia to the courtyard with his

arms tied behind him. As he passed under the balcony he raised
his face and looked at me from behind his dark glasses. A bitter,
dead smile made lines around his mouth. The parallel shadows of
the railing striped his face. I couldn't read his thoughts and I had
no idea what he was thinking about. Somehow, making a connection with him was impossible.

They had filled the grave of my Khan Papa Doctor. They
sprayed water on it and covered it with a black cloth and put a
tulip lamp and a Koran at the head. Meanwhile, my Khan
Brother Zia sat beside the grave and didn't make a move. He
rested his forehead on his thumb and middle finger and cruised in
another world, as if he had just awakened and couldn't tell the
dawn from the twilight. That expression of his made me doubtful.
I wanted to say something but I was afraid he'd become cross and
scream at me. Finally, I put my arm around him and rested my
head on his shoulder. I murmured, "Khan Brother Zia, I love
you."
    He put his arm around me too and, with a softness I hadn't
expected, he said, "Thank you very much."
    His answer upset me. I pulled back a little and said, "Why are
you thankful, Khan Brother Zia?"
    "For thinking of me, for not forgetting me."
    "Did you recognize me?"
    "How could I not, warbling nightingale, lastborn?"
    I burst out crying. My Khan Brother Zia smiled. His smile, like
the smile of a blind man, lacked focus. His gaze was on my Khan
Papa Doctor's prayer reciter, who was singing the elegy for the
funeral escorts: " 'Behind the veil, there's a conversation between
you and me. When the veil is pulled away, there will be you and
me no more.' "
    I turned and looked around at the crowd so they would under-
stand that my Khan Brother Zia was really here, that it was he
and that he was conversing with me. The crowd took some reas-
surance. They were satisfied that Agha Zia had not been completely transformed during those eleven years, as they had imagined. He was still capable of performing the rituals of my Khan
Papa Doctor's funeral service. He could still exchange the tradi-

tional pleasantries with relatives and inquire as to how the cousins were doing. He not only failed to scream or beat his breast like Tarzan; he didn't even climb on a stool to give a two- or three-hour political speech to all present.

Gradually, the ladies grew bolder. They scurried from the garden to the french windows. They put their covered faces and curious eyes to the glass. The men feared the ladies would suddenly burst out wailing—the type of wailing that makes your hair stand on end and reminds you of the first night in the grave and the Death Angel's awesome interrogations. Fortunately, the ladies displayed a sensitivity to the moment and they didn't make any noise. Perhaps they couldn't yet accept the reality of my Khan Brother Zia's presence. Perhaps they hadn't yet found the time to give wings and feathers to the story of his return. It was only Zahra Soltan who started crying bit by bit and broke the silence. "Oh, Agha Zia, Agha-jun, let your beautiful face take me, little Agha. I was afraid I would leave this world without seeing you. But my Lord, the Moon of Bani Hashem, had pity on me and answered all my prayers and all my votive promises."

Still the crowd didn't make any noise. The ladies didn't mistake the crying of Zahra Soltan for a signal to start wailing. Everyone listened quietly till Zahra Soltan's sobs gradually faded.

I could not calm down. It occurred to me to get up and get myself out of that crowd. But if I were to do that, they would no doubt start gossiping that, yes, you have to expect this kind of thing from these autocratic and unfeeling Heshmat Nezamis. The things they do don't have any relevance to the world and its people. I turned to my Khan Brother Zia and asked, "Would you like to go together to the garden to see your Iran-jun?"

He said, "I'll go there alone."

I rose and went to the middle cloister. It was empty and its walls had recently been whitewashed. When you walked on its brick floor, it sounded like a hundred scissortail pigeons fluttering nervously under its honeycombed dome. From a distance I saw my Khan Brother Zia get up. He looked around. He jumped through the french window to the cobblestone floor of the night porch. The ladies backed up and made way for him to go kiss my Bee Bee. Although my Bee Bee still couldn't speak, she managed to stretch her arms toward my Khan Brother Zia. He paid no heed and went to stand on the grave of Homayundokht, God forgive her soul.

The Sardar Azhdari ladies believed that my Khan Brother Zia's behavior wasn't so farfetched. They couldn't blame him. Eleven years of living in a dark and damp four-walled cage is no joke. It is frequently the cause of all kinds of mysterious and incurable forms of arthritis. In prison, your company consists only of a handful of cockroaches and vermin. Of course, in such a situation you would think of your mother. Surely my Khan Brother Zia had wished to see the late Homayundokht, God forgive her soul, coming through the door as in the years before she had gone astray, and sitting on the kitchen bench all tired and thirsty. She takes off her straw hat and fans herself with it. She asks Zahra Soltan to bring her chilled rocket seeds and Shirazi pudding to cool off her heat-stricken liver. After her sweat has dried she goes to the basement and plays her sitar.

But my Khan Brother Zia, his hands clasped behind him, held up his head and passed his gaze over the funeral escorts as though he were inspecting a military parade in spit-polished boots, a baton under his arm, his face newly shaved by a barber. Sayed Jaafar stepped forward. He fiddled with his hands a little, swallowed, scratched his beard beneath his chin, pushed his felt hat forward. Then he plunged in and said, "Little Agha, how come this once you arrived on time? We didn't expect this at all. We thought the chance for your return was one in a thousand."

My Khan Brother Zia, without turning his head, said, "Sayed Jaafar, the heavenly verses haven't decreed that you understand everything and put your nose in business that's not yours. Go fry your own fish."

Nobody breathed. Sayed Jaafar coughed a little and said, "If I caused any offense, please forgive me. It was pure ignorance."

He turned his head to the ladies and raised his shoulders. He circled his peasant pipe in his tobacco pouch to fill it. He followed with his eyes as my Khan Brother Zia vanished among the orchard trees.

With my brother's disappearance, Sayed Jaafar motioned to the crowd to leave my Khan Brother Zia alone. They would have to be satisfied with viewing him from afar.

Now the funeral escorts were getting into their private cars and chartered buses in small groups and returning to the city. Still a few Sardar Azhdari ladies stood under the trees in the garden. They were smoking cigarettes and pointing to the cloisters with their curious, interfering fingers. They were asking on what basis the left cloister belonged exclusively to the children of the late Heshmat Nezam. By what right had the Heshmat Nezamis confiscated half of the endowed mausoleum and put their name on the deed? Any thick-necked country bumpkin knew that in one year the price of the land would skyrocket and every tuman of it would become a thousand tumans. According to the original deed, custody of the mausoleum should go generation after generation to the male descendants of Mirza Solayman, the Grand Secretary of the Army. In this deed there was no mention of the Heshmat Nezamis and Sardar Azhdaris.

I walked down the avenue of trees and reached a short, hedge-topped wall that separated the mausoleum garden from the field outside. The garden was taking on a strange aura. Evening was arriving and the air was growing pale.

The leftover mourners, those who couldn't leave the prisoners of the dust behind, gathered around each other. Not a soul made a sound. They went toward Iran.

In the photo, Iran is sitting on a log by the stream, facing my Khan Brother Zia. My Khan Brother Zia looks vague and it's impossible to see the details of his face. He rests one foot on the log and holds a thin branch with three leaves on it. It's not clear whether he wants to offer the branch to Iran or is just twirling it between his fingers. I myself am standing in the lower part of the photo, so my back is facing the camera. Only my profile shows.

In the second photo, my Khan Brother Zia holds his sunglasses up to the sky and examines the lenses. His head is raised. Under his chin, a line like the scar of an old wound stretches down to his chest, to the opening of his shirt. It's not easy to say exactly what that line is. The crowded shadows of the trees and the paleness of the old photo don't let us trust our perceptions.

The picture was snapped at the moment when my Khan

Brother Zia took out his handkerchief and unfolded it. Afterward, he cleaned his sunglasses with the handkerchief and put them on again. Then he grabbed Iran's shoulder and shook her hard. Nobody breathed. The mourners gathered around and stared. My Khan Brother Zia shook Iran like a mulberry tree—as though he wanted to bring her to consciousness, to wake her up and ask, "Uncle Memory, are you asleep or awake?"

Iran's body was as soft as a piece of wax in my Khan Brother Zia's impatient hands. She didn't resist at all. The more he shook her, the less responsive she became. Apparently that doggish temper of his had surfaced. He shook her like a piece of raw meat from the butcher shop. The leftover mourners were praying that somehow Iran would start talking. Maybe that would stop his fury. He had scared everyone. Impulsively, he shouted to Iran that she must open her mouth and sing Uncle Abdolbaghi's song. The Sardar Azhdaris said: Suppose Iran opened her mouth and gibbered two words of nonsense for my Khan Brother Zia. Well, what then? What kind of wounds can be healed by the singing of that poor girl?

But I knew too well what was troubling my Khan Brother Zia. I said in my heart, What if Khan Brother Zia could cry a little, what if eleven years in prison have not turned his heart into stone? I went and grabbed his shoulder from the back and kissed his cheek. He turned his head and was surprised to see me. He smiled nervously, so that I thought we were back eleven years ago.

Then, suddenly, Iran showed a little movement. She sat up straight. She raised her chin as if about to burst into song. My Khan Brother Zia grew happy. In his eyes a spark of hope flickered. With rapid nods, he encouraged her to sing.

But when you examine the photo from close up, it's obvious that Iran is holding her breath and has fixed her worried eyes on Khan Brother Zia. The shadows of the trees have striped the two of them like the bars of a wrought-iron window. In front of them, a row of mourners is frozen, exactly as if sitting in a movie theater, cracking watermelon seeds and watching a movie full of suspense. In the right corner, the Sardar Azhdari ladies are pressed against each other, are covering their faces tightly and looking at someone far away. Maybe they're looking at me, asking why now I am saying good-bye, why I am jumping over the hedge-topped wall into the field behind the garden. No matter how you figure it, stepping into that strange field at sunset is absurd. You have to be prepared to face strange faces and even stranger events on every curve of that road. They are afraid that I've been hit again by the dream of following Homayundokht, God forgive her soul—with that straw hat of hers, with that head-shaking of hers, as though nothing will come to her mind and her memory is not much help. She seems to be saying one should not give her a headache with all sorts of silly questions.

She is sitting to rest a little. It's as if she has walked a long way and is tired. She has taken off the straw hat and her pitch-black hair is spread on her shoulders. She tilts her face upward. Above her head, the dawn has made cloud castles of hills, valleys, and fields. Seams of light have appeared in the sky. You can imagine that the God-forgiven is thinking of my Khan Papa Doctor, or else she's listening to the warbling of a nightingale, coming from far, far away.

A young man took the last photo of me in the airport. He would stop the passengers and ask them whether they wanted him to take their photos with his Polaroid camera and give them to the well-wishers seeing them off. Of course, except for Azra Hamedani, no one had come to see me off. She was against having the photo taken. She frowned and said, "What would I want it for? And if you need something as a reminder yourself, the new sketch I brought you is enough."

When I saw her sketch first, I thought it was a sundial. It showed a white circle on a blue background, and the circle was divided into sections by a few spokes. A slanted line divided the circle. Azra explained it: "This slanted line is the stretch of an ice dancer's leg, a woman dancing on a floor of ice. After the balloon-man sketch, this is my new one. You know, the balloon man's problem is his position in space. He doesn't know how he can safely land. But the dancer wants to entertain her audience so they won't disturb the privacy of her mind. I mean she worries about the privacy of her mind."

Then she talked about Homayundokht, God forgive her soul, and how I'd always said Homayundokht liked dancing on the ice in Petersburg. Whenever she danced, Azra said, the Heshmat Nezamis probably thought she was dancing for her friends' amusement; but really she was creating a kind of privacy of the mind that allowed her to spin around and become the characters of her imagination. Azra brought her face close and said, "Why do you want to stand in front of the camera and disturb the privacy of your mind?"

I said, "But, Azra, getting your picture taken is just like dancing on ice. Maybe it amuses the viewers, but you're still in your private self. When you send your photo to someone, it's not really you you're sending. You're always absent from your own photo."

She smiled and said, "Homayundokht, God forgive her soul, had a lot of dreams about dancing on ice. But when your Khan Papa Doctor stopped being just an audience and entered her private life, she couldn't take it. Rokni, don't forget."

She backed up gradually and, as she disappeared among the crowd, she waved good-bye. I was picking up my briefcase when the young photographer stepped forward, raised his camera, and said, "It's a shame. It will be a reminder."

He took the last photo in front of a poster advertising the Iranian National Airline. My serge suit looks a bit big on me and I'm holding my briefcase in my left hand. With that forced smile, I look like an exporter of Persian rugs. Behind me, the airline poster shows the enlarged face of a stewardess. She holds one corner of her sunglasses in her delicate, leather-gloved fingertips. Exuberant and inviting, she looks directly at us. One lens of her sunglasses is actually a watch, and its hands show the time of the daily flights.

Who knows? Maybe already they're wondering how I am and where I've gone. Am I alive, am I dead, what if I've been done away with, what if I, too, have joined the world of absent people? But now I think of other things. I loiter in the streets and stand in line at movie houses. If they stopped me and asked, "Rokni, what for?" I would only shrug my shoulders.